Key of CUNNING

Key of CUNNING

KATIE LOWRIE

*To me, myself, and I
I did this shit.
Even when it didn't look like I could.*

Author's Note

I wrote this book for me. A true passion project.

It was a story that was in the back of my mind for some time, and honestly, I needed to just get it out there.

Key of Cunning is a dark book with mature themes and violent-ish scenes.
Please feel free to reach out to me via social media or email if you wish to know more.

P.S. A quick heads up; the vocabulary, grammar, and spelling of *Key of Cunning* is written in British English.

Part One

Embark

THE WORLD PASSED BY THE TRAIN WINDOW; THE TREES blurring and the clouds zooming. Nothing made much sense as it whizzed by, but I looked out on it regardless, taking it all in as much as I could. The splendour of the countryside. The sharp green of the expansive fields.

The journey into the city always took forever, and it wasn't helped by the quality of the air on the train, which was stifling and uncomfortable. Suffocating.

I rearranged my blazer, trying to prevent it from sticking to me, hoping that I would still look presentable when I arrived. What a pitiful first impression wrinkles would make. I wouldn't get the job if I showed up looking like I'd been dragged through a bush backwards, would I?

Graduation had only been a month ago, yet already I knew I needed to get a job that paid well. A high paid job would mean that I could provide for my family and never be poor again. I had enough of that growing up, thank you very much.

We'd always lived in squalor—or my idea of it, anyway. A two-bedroom apartment, a tiny living room, everybody sharing the one bathroom. It was my idea of hell. Or at least it belonged in one of the circles of it. Not sure which one, though. I'd never thought to learn them by heart.

School was always hard for me. I hadn't graduated with the best grades, but they were solid enough that I believed I could obtain an entry level position and work my way up the corporate ladder. Surely, there was a fast-track programme somebody like me could slot into.

It wasn't what I wanted to do, though. I wasn't really sure what I wanted to do. Not in the long run.

Many people growing up had dreams and ambitions. Aspirations. Something they wanted to be, or a job they wanted to pursue. I had none of that.

As I said before, just getting out of our crowded two-bedroom apartment would be a dream for me.

I had to share the second bedroom with my younger sister and, before they left home, our older brothers as well. At one point, that bedroom had been occupied by the four of us, and I never got a good night's sleep, what with all the snoring and tossing and turning that took place.

So, I needed a job.

A proper job.

I'd scored this interview, and I knew I had to put my all into it. Had to get the position, even if it was just as a low paid member of staff at the mansion across town.

In the town of Beurre, everybody knew the mansion hidden by the trees of the woodland on the outskirts. Everybody had heard the rumours. The whispers.

The building itself was large, imposing and made of grey brick. It had needed repair when I was growing up, but around seven or so years ago, it was bought by a wealthy man and given a new lease on life.

He rarely showed his face around town. Rarely attended any events. But everybody knew his name.

Baron Henrick.

It was the kind of name that sat on everybody's tongue. Juicy and filled with promise.

One that all the housewives loved to gossip about, and one that all the teenagers at school couldn't help but whisper in their dreams.

I didn't care much for men, but this one intrigued me.

He was the man I wanted to go work for. Or at least, I wanted to work for his household. A rumour had floated around that his staff were paid well, and that ever since his last wife disappeared, he was rarely home, so it was a relatively easy position to fill.

I'd learned little of his ex-wife.

I glanced back down at the newspaper I'd placed on the table in front of me and reread the headline on the front page.

Wife of 'Baron' Still Missing. Search Enters Sixth Week.

The article itself was filled with mostly nonsense. Some rag reporter trying to spin a tale where there wasn't one. Well, wasn't one that people knew, that is.

Baron Henrick was adamant that his wife had been taken during a break-in at his mansion two months ago, and that they should search for the criminals, as opposed to searching the surrounding woodland for his wife's dead body.

I startled from my thoughts as a voice called over the speaker, *'London Liverpool Street,'* and everybody around me shuffled, moving around the carriage, ready to alight at the station.

The interview was being held in the city—something to do with the fact that Baron Henrick had multiple properties, and it wasn't a guarantee that I would get a position in one so close to home, like the Beurre mansion.

Once the train pulled into the station, I waited for everybody else to leave first, before following them. Being in crowds wasn't fun for me. Part of the claustrophobia I suffered from. It was why I avoided the city as a rule.

But here I was.

I must want this job a lot. Or so I told myself.

The interview was taking place at a small coffee shop near the station, and it only took ten minutes to walk there at a fast pace. The first thing that hit me when I entered was the smell. Rich coffee and baked goods, enough to make my mouth water, filled the senses. It was relatively small inside, with only a few tables and chairs dotted around, most already taken. Two sofas were placed in the furthest corner from the counter, but one was already occupied by a man with dark hair who had his back to the shop.

Making my way to the counter, I wondered how I was meant to know who I was meeting. The instructions had been quite vague: Meet at Small Talk Tearooms at one p.m. sharp. Don't be late.

Nobody seemed to be seeking me out. Everybody was minding their own business, or talking to the person in front of them.

Unsure of what to do, I walked up to the counter and perused the large menu board on the wall. Coffee wasn't really my drink of choice. Neither was tea. I'd much rather have a refreshing glass of water with ice than anything flavoured.

My sister always told me it was because I was plain—my older brothers told me it was because I was boring. Either way, people generally found it odd.

Not that I cared.

'Anything I can help you with?' asked the young girl behind the counter. She was probably my age. Maybe it was a part-time job.

Maybe she was here for her gap year. Or maybe she had no aspirations. No goals. Maybe she wanted to work here forever.

I shook my head, clearing away the tangent my brain had taken me on. Why did it matter *why* the girl was behind the counter? The fact of the matter was that she was there, and she was asking if I wanted anything.

'Could I have green tea, please?' I asked, my voice small. I'd always been the quiet one. Maybe it was because I was the middle child, sort of, and my older brothers had always talked for me. Had decided everything for me. Or at least they did before they moved away.

'Coming right up,' the girl replied, a kind smile on her face. She pointed at the card reader in front of her, and I put my card in, entering my pin. It may seem old-fashioned in this day and age to insert a card into a reader, but I worried about tapping my card or phone. It was easier to spend money that way. And because of my family's financial situation, I didn't like to spend more than necessary.

My hands were wringing in front of me, my nerves on show for everybody to see. Not that they'd notice, though. Nobody was looking at me. I was invisible. The way I liked it.

I took another look around the cafe, wanting to see if there'd been any changes. Any new arrivals.

I was sorely disappointed.

'Here you go, Miss,' said the girl at the end of the counter, a large white ceramic teacup and teapot on a tray. Once I'd moved closer, about to grab the tray, the girl looked at my outfit, then back to my face. 'Are you here for the interview?'

'Erm.' I hesitated, wanting to answer in the affirmative but also wondering whether I should. *The interview* was pretty vague, wasn't it? But then again, what were the odds that many people came here for interviews daily?

'Sorry,' she said with a laugh that sounded like tinkling bells. High pitched and happy. 'The interview for the Henrick household position.'

I nodded, and she gave me a small, sympathetic smile in return.

'Over there'—she nudged her head towards the far corner, where the sofas were—'the man's waiting for you.'

I glanced over at the sofa again. The man sitting with his back to us hadn't moved since I entered. For some reason, I'd been expecting my interview to be with a woman.

How sexist of me.

At no point in any communication with them was I told who the interviewer would be. It was just me assuming. Maybe it was because of the rumours I'd heard about Baron Henrick. He seemed no-nonsense. He also seemed like the type of man who would believe his household needed to be run by a woman.

On shaking legs, I made my way to the sofas at the back. To the man waiting there for me. My hands—much like my legs—were shaking, causing the teacup and teapot on the tray to rattle loud enough that I fully expected him to turn around and judge me.

He didn't.

Which made it even harder to approach and introduce myself.

'Hello,' I started, bending at the knees to place the tray down in a polite and practised manner. 'I'm—'

'Hello,' the man addressed me before I could continue, glancing up from the newspaper gripped firmly in his hands. 'I know who you are.'

I swallowed at the smooth rumble of his voice. My mind was racing a mile a minute. The man in front of me was beautiful. His hair was the colour of the darkest night sky, and he had a trimmed beard with a slight bluish tint to its black. His eyes seemed to match his hair, with dark, long eyelashes framing them.

He stood and held out his hand, waiting patiently for me to

shake it, and in a robotic motion, I did so. My palm was sweaty, and I worried he'd pull his hand away, repulsed by my touch. I felt small with my hand in his. Like a child. Like a young girl that was attempting to enter a world she didn't understand.

My breathing picked up, and it took great strength to stop myself from becoming too anxious and having an attack right there and then.

'Please,' the man said. 'Sit.'

He let go of my hand and gestured to the sofa opposite the one he'd been sitting on when I approached.

Like an awkward fawn, fresh from its mother, I moved on precarious legs to the sofa and took a seat. The moment I touched the cushion, I let out a long breath, then stopped and trapped the rest of the exhale before it could leave my lips. The imposing man sat down again, across from me, the small glass coffee table the only thing stopping our knees from grazing.

'So, Miss,' he began, grasping his hands in front of him, seeming deep in thought. 'Why don't we start with you telling me a little about yourself.'

I coughed, surprised. I'd expected questions, of course. It was an interview. But that definitely wasn't the starting question I'd prepared for.

'Err,' I murmured, before closing my mouth with a snap. There was nothing worse than a gormless interviewee. To distract myself, I lifted the teapot and poured the hot green tea into my cup, but because of my nerves, I nearly missed it. For a split second, it looked like the hot tea would splash down onto this man's expensive looking slacks.

Wouldn't it be just my luck if I gave him third-degree burns within the first five minutes? Doubted I'd get the position then.

'Sorry,' I breathed out, putting down the teapot abruptly with a loud clatter. 'I promise I'm not usually this nervous.'

'That's okay.' A small smirk formed on his lips as he watched me. 'No harm, no foul.'

I smiled back, warmth filling my gut at the look of kindness that flashed in his eyes. The pupils may be nearly black, but in the soft coffee shop lighting, it looked as if there were flecks of silver swimming near the centre.

'What would you like to know?' I asked, sounding like the naïve schoolgirl I'd wanted to avoid sounding anything like. Ever since I took a seat, it hadn't felt like any other interview I'd taken part in. Not that I'd taken part in many. But it also didn't resemble those I'd seen on television, either.

'Your hobbies. Interests. What makes you suitable for a position in one of the Henrick households?'

'Okay.' I inhaled through my nose before exhaling slowly. 'My favourite way to spend time is reading while listening to classical music. That's my greatest love. Until last month, I was studying at Hollowdale High, so that occupied most of my time. I've never really had much time or money for any other hobbies.'

While talking, my gaze had migrated down to my hands, that were once again wringing together, in my lap. At the realization, my eyes snapped up again, knowing I should keep eye contact with this mysterious man. Should be trying to impress him. Couldn't do that with my eyes on the ground, could I?

'Any family?' he asked, his kind smile endearing me to him. He wasn't giving much away, but I didn't sense that he was annoyed by my lack of eye contact. Or irritated by my answer.

'I have two older brothers, but they left a couple of years ago. Then one younger sister.'

He nodded, moving his hands from their grasped position, to lift his cup to his mouth. The way his lips wrapped around the edge of the cup made my insides squirm. There was something so sensual about his lips. Full. Pink. Plump. But still masculine and strong.

'And you're happy to leave your sister,' he said, placing the cup down. The thud of it hitting the glass table made me jump. His eyebrow quirked up, drawing my eyes to his forehead. There were some wrinkles there, but only a few. I wondered for the first time how old this man was.

Then I wondered *who* this man was.

I'd been so nervous. Preoccupied with not tripping, not spilling my tea everywhere and scalding him, I didn't think to find out his name. His position. He hadn't introduced himself.

From the way he carried himself, I could tell he was an important member of the household. Somebody that people listened to. Somebody I needed to impress.

'Not happy, no,' I replied, deciding to be honest. To stay true to the ethics, I believed in. 'But this job will help her. Help my entire family. Working for Mr Henrick could be the change my family needs.'

'Please.' A wolfish grin plastered on his face before he continued. 'Call me Baron.'

Objective

My mind couldn't catch up with the words that had left his mouth. Why was *Baron Henrick* sitting across from me? I wasn't anybody of importance.

'B-baron?' I stuttered, regretting the mishap the moment it happened. By mishap, I meant the stutter that came out of my mouth. The one that made me sound weak.

The look on his face changed in a split second. His smile barbaric. Teeth on show. 'Pleasure to meet you, Sir.'

'Didn't you just hear me say that you can call me Baron?' he asked, his tone dark, treacle-like. Syrupy. Thick.

I nodded. Mute.

What could I say? I didn't want to make a mistake. Didn't want him to think me inept. Or unsuitable for a position in his house.

My eyes lingered on his. Those dark pupils with specks of silver reaching into my soul. Pulling me out of the haze, I was walking around in.

'Your family needs a change?' He rested his elbows on his knees, leaning forward to look at me better. His darkened eyes smothered me with their stare. The air from the room being sucked into their depths.

Was he looking for anything in particular? Flaws? Desperation?

I didn't know. But whatever it was, he sought, I wanted to provide. Maybe if he saw what he was looking for, he'd hire me. Give me a good wage, a good position.

'Yes, S—' I stopped myself. If he wanted me to use his name, then I should, right? I didn't want to upset him. Displease him early on. 'Yes, Baron.'

'See,' he said, raising his top lip into a smile of sorts. 'That wasn't so hard now, was it?'

My tea was cold, but I drank some, anyway. A desperately needed distraction.

Ever since he told me his name, my nerves had grown. There was enough riding on the interview before I knew the interviewer was the man himself. But after he revealed his true self, my nerves went into overdrive. My brain was running in circles to find the best way to talk to him. To answer his questions. To not seem stupid.

'I'm sorry,' I replied, my eyes cast downward. 'What position would you like to interview me for?'

'All in good time. I'd like to get to know you a little better first. Then I'll know what position is best for you,' he said, sitting up straight once more. His tie was expensive. I could tell. The way the material shined in the light. Everything about him reeked of wealth. Of more money than I'd expect to see in my lifetime. It just made him even more intriguing to me.

Ever since I could remember, The *Beurre Banner* had written articles about Baron Henrick. They rarely published photographs of him, and if they did, they were taken from behind, or from the side. Or they were so blurry, you weren't sure who the subject of the photograph even was. The reporters wrote about his obscene wealth, his extravagant lifestyle—and the fact he had six ex-wives, dead or missing, like some modern-day knock-off Henry VIII.

He was elusive. Rich. Powerful. An enigma.

He wanted to know me a little better first, but I wanted to know him, too. Reporters lied often. But missing people were a hard thing to lie about. Dead bodies were even harder.

'Okay,' I said, twiddling my fingers in my lap, making eye contact with him. The clock on the wall told me only fifteen minutes had passed since I entered the coffee shop.

It felt like it had been a lot longer.

'Your application tells me you're eighteen.' I nodded. 'And that you live in Beurre.' I nodded once more. 'But what it didn't tell me was how beautiful you are.'

A slow flush crept up my neck. How was I meant to respond to that? What words could I say that didn't sound self-involved or indulgent?

I didn't agree with him.

Beautiful wasn't a word people used to describe me. *Odd. Quiet. A loner.* They were the things people said about me. *Plain.*

My cheeks blushed. My eyes fluttered shut as I took in his words. Baron thought *I* was beautiful.

'Thank you,' I whispered, looking down at my teacup, wishing I had more green tea to drink so I could focus on anything else. 'You're the first person to ever tell me that.'

He smiled, his eyes darkening with emotion.

'That's a pity,' he drawled. 'You clearly don't have the best people surrounding you.'

'The only people surrounding me are my family,' I told him,

embarrassed at my truth. When had he flipped the switch so drastically? And why was I letting him?

A job interview required questions about experience. About why you were the right fit for the job. Not whether an employer thought you were pretty enough for the position.

Baron raised his hand in the air and curved his finger, beckoning somebody to come to us. It was self-assured, and a little rude. We were in a coffee shop where you ordered at the counter. No waitress service in sight.

'Yes, Mr Henrick,' the girl from earlier asked, having run from her spot behind the counter when she saw him beckon. I wondered how often he came here to have the staff so well trained.

'Another round of drinks, please, Louise.'

She nodded, her smile practically reaching both sides of her face. I could understand. He'd said her name. Had acknowledged her.

There was a lot in a person's name.

A currency of sorts.

A name held power, meaning.

'...this place.' Baron finished his sentence. His lips turned up into a friendly smile, and all I could do was stare at them.

'Sorry?' I stammered.

'I own this tearoom,' he repeated.

That made sense. The familiarity he had with the staff. The way the girl behind the counter had known what interview I was arriving for.

'And do you own many properties?' There were the ones everybody knew about, of course, like the mansion on the outskirts of town. I also knew he had a penthouse in the city, and a couple of places abroad. But nobody knew the true extent of his empire.

'Several,' he said, his white teeth showing in his bared smile. 'I'm certain you'll get to see some of them one day.'

My heart flared with hope. Did it mean he was considering me for a position?

I didn't want to get my hopes up yet, but it was looking promising. Even if his answer was vague.

'I would love to work in whichever home you choose.'

'Ah, yes,' he said thoughtfully, rubbing his finger underneath his chin, scratching at his short beard. 'And what skills do you have? Ones that would recommend you for a position.'

'For which position?' I tried to remember if I'd missed something. If Baron had mentioned a role, anything, but I felt positive he hadn't. In the same way the application online didn't give much detail.

'For *any* position.'

I blinked at him, but he seemed unperturbed, blinking back at me. The young waitress came over and placed a tray with new drinks down on the table before collecting our old ones.

'I'm good at working in a team,' I said, even though it was stretching the truth. I'd never really been much of a team player. Back at school, the other kids would bully me, and I was always picked last for team sports or projects. It had never bothered me, though, because who wanted to be on a team with horrible kids? Not me. 'I'm a good listener.'

Once again, I wasn't sure if that was completely accurate. But it seemed like something a prospective employer wanted to hear. Especially one as commanding and powerful as Baron.

'Are you good at following orders?' he asked with quiet emphasis. 'Obeying those above you?'

I shivered. His words were like honey, trapping me. Many people had agreed to obey Baron Henrick in wedding vows—six people, to be exact—and I wondered how they'd all felt handing over their obedience to the overpowering man sitting before me.

Did he fascinate them the way he did me?

A man with six previous wives was either doing something wrong, or wanted to find something, or someone, *right*?

'I like to think I can obey orders well,' I whispered, then coughed. My next words came out clearer. Less breathy. 'I've never had any complaints.'

'Have you had much experience?'

Were we still talking about work? Or had I somehow stepped into unknown territory. A no-man's-land that I knew nothing of how to navigate.

My mind racked for a way to answer his question in a satisfactory manner that answered both versions of it. If he was indeed making some kind of underlying innuendo, I wanted to make sure I didn't come across as a simple, naïve, town girl. But if it was solely work-based, I wanted to make sure I hit that mark too.

'Very little,' I said. 'But I'm more than willing to learn.'

'That's what I like to hear,' he murmured, adjusting his position. 'Somebody eager to learn.'

Baron looked me over, and my heart jolted. My stomach fell away from me, and I squirmed a little under his sensuous gaze. For most of my life, I wanted to be invisible. And a lot of the time, I got my wish. People didn't pay much attention to me. And when they did, it was always negative. It was some bully picking on me for the way I looked, or the fact that my clothes weren't as expensive as everybody else's. Or maybe a teacher frustrated that I couldn't understand the basic math equation they were showing on the whiteboard.

At that moment, I felt the opposite of invisible.

Seen for the very first time.

And I didn't hate it as much as I thought I would. No, if anything, it was invigorating. The way his eyes roamed, the way his pulse thrummed away in his neck as he stared, and the way he had to adjust himself.

Would it be delusional to think that he wanted me?

Of course it would.

No man with the world at their fingertips would want a plain, brown-haired, blue-eyed mouse like me.

'What's going through that brain of yours?'

'I really don't know what to say,' I said with as much poise as I could summon, flustered at the attention. Unsettled by his question. Nobody ever wanted to know what was going through my mind. My brain was a lonesome place a lot of the time, and the people that knew me avoided trying to understand it. I decided to go with honesty again, because for some reason, he made me feel secure enough to do so. 'I've never had anybody care enough to ask me that before.'

He laughed, a low, deep chuckle. Was he laughing at me?

I clamped my lips together, not wanting to say another word. Not if it meant ridicule.

'Don't get all shy on me now,' he whispered, reaching out his hand to touch mine that was placed on the table, about to pick up my teapot to pour myself another drink. The china rattled underneath our joined fingers, and I shivered at the electric pulse that travelled through us.

It was rare that my skin touched another's skin. I had no friends. And my family wasn't the affectionate kind.

My eyes stayed fixed on the point where our hands met. I worried that if I looked away, it wouldn't be real. That his hand had never grazed mine, and it was all something I imagined.

'I don't know what to say,' I whispered, still looking down. 'I don't want to mess this up.'

Without the job, I wouldn't be able to provide more money for my family. I would have to search for other suitable positions and that could take weeks. Months even.

All the summer jobs would be filled already.

'On the contrary.' Baron's deep baritone voice interrupted my thoughts. 'You're doing everything right.'

My head flew up, catching his eyes, and I pulled my hand out from underneath his in my shock.

'I am?' I blinked. 'I never do anything right.'

'Today you have,' he stated simply, reaching across the table to place his hand on my face. He brushed my cheek with the backside of his hand; reverent, gentle.

'Really?'

'Really.' He nodded, removing his touch and leaning back on the sofa. 'Which brings me to my next question.'

I stayed silent, toying my lip with my teeth in anticipation. The next words out of his mouth could be an offer of a job. That was what I wanted them to be.

But what came next was something vastly different from what I expected. Something I would've never fathomed in my wildest dreams.

'How would you like to go on a date with me?'

Warn

MY SISTER AND I WEREN'T OVERLY CLOSE.

But growing up with little money gave us little choice when it came to spending time together.

Sharing a bedroom meant you shared so much more than space. Whether you wanted to or not, the person you shared with knew everything about you. Every detail you wished would stay hidden.

'And you're going?' my sister asked, looking confused. 'You *want* to date *Baron Henrick*?'

It was easier to avoid her question.

'He's very rich, you know?'

'I'm aware,' she said. 'Still doesn't mean you should go on a date with him. You've read the articles. Seen the news.'

She had a valid point, but I wasn't going to let her know that a large part of me agreed with her. My sister was one of *those* people.

Some would call her a know-it-all.

I just called her an insufferable brat. Which meant the same thing, really.

'I want to,' I replied clearly, hoping she'd get the message to back off and leave my decision alone. Step down off her high horse—a position she found herself in often—and see the situation for what it really was. A way out of squalor. A way for me to leave this wretched apartment, and eventually, take my family with me. 'He seemed nice. Impressive.'

'Of course he did,' she scoffed. 'He wanted to impress you. He arranged a fake interview to get the chance to do just that.'

'There's no proof the interview was fake.' I sniffed, getting more frustrated with her the longer she talked. 'A man like Baron Henrick could date anybody. Why would he need to go to such lengths?'

'Because nobody in his circle will date him,' she said, narrowing her eyes at me. She held up her hands, six fingers pointed skyward. '*Six* wives, sis. Six! And all deceased, or missing, *or worse.* Please tell me you see the issue with that.'

'We don't know how they died,' I replied. 'All we know is what the tabloids have told us.'

'Right!' she asserted. 'And none of it's been good.'

I shrugged. It was a losing battle. There wasn't anything I could say for her to see it the way I did. Being the youngest, she'd never had to struggle the way the rest of us did. She was the baby. If food was scarce, it went to her. If warmth was needed, the blankets were hers before they were anybody else's. That was the way of families living on the poverty line.

Our mother worked hard to pay the bills. But it was never enough.

Would never be enough.

'Mama could leave her job,' I told her. That gave her pause. She stopped folding her clothes, sitting on the edge of her bed, and stared at me. Her mouth opened and closed, before she bit her bottom lip in anguish. More than anybody, she wanted our mother to quit her job.

It was her Achilles' heel.

'I'd love that. I truly would,' she whispered, toying with the ratty knitted jumper in her hands. It was a hand-me-down from our oldest brother, making its way to her. 'But let's be sensible here. The man's seventeen years older than you, for starters! What do we know of the six wives?'

'Well, the last wife is merely missing,' I pointed out, purposely acting obtuse. Because missing for six weeks or more basically meant dead, didn't it?

I also chose to ignore her pointing out the age difference between us. Many couples had an age gap, and I never thought there was anything wrong with it. Baron was thirty-five, not eighty-five, after all.

'What was her name again?' She went back to folding her clothes.

'Violet Brown.' I glanced down at my old phone, wondering when I'd hear from Baron about our upcoming date. He already had my number from the interview application I filled out, and he seemed no-nonsense enough that he'd use it. Surely, he wouldn't surprise me by showing up unannounced.

What was I even meant to wear? My best clothing was my interview outfit, and he'd already seen that. Plus, it wasn't exactly designer-looking enough to be seen out in public with him.

Although, if people didn't know what he looked like, then maybe it wouldn't matter.

'...right?'

I nodded in reply to my sister's question. She would never ask a question ending in the word *right* if she didn't already know the answer. Even if I didn't hear the start of her sentence, I knew the answer she wanted from me.

'Do you know the names of the other ones?' she asked, as if I was going to reel off the list with both first and last names, including occupations.

I shrugged, casting my mind back to the many articles I'd read since meeting him.

'I remember reading about Olivia, but she died in childbirth. Naturally. So that can't be blamed on Baron.'

'No, but there were four others. Are you telling me you know nothing about them? That you haven't searched online since you met him?'

My lips stayed shut. Of course I had, and she knew I had, otherwise she wouldn't have asked. She would've just looked him up herself. Bet she had already and was testing me. Seeing if I lied to her.

'And you're saying you haven't either?' I asked, calling her out on my suspicions.

She sniffed, raising her nose high in the air, giving me a view of the inside of her nostrils. Two dark tunnels that led to her brain—according to Egyptians and their hooks. Just what I needed.

'Of course I have,' she admitted. 'The moment you applied to work for him.'

'So, you can tell me, then, can't you?' I raised an eyebrow, waiting for her to spill all she'd learned about Baron and his ex-wives from random online articles written by people who had probably never even met him.

'His first wife was named Elena. They got married straight out of high school at eighteen.'

'Okay...'

'She drowned in their swimming pool.'

I nodded, not giving her the satisfaction of seeing me sweat.

From the look she was giving me, I knew she wanted more of a reaction from me. Wanted me to gasp or ask for more details. For literally anything more than what I was giving her.

'Then there was his second wife, but you've already mentioned her. Then the third wife, there wasn't much information about. She was older, and she took her own life only a year after marrying him.'

'Maybe there isn't much information because they want to respect her privacy?'

'Oh, yes,' my sister hissed. 'The *Beurre Banner* has been known to care about the people of this town. I forgot.'

I rolled my eyes at her dramatics. My sister had a problem with the way the local newspaper was run, and I think it had something to do with the time they'd posted an unsavoury article about our family. It led to some jibes at school, and people weren't very nice to us for a year afterwards.

'Then there's the fourth wife. Even less information about her and their time together. The only thing I could find was an article about her admittance to a rehab facility after she suffered from a mental break.'

That one caused me to wince. For some reason, I didn't want to look too deeply into her. I felt more sympathy for the wife trapped in her mind than the ones who were no longer on this plane. There was something saddening about the fourth wife, whoever she may be.

'And the fifth?' I asked, moving the topic along. My sister narrowed her eyes even more, but continued on. She was bloody loving it, I could tell. Her face may be sour, but she got off on teaching somebody anything. It was a power play for her. Having knowledge that those around her didn't have.

'Emmeline Sanders,' she stated, going back to folding the clothing, not looking at me anymore. 'Nobody knows what happened to her.'

'What do you mean, nobody knows?'

'I mean what I said,' she said, her tone sombre. 'She's presumed dead, as she's been missing for over seven years now. She went missing around the same time that he moved into what is now called Henrick mansion. That was why Baron had such a big gap between wives. He couldn't remarry without Emmeline showing up, dead or alive.'

'What was the gap between his other marriages?

'Two or three years,' she replied. 'The moment Emmeline was declared legally dead, he married Violet.'

Seven years seemed such an odd amount of time to me for somebody to be presumed dead. You would think that five years would suffice, or that in cases of marriage, there could be exceptions to the rule. A person should be able to remarry if their spouse goes missing, no matter the time apart.

Although, I suppose they would just assume that you'd offed your partner if you wanted to remarry *too* fast afterwards.

Swings and roundabouts and all that.

'...divorced.'

'Huh?'

'He divorced his ex-wife prior to her going missing,' my sister told me. I uncrossed my legs and placed them over the edge of the bed, leaning forwards to hear what she had to say. The fact that Baron had divorced his last wife intrigued me the most. The others could all be put down to sad circumstances that had nothing to do with Baron or his actions. But for him to divorce a wife, something had to go drastically wrong. 'Or they got the marriage annulled. Not sure which. But they're not legally married anymore.'

My heart leapt, and I tried my best to keep my face straight. When Baron had asked me on a date, I hadn't thought about whether he was still legally married or not, as I was too excited to have been seen as desirable by a man as wealthy and powerful as Baron Henrick.

'That's good,' I said, my voice low. Dating a married man would've given me a short thrill, but after one date, I probably would've questioned my morals. Maybe him being a single man was for the best. 'Maybe he's eyeing up a seventh Mrs Henrick.'

I wagged my eyebrows, trying to joke with my sister, but she scowled back at me, finding my joke distasteful. The way she found pretty much everything I did in life.

'Could you be even more classless?' she spat. 'Why would you want to become that man's next wife after hearing about what happened to the others?'

Her tone was incredulous, and I felt something sit low in my gut, sinking with every second. She was judging me. My little sister. The person I wanted to save from the life she was handed. The reason I'd even headed off to the interview in the first place.

It wasn't her place to judge me for my decisions.

She'd never judged our mother for hers.

'That's not fair,' I pressed, looking back at her, holding back the tears that filled my eyes. 'I'm just trying to get us out. Change our situation. What's so wrong about that?'

'There are so many ways to change it, though! You don't have to date a psychopath, sis.'

'What ways?' I stood up, my anger getting the best of me. I hated losing my temper with her. She didn't deserve my anger, not when it was aimed at somebody else. 'Like Mum? I should go and do *that* and still not make enough money to cover bills?'

'That's not what I meant,' she implored, standing up and grabbing my hands with hers, stopping me from pacing the room. 'I meant something like a job at the local supermarket. Or maybe you could look into university courses and get out a student loan? Study for a degree in a highly sought-after field.'

'You know I can't do that.' I pulled my hands backwards to get out of her grip, but she just held on to me tighter. 'I didn't get good enough grades at school to be accepted into any decent universities. And I wouldn't even know where to start. I didn't pay attention at school when they were talking about that stuff, because I knew it wasn't for me.'

'Well, then, an apprenticeship?'

'They don't pay anywhere near enough money! Did you know the average hourly pay of an apprenticeship in the city is less than five pounds? Five pounds! We'd never survive on that.'

'Maybe Mum could take on more hours.'

'You know she can't do that. She's already washed up enough as it is. She barely gets any work anymore.'

We both went silent, hands still held tight together, while we thought about our lot in life. I wondered if everybody felt the same way. Did they do everything they could to get out? Or did they accept it, and go to work unsavoury jobs, just to get by?

'So...' my sister said, depleted, looking up at me. I may only be a couple of years older, but I was a lot taller than her. Ever since she was young, she'd been small for her age. It was one of the reasons bullies had picked on her at school. She was petite, slim—read as underfed—and had the most spectacular blue eyes and blonde hair. She was picturesque, really. And I'd always said that if we were wealthy, she'd have had friends and boyfriends galore. Everybody would have queued up to date her or go shopping with her. I just knew it.

'So...' I studied her intently, looking for any sign of what would come next. Would she approve of my plan to go on a date with Baron? Or would she still disapprove but allow it anyway, knowing it really was our only choice at something more than the life we were living.

'So, I guess you're going on this date,' she conceded with a sigh, her eyes searching mine. I nodded. 'There must be something we can find for you to wear.'

I scoffed.

'I highly doubt we have anything that's up to his standard. The dress I wore to the interview was the nicest thing I own.'

'But for the interview, you never went through Mother's wardrobe.'

I narrowed my eyes at my baby sister.

'Because we're not allowed.'

Back when we were younger, and we didn't know the darkness of the world yet, we used to enjoy dressing up in our mum's long evening gowns and large fur coats. It was a fun game to play. A way to pass the time together, seeing as neither of us had any friends inviting us out to play or to birthday parties.

'She'll never even notice.' She scratched her wrist, causing little red nail strokes to appear on her pale skin. I didn't point it out to her. It was something she did whenever she was agitated. Thinking about the past. It was easier to let her come out of it on her own.

'If you're sure,' I said, not feeling sure at all.

'I'm certain.'

First

The dress wrinkled as I ran my hands down the front, the material smooth to the touch under my fingertips. It was a garish blue colour that did nothing to accentuate the small curves I had going for me, but there wasn't much choice. It was that or a bright neon pink monstrosity that looked like it should've been burned in the 80s.

'Stop rubbing your hands down it. You'll ruin it,' my sister snapped, slapping my hand away from the skirt. 'You look fine. Calm down.'

My sister and I had rooted through our mother's closet for hours, hoping she wouldn't return home to find us with our "grubby paws" all over her clothes, and eventually, we found a dress that we both thought was suitable for a fancy date with Baron Henrick.

I had a pair of lace black gloves on, too. They were mine. They weren't hand-me-downs, and my mother hadn't owned them before me, either. It was one of the clothing items that was truly mine. An old acquaintance had given them to me, way back in the day, and I was just lucky my hands hadn't grown much since I got them.

'You're right,' I snapped back. 'I look *fine*. Nothing more.'

Should I have snapped at my sister, who meant well for the most part? Not at all. But it was as if a demon was crawling underneath my skin. Taking me over. Possessing me and commandeering my actions.

And I couldn't stay 'calm'. No. I was freaking out.

Baron hadn't said where he was taking me. I just hoped it wasn't something more than I could handle. Having little to no friends growing up meant I wasn't very good at the social aspect of life.

What if we bumped into somebody he knew that was important, and I messed it up for him? Embarrassed him and myself.

I would die from shame.

Maybe it wouldn't even be a date in front of other people. Maybe I wasn't worthy of that yet. Or maybe it wasn't even a true date, and I'd worked myself up for no reason.

Anxiety was a bitch. It crippled you until you couldn't see through it anymore. Couldn't see through the foggy haze that your mind had become because of it. Putting myself out there—dating somebody—was one of the hardest things. Once I started, I was jumping in headfirst. Of course, I couldn't start by dating somebody average.

A knock came on the front door, shaking the wood so hard, it looked like it was about to fly off its hinges. I wouldn't blame the door if it did.

Everybody flew off their hinges at some point in time.

It was always a question of *when*, not *if*.

'Coming!' I called, taking one last look at my sister before I opened the door. Even though I knew she was worried for me, she still gave me a tentative smile and a wink before slinking back into our bedroom. Out of sight, but able to hear us.

I opened the door to find Baron standing on the other side, looking more handsome than he had at the coffee shop—something I hadn't known was possible.

He was wearing a suit, and the instant I saw how suave he looked, I knew my outfit wasn't going to cut it in his world for long. Ignoring my sister's advice, I ran my hands down the skirt once more, hoping to straighten out the wrinkles.

'Evening,' he said, his tone low and full of sin. It tickled me *there*. My pulse quickened as sweat began to form in my hairline. 'Are you ready to go?'

I nodded, embarrassment covering me from top to toe.

When I agreed to the date, and agreed to Baron picking me up, I hadn't fully thought through the fact that he would be coming to my apartment. That he would be seeing the squalor I lived in. The dire situation I wanted to leave so desperately.

'Y-yes,' I stammered, picking up the black clutch bag I'd placed on the kitchen counter to complete my outfit. Now that Baron had arrived, my shame was hitting its peak. I felt foolish. A cheap, black clutch bag wasn't adding anything to my outfit—except for maybe an arrow above my head pointing at me, with a neon sign above it that read *poor and desperate*.

'I hope you don't mind, but we're heading into the city tonight.'

My heart dropped to the floor.

Was a date in the city better than staying within the town limits of Beurre? I couldn't decide. For starters, if we stayed in town, we may see people I knew from school, and I wasn't ready for that. They would judge. Maybe even repeat some of the horrid words they'd hurled my way at school, and I didn't want Baron to see or hear any of that bullshit.

'Where are we going exactly?' I asked, hoping he'd tell me.

I hated surprises.

That was something I avoided at all costs. It seemed odd to me that people loved them—even went out of their way to have them —as if they brought genuine joy and not anxiety-ridden spells.

'An art exhibition.' He reached his arm out towards me, for me to place my gloved hand in his, and I fell into step with him, letting the door of my home slam behind me.

My natural reaction to his words wasn't pretty, so I didn't let it out, not wanting to upset him. Art wasn't one of my favourite things to look at. Or talk about. Or basically have anything to do with.

I was one of those people who looked at a painting, or a photo, or whatever medium of art it was, and decided whether I liked it or not. It wasn't in my nature to study composition. To focus on the colour scheme, or the brush strokes, or the lighting.

My heart and my head both came to a decision and stuck to it. Unable to be swayed in either direction.

Hopefully, Baron wouldn't want much from me. Need me to give him anything more than a nod or a shake of the head. A quick 'lovely' or a brief 'not for me'. And fingers crossed, he didn't want to introduce me to any gallery owners, or worse, any artists.

'Fun.'

The two of us made our way down the stairs of the flat block I lived in, and went to the waiting car that was idling at the kerb.

Baron let go of my hand, leaving it cold, and opened the door for me. It was a complete gentleman move, and I swooned. It was one of those gestures you read about. Saw on TV. Not one that you ever thought you'd experience.

And believe me, experiencing it was so much more.

The interior of the car was dark, luxurious, and even though it wasn't small, it still felt intimate. Like I was basically sitting on his lap while he told me a little more about himself.

'I moved to Beurre seven years ago,' he started. 'The moment the mansion went up for sale, I knew I had to have it. Make it mine.'

'What made it so special?' I wondered aloud. I'd never seen pictures of the mansion, so I wasn't sure what appealed to him the most about it. Clearly something had.

'Maybe one day, I'll get to show you.'

'That would be nice.' My tone was a low hush, an excited whisper. 'I'd love to see your homes.'

If he thought I was being too presumptuous, he didn't comment on it.

When he didn't reply, I spoke again, the words flying out of my mouth without much thought.

'I told you a little about myself at the coffee shop,' I murmured. 'I'd like to get to know you a little bit. Can I ask you about the past?'

'No,' he bit out, his fist clenching on his knee, the only outward sign of irritation at my question. 'You cannot.'

The two of us fell into an uncomfortable silence, and I watched the world pass by outside the car window. Like a heroine in a movie, I imagined I was embarking on a new adventure with the love of my life beside me.

Even as I acted like the main character in the story of my life, the hour drive into the city passed by slowly.

We stayed quiet. The only sound in the car was our breathing mixed with the classical music playing through the speakers. I wondered if he always listened to that particular station, or if he'd requested it after I told him I loved classical music during my "interview".

The car pulled up outside of the exhibition centre and I took a deep breath to steady myself. Drawing in the stifling air to calm down and prepare myself for the evening ahead.

The voices in my head were at war with each other.

Why did we need to prepare? One asked, confused at the flight or fight sensation that trickled through my veins as I waited for Baron to open my car door.

Didn't you see the exhibition title? Another said, pissed off at Miss Confused.

I *had* seen the exhibition title, and the moment my eyes read it and my brain computed the words, my heart rate sped up, wondering what I'd got myself into.

The title in question: *The Art of the Tease, an Erotic Art Exhibition.*

Baron had taken me—on our first date—to an *erotic* art exhibition. Me. A virgin that had never once had a boyfriend. Had never even experienced a first kiss. I couldn't decide if that told me a lot about him or if I came across differently from how I saw myself.

Cold air covered my skin, goosebumps rising to the surface the moment Baron opened the door and held out his hand for me to exit the vehicle.

'I know this isn't what you expected,' he murmured, holding my hand to walk beside me to the entrance. 'But I promise you, it will be rather enlightening.'

We handed our coats to the person working the coat check and I once again felt out of place in my dress. Vulnerable. Insecure.

The only reason I wasn't wrinkling the skirt of the dress was because Baron had my hand in a tight grip again—well, less my hand and more my wrist. I winced when his hand squeezed tighter, a sharp pain travelling up my arm.

'If you say so...'

My voice quietened as we entered the exhibition hall.

I didn't know where to look. What to focus my eyes on. There was art on every available surface. The low hum of voices flowed through my ears, and I tried to ground myself so as not to be overcome by all the senses at once. It was a stimulation overload. Sometimes they didn't bother me, but then there were the times where it all became too much. Too loud. Too busy.

'Where would you like to start?' Baron asked, taking a glass of champagne off a tray for us both before handing one to me. 'The photographs?'

I nodded, unable to say much. I had no idea where I wanted to start. Or even *if* I wanted to start. Just being there felt wrong. Sordid. Like I was doing something I shouldn't be.

Deep down inside, it made me feel... sort of... excited?

The first photo my eyes fixed on was of a woman on her hands and knees, masturbating with a bedpost. The plaque beside it told me that it was taken in 1887 and it amazed me that pictures like *that* existed from such a long time ago. In every time period, lewd and forbidden sex existed, or at least that was what the pictures on the wall led me to believe. There were depictions of so many things I hadn't expected to see. There were pictures of men pleasuring other men and one of a dominant hitting another's backside with a birch rod.

My insides squirmed and I could feel myself getting wetter the longer I stared at the images in front of me. The age of the photos added to the taboo quality of it all. Those pictures were taken at a time when those acts weren't socially acceptable—or even legal.

'Aren't they something else?' Baron's deep voice startled me. I'd been so lost in looking at the photographs that I'd forgotten my surroundings and had completely blanked that I was here with Baron Henrick, of all people.

Not that I would have come here alone.

It really was a surprising destination for a first date. That thought still lingered in my mind since the moment we arrived. But maybe he knew one of the artists?

Or, more likely, the owner of the exhibition centre?

Either way, I didn't want to delve too deep into the inner workings of Baron. Not so early after meeting him, anyway.

'They are,' I replied, my tone low, filled with awe. These photographs were something special. A relic of a bygone time and what was going on behind closed doors.

The two of us moved slowly around the room, taking in everything.

Turned out that maybe I *could* look at art for longer than a second and enjoy it. More than I ever had before. My old art teacher, Miss Simpson, would be so proud.

We stopped at a painting that captured our eye, experiencing it together.

The painting in front of us was... colourful. And I didn't mean the colours the artist used.

It depicted a naked lady, splayed out for all to see, with a lover between her thighs. My heart rate sped up. My pulse thrummed in my neck at breakneck speed, and I was certain my face was as red as a telephone box. It wasn't a cute flush. It was a full-blown problem.

'My dear,' Baron said, turning me to face him, his eyes alight with mischief. 'Have you ever heard of a book called *Histoire d'O?*'

'No, I haven't.' I shrugged, playing down my embarrassment. I was working hard to ignore that I felt ignorant. Or naïve. Or stupid. Or maybe all the above. 'Is it an old book?'

'Written in the 50s. French, of course. No way a book like that in that time would've been anything else,' he said with a chuckle. I chuckled back, because if Baron thought it was funny, then so should I. 'It was made into a movie too in the 70s. Pretty wild stuff for its time. Banned in the UK until 2000, actually.'

My ears pricked up at the word *banned*. What was it about

human nature that caused a spark to ignite when they heard of the forbidden?

'What's it about?' I asked, giving him my full attention.

'A submissive's training.' He took a step closer to the fireplace. The press of a button caused a fire to start. Small at first, but building.

'What kind of training?' I asked, not sure what he meant. I knew what a submissive was, of course. After the phenomenon of 2012, everybody did. I was only ten at the time, but Mum mentioned it often enough. So did some of her clients.

I shivered, then shook my head to rid myself of the nasty images that plagued me whenever I thought of *that*.

'All sorts of things,' Baron replied. 'Mainly how to be a slave. Open for all, so to speak.'

I gulped. I hoped he wasn't about to ask that of me. He had to know I was a virgin. Right?

'No need to look so frightened.' He took a step closer to me as I surveyed the painting before us. 'I think you should read it.'

Goosebumps covered my arms once he stood beside me, close enough that our arms were touching. I felt frozen to the spot. Trapped, staring at the painting, wondering where he was going with it all.

'Read it?' Relief filled me. Reading it was a lot better than experiencing it. But then again, I had no way of knowing if I'd hate it. 'Sure.'

'That was easier than I expected,' he said with a chuckle. 'I was expecting you to put up a little more of a fight.'

'Why would I do that?' I asked, confused. He wanted me to read a naughty book, not go off and live it. And I wanted him to be happy with me. That was the point of all this, anyway. To make him happy. Make him want to keep me around. 'I want to please you.'

'And you do.' He put his hand on mine. 'Immensely.'

His words warmed me, filled my heart with something new and foreign, and the way it made me feel meant that I would seek out more of it. More of his attention. Because it felt good to please him.

Maybe being submissive to *him* wouldn't be as bad as I thought. The women in the images dotted around the walls seemed to enjoy it, and unless I experienced it, I wouldn't know.

Baron exuded power, and my stomach clenched, thinking of him being in a position of power over me.

Softly, he fingered a loose tendril of my hair that had fallen into my face before his fingers curved underneath my chin, tilting my face up to look into his. His fingers on my skin sent a chill down my spine. Did I want him to make a move on me? I wasn't sure. But what I did know was that he looked handsome, with his gaze solely on mine.

His tongue poked out and swiped at his bottom lip.

Watching his tongue, I blinked, my mind running away with me. Maybe I was lying to myself. Maybe I did want him to make a move.

'I'm going to kiss you,' he whispered, his eyes a question.

I nodded, briefly. I wanted nothing more than his kiss. Nothing more than his lips firmly planted on me.

He leaned into me, his face tilted towards mine, and I blinked. Was it real life? Or was I in my bed, dreaming of a date with the most mysterious man in town?

When I opened my eyes, I smiled. The vision remained.

His lips were persuasive in the best way as his tongue sent shivers of desire racing through me, his charcoal eyes boring into my soul.

The kiss awakened a blaze. A fire burning deep inside.

And I knew that I wanted more of it.

No matter what happened.

Virgin

BARON

She was untouched.

Pure.

Innocent.

And everything I wanted in a new bride.

Over the last couple of weeks, she'd got mighty attached to me very quickly. And I relished in it.

Wanted more of it.

The moment I met her at the coffee shop, I knew. I'd known when I read her application for the job. I hadn't meant to see it. It wasn't for me to get involved in the hiring of staff, and I usually left it up to the trusty head of the household, Mrs Peters. But I happened to be in the kitchen when Mrs Peters had the applications piled up on the counter, going through them with her meticulous eye. I glanced at the top of the pile, and I saw three details that told me all I needed to know to want to meet the candidate.

18.

Lived in the poorer district of Beurre.

Fresh graduate of Hollowdale High.

What more could I look for? She'd get to be lucky wife number seven—a privilege enough on its own—but she'd also be my last if all went well.

The previous six were all disappointments. Each of them had let me down in some capacity or another, and I wasn't about to make that mistake for a seventh time.

The next bride I chose had to be perfect. Had to be *the one.*

'Baron?'

'Yes, sweetheart.'

'Where will we live when we're married?' she asked, fluttering her eyelashes at me.

One thing I'd noticed from the day I met her was that she wasn't very good at flirting. Or understanding flirtatious advances. I intimidated her, but not for the reasons I intimidated others, and that gave me a thrill. A powerful man doesn't get there without enjoying the power of intimidation. Without stepping on some enemies' toes and making people uncomfortable.

The day after our date at the museum, I'd asked her how she felt about marriage. Sowing the seed, as it were. And every day since, I'd dropped a sentence or two about what being married to me would be like. How much she'd benefit from it.

Clearly, she was on board.

I smiled at her question, proud of her for asking.

'The mansion, of course.' I looked at her square-on. 'That address is my main one. My favourite one'

She gulped and nodded, brushing her hair away from her face, wanting to distract from the flush encroaching up her neck. Travelling up from her decolletage to her cheeks, resting there, a defined dark red. Just ready for biting.

'I can't wait to see why,' she murmured. 'I've heard so many things about it.'

'I'm sure you have, my dear.' I ran my fingers up and down her bare arm, feeling the goosebumps raise underneath my fingertips, savouring the delicious feel of her skin.

Her unharmed skin. Unblemished. Perfect.

Like a plucked turkey ready for Christmas dinner.

'Is it really as large as people say it is?' Her eyes were as wide as saucers, the bright blue of them glazed over. Her cheeks went even darker. Her pulse thrummed in her neck, and I focused on it. What a beautiful neck she had. Slender. Defined.

One that showed enough of what was happening underneath to excite me. The blood in her veins was on show through her almost translucent skin.

'Depends what you've heard,' I replied, and licked my bottom lip. I hoped she could hear the double entendre underneath our words. I used them frequently enough, but only on a couple of occasions did I think her response was a knowledgeable one.

Innocent or not, she was old enough to know about sex. To know how her words sounded in my ears.

And if she didn't know much at all... well... I'd be happy to teach her.

None of the wives that came before were virgins—except for my first wife, Elena. But of course she was. We were high school sweethearts, or so everybody called us, and were in a relationship from the age of fourteen until she died at twenty-one. Her passing was a sad affair. Mainly because I had to drain the pool out afterwards and have the tiles completely redone. It really rather spoiled the ambience of the house.

'Well, not many people I know have seen it,' she replied, and I wondered if she was talking about the house or my cock. The response worked for either, but her blank gaze always made me doubt.

'True. True.' I smiled, reaching out my arm for her to lean into it. We were sitting on the sofa in my penthouse in the city. The view from here was spectacular, and I knew she'd never seen anything like it before.

Coming from the poorer side of Beurre meant that she probably rarely visited the city. Not for pleasure. And definitely not to have dinner in fancy restaurants at the top of the tall buildings that littered the city skyline.

Her clothes had been a problem, and for our second date, I arranged for her to go on a shopping spree with my credit card and a personal shopper.

She couldn't be seen on my arm looking like trash.

'What time's our dinner reservation?' She pressed herself into my side with her question. Her palm rested on my chest, and I smiled.

'Not until seven, so we have plenty of time.'

'To do what?' she asked, biting her bottom lip. It was a gesture she made when she was feeling self-conscious about something.

My hand squeezed her shoulder before trailing up to her ear.

'To do whatever we want.'

'And what is it that you want to do?' She bit down so hard that a tiny prick of blood rose to the surface of her plump bottom lip. Her tongue flicked out quickly to swipe it away, and I wondered what it tasted like. What *she* tasted like.

Putting a hand to her waist, I pulled her closer to me on the sofa and whispered in her hair, 'I think you know.'

My fingers moved her fringe from her eyes, and I looked into the baby blues that were staring back at me, filled with wonder and apprehension.

Our faces at the same level, I leaned in, my tongue tracing the soft fullness of her lips, the faint tang of copper and metal still there.

My hand moved to her thigh and trailed its way up her leg until it was resting underneath her skirt on her bare skin that was cool to the touch. The feel of her smoothness on my calloused fingers elicited a reaction in me. One that was foreign.

With every breath she let out in anticipation, my cock grew harder, wanting to be touched by her. To have her small hand gripped around him in a tight fist, opening up her world further.

But that was for another day.

The moment wasn't about me. It was about *her*.

I'd hoped by taking her to the erotic art exhibition, she would have opened herself up to me a little more by now. That by reading the copy of *Story of O* I handed her in the car on the way home, she would understand more about herself, and her desires.

My finger traced the edge of her cotton underwear. The fact she wasn't wearing lace wasn't lost on me. Every wife before her would never have dreamed of wearing such plain underwear. Not for a man like me. I stayed still, watching her pulse as it thrummed in her throat, letting her adjust to what was happening.

I wanted her to know my next move before I made it. Wanted to give her the chance to say no, or to tell me she wasn't ready for that yet. We'd only been dating for two weeks, and she was a naïve eighteen-year-old alone with a thirty-five-year-old man.

When she made no move to stop me, my finger moved her underwear aside, and with gentle movements, I ran my finger up and down her wet folds, basking in the feel of her slick skin.

A single digit inside of her and she gasped, the sound travelling straight to my dick.

'Fuck,' I hissed. 'You're so tight.'

'Is that o-okay?' she stammered, the shame in her eyes

evident. So innocent, that to her, it could be something to be embarrassed about. I never wanted her to feel embarrassment again. Not about anything, but especially not about her body's wants and needs.

'It's more than okay,' I told her, removing my finger so I could lay her down on the sofa. Make her more comfortable. 'It's perfect. You're perfect, princess.'

The nickname rolled off my tongue. Into the atmosphere. It felt right for her.

She was the princess locked away in the tower, waiting for a prince to rescue her. But sadly, for her, I was less the prince of the tale and more the... villain.

Her back touched the cushions, and she stayed super still, but whether it was due to nerves or fear, I wasn't sure.

I pushed her legs apart, trailing my fingertips up until they were back on her thighs. Moving her underwear to the side, I inserted my finger inside her tight passage once more.

Her hips tilted forward, bucking up off the sofa in an involuntary response, and it encouraged me to push her further. To test her limits. I added another finger and kept moving, feeling her tight walls grip me. *Fuck.* The more she writhed beside me, the more I wanted to be inside her. Show her what she could expect in the future if she decided to marry me.

Without breaking my concentration, I moved so I was hovering above her, my face in line with hers. I bit her bottom lip, moving my thumb to rub over her sensitive clit, until she whimpered beneath me. If my senses were correct—and they usually were— then it was the first time anybody had touched her in that way. Had caressed her skin and caused goosebumps to rise along her body.

Her response to my touch thrilled me as a moan of ecstasy slipped out from between her lips. Her moans grew, and I knew the moment she had reached her peak. Revelled in the way her skin flushed, and her face contorted with sheer arousal.

'Ah,' she moaned, and I placed my lips on hers, our foreheads colliding as she came around my fingers.

Our kiss was savage. Filled with an intensity I had only experienced once before.

I wanted more from her.

And one day very soon, I would be taking it.

A month of being with her, and I still couldn't believe my luck in finding her. Every day, she opened up to me more. Showed me something new. Something that kept me on my toes. And now it was time for me to surprise her.

All the way through dinner, I'd been keeping a secret.

One that my young date was none the wiser to, or if she was, she pretended she didn't know it. As always, her acting surprised me—in a good way.

I hoped it wasn't a coincidence. Hoped that she could act through her teeth no matter the event or situation.

With every powerful businessman that we met, she made a good impression on them, and I felt proud to have her on my arm.

Since her wardrobe reboot, she looked exactly the way a trophy wife should. Coiffed. Perfect. Poised. And sexy.

'Can I get you two anything for dessert?' the waiter asked, having snuck up on our table while I was lost in my thoughts.

The table the two of us were seated at overlooked the city skyline, the wall a floor to ceiling pane of glass, but because of the lighting inside, we could mostly just see our reflections.

Mine looked dapper. My bespoke suit cost more than anybody

should spend on one, and I looked the epitome of a wealthy businessman.

My date, on the other hand, looked like a newly found diamond. Still rough around the edges. Not quite polished and cut into its desired shape. But workable, even if not quite malleable.

The waiter waited for a response.

She looked at me with a questioning brow. A tilt of her head.

I nodded, and said, 'The chef's special please.'

'Coming right up, Sir.' The waiter took the menus away from the table and briskly moved off to his station.

When arranging our reservation, I told them of my proposal plans. The chef's special was code. Not that my dear date would know that. She'd never eaten at such an extravagant restaurant before—not even since *dating* me. No. I'd saved the best for last.

Unlike with my previous wives, I wasn't entirely sure that my princess would say yes. The ring I picked out was relatively subtle compared to the rings I'd given out in the past. Or at least for the other women it would have been. I felt certain my princess was going to love it, though. It was a platinum pave band, with the main diamond in the centre being an oval cut three-carat black diamond.

Most women wouldn't appreciate a black diamond, but if I knew her soul the way I thought I did, then it would be the perfect ring for her.

'Thank you for the wonderful dinner,' she said, her eyes bright and wide. A certain sparkle shone in them that made me smile in return. 'It was amazing.'

The bright lighting of the restaurant framed her well, and with the city skyline beside her, I saw the future. Or what would be our future if she said yes.

'Thank you,' I started. 'For the last four weeks. They've been magical.'

She nodded. A slow blush covered her cheeks and travelled down her chest and over her prominent collarbone.

In my peripheral vision, I saw the waiter heading back with a tray, and behind him was another waiter pushing a trolley with a champagne bottle, bucket and two flutes.

I continued talking.

'I know we've only been together for a brief time, but there's something about you that I can't get enough of. As a man who's been in this position a few times'—I laughed and she gave me a shy smile in return—'I can now safely say that I never knew what love felt like. Because *this*, between me and you, is love.'

The waiter had reached our table and placed the dessert down in front of us. It was a large chocolate lava cake, and on the top, rested a black velvet ring box

My eyes never left her face, wanting to gauge her reaction the moment she spotted it.

The flush on her cheeks darkened, and tears glistened in her eyes, a look of shock covering her features.

'Darling,' I began, keeping my eyes locked with her baby blues. 'I know we haven't known each other long, but you have the chance right now to make me the happiest of all men. Will you do me the ultimate pleasure and become my wife?'

'Yes,' she whispered, the tears leaking from her eyes creating a trail down her face, disrupting her makeup. 'Yes, I will.'

Splendid.

Three Months Later

My wedding day brought lightning and thunder. A dark sky, with an even darker cloud that stayed atop of everybody, shading every corner. Every small piece of happiness that existed.

A young girl dreamed about their wedding day for years.

Well, most young girls that weren't me did, anyway.

I was just lucky enough to be leaving my family home behind and moving into the Henrick mansion I'd heard so much about. Even though I hadn't seen inside yet, I knew I was going to love it. Be wowed by its magnificence and grandeur. I would meet the staff and form a lifelong employer/employee bond with them, just like the ones I'd seen take place in my favourite television shows. Even if those shows were period dramas based in the early 1900s.

Baron's other properties—the ones I'd been lucky enough to

go inside—were beautiful, much like the man himself, and I knew that his largest and most discussed home wouldn't disappoint.

'Are you sure you're ready?' my sister asked. A frown marred her features, causing her makeup to wrinkle around the edges and in the creases. The foundation cracked.

'Of course I am.' I adjusted the tiara on top of my head, staring at myself in the large ornate silver full-length mirror in front of me. The bridal suite was spacious, and more than enough room for me, my mother, and my sister.

They were the only party I needed.

Not like I had any friends to stand beside me—even on a day as important as a wedding. I'd invited them, though, to attend as guests.

Marrying Baron Henrick was the most noteworthy thing I'd achieved in my short eighteen years of living, and I was going to reap the benefits of it while I could.

'You can back out now, you know? We can walk away from this. Pretend it never happened. Nobody would blame you.'

'Why would I do that?' I asked, my fingers pausing in their fiddling as I stared at my sister in the mirror. Her reflection was pale, and if I didn't know any better, I would think she was scared for me. Scared of the life I was willingly walking into.

But she was being silly, as usual. There was nothing to be scared of. Baron was a good man and would look after me. And with the wealth I was marrying into—with no prenup in place—*I* would look after me if he failed. I'd have the funds to do whatever I liked. Live my best life. Be whomever I wanted to be with no fears of falling into the life my mother existed in.

'Because you've only known the man for three months. Because you're marrying somebody with a trail of dead bodies strewn behind them.'

'That's not very fair!' I shouted, losing my cool with her for the first time.

For three whole months I'd listened to her talk badly of the man I loved. Every time I told her something positive about our time together, she'd spin it into something nasty. Something twisted.

'It's true, though!'

'Girls,' my mum called from her spot on the chaise lounge. 'Stop the bickering, please. I've got a headache.'

Her words were enough for me and my sister to stop our fight. Truly, our fight shouldn't be with each other. We should be united against the woman lounging on the chair, with no worries in the world. She didn't care about either of us.

All she cared about was the fact that Baron was mega rich and was taking her eldest daughter off her hands. With me gone from the tiny apartment, my sister would get her own room and maybe they'd be able to afford it with the help Baron said I could give.

The moment I became Mrs Henrick, I would be given a monthly allowance to spend on whatever I wished. The amount he was giving me per month was more than my mother made in a year.

'I'm sorry,' my sister whispered, and I turned to face her full on, so we weren't dishing out apologies to a reflection. 'I just want what's best for you.'

'And I want us both to be happy. Maybe one day you can live with us. There must be enough space at the mansion for you to have a set of rooms there.'

'Do you really think he'd let me?' she asked, unsure. I wasn't certain he would, either, but I knew that one day I would make it my mission to ask.

'Worth a try, isn't it?' She nodded. 'But I thought you didn't like him? Why would you want to live with him if you don't even want me marrying him in the first place?'

'Honestly, sis? Anything has to be better than this.'

'Well,' I said with a brisk nod. 'That's settled, then.'

The two of us spoke no more as I put the finishing touches on my tiara before attaching the veil.

The dress was a princess gown, and I felt like I belonged in a fairytale. And maybe with Baron, that was exactly the happy ever after ending I'd be getting.

The wedding went fast.

The honeymoon came even faster.

The moment the wedding reception ended, Baron whisked me away into a waiting car, and onto a private jet. He hadn't told me where he was taking me, but seeing as I'd never been out of the country, it didn't matter. I was happy to be leaving England, even if only for a week.

But it was the start of something bigger, wasn't it?

Baron had properties all over, and as his wife, I would be afforded the luxuries that came with marrying him. The travel. The wealth. The opulence.

My eyes were wide as boulders every time he showed me something new.

Showed me how my life would be from then on.

For the last three months, I knew what Baron was hoping for on the trip. Knew what he yearned for more than anything. And I wanted it, too.

I was still a virgin. Something I'd made clear over the three months I'd known him. The first time we had the conversation, things were stilted between us. But after I explained my reasons, he came around.

"I've never," I told him. "Never done that."

"I know, princess," he whispered. "And I can't wait to be the one to teach you. To show you one of life's greatest pleasures."

"I need to tell you something." I took a deep breath, worried about his reaction. I just needed to spit it out and get it over with. I exhaled and said, "I would like to wait."

"Wait?" His tone was hard. Cold. His eyes darkened, and he moved an inch away from me, to get a better view of my face.

Maybe he thought I was lying. Or joking around.

I was doing neither.

My words were my truth. I wanted to wait until marriage—or at least until I knew the person I was gifting my virginity to was worthy of having it. Watching my mother navigate her relationships had changed the way I saw the world. The way I saw people.

The way I saw men.

One second, they'd be fawning all over her, wanting her attention and time. Then the moment they were done with her, they dropped her, as if she was the one that was lucky to have them and not the other way around.

Sex was a bargaining chip to them. A currency.

And if I was going to sell myself in that way, I wanted to make sure it went to somebody who could afford it.

Baron Henrick certainly could.

"I'd like to wait," I repeated, gulping at the murderous expression that covered his face.

"Because of religion?" he spat, and I winced at the venom in the question. I wasn't religious, not one shred, but would it matter if I was?

When it came to religion, I had no issue with it. Believe what you want to believe and all that good stuff. I only had one request: don't shove it down my throat, and don't try to convert me.

But the way Baron had spat the word made me pause. Clearly, he didn't share my sentiment.

"No," I replied, keeping calm. "It has nothing to do with that. I just want to be sure. I don't want to mess anything up with you."

Baron's face softened, and his grin flashed briefly, dazzling me with his beauty. Since the coffee shop, I'd tried to come up with another word for it. Something other than beautiful. He was too masculine for the word beautiful to do him justice. He was that and more. Something I couldn't define.

"You won't mess anything up," he said, "but if you're certain that's what you want, then I can respect your wishes."

"Thank you," I whispered. "You won't regret it."

Now my whispered promise worried me. It was only a week later that he proposed, and part of me wondered if we were rushing our marriage just so he could have his way with me. Not that I could ask him.

Especially not now that the deed was done—the wedding deed, that is.

The cool beige leather seat underneath me grounded me. And I looked around the jet, taking in the sights and sounds of how the other half lived. Or at least how *my* other half lived.

'Are you okay?' he asked, sitting in the chair opposite me, putting the newspaper he was reading down on his lap. His black hair gleamed in the bright fluorescent jet lighting, all dishevelled and perfect.

The bold headline of the paper jumped out at me.

First pictures inside: Henrick and his bride

The *Beurre Banner* struck again. It wasn't the first headline they'd written about us, and I felt certain it wouldn't be the last. An article had run after our engagement party, highlighting how fast Baron had got engaged—pointing out that his ex-wife was still missing and that the police force was getting less hopeful of finding her alive as each day passed.

I never asked Baron about her. The information I knew was from a time he chose to speak a bit about his past—and from what the internet and my sister had told me back before our first date.

Was that only three months ago?

It felt so much longer. Like a whole lifetime had passed.

'I'm good,' I replied, toying with the lace on my skirt. After the ceremony, I changed into something easier to socialise in. From what my boutique told me when I went dress shopping, that kind of thing was becoming extremely popular. Removing the princess gown had hurt, though. The time I spent wearing it was too short.

I should have savoured it more.

'As long as you're telling me the truth,' Baron pressed, narrowing his gaze. I smiled brightly, teeth showing and all, not wanting to sour the moment. Sour the day.

'Of course.' I reached out to put my hand on top of his. His skin was similar to worn leather, and it filled me with warmth. His touch was a comfort to me. 'Why would I lie to you?'

'You wouldn't.' His tone was brusque, dismissive. As if I would never lie to him. Could never lie to him. But if he was so sure, then why did he ask?

'No, Sir,' I agreed, a coy smile covering my face. Baron may not have wanted me to call him *Sir* back when we first met, but he didn't oppose it now. The moment the name left my lips, he sat up straighter in the leather seat, puffing out his chest in a show of manly pride. He loved it when I showed my inferiority to him.

Inflated his ego by making it clear that he outranked me, and that I was his pretty little wife who would always obey.

Submissive.

Meek.

Subservient.

When I met him, I was in awe. That awe had only grown as time passed and I got to know him more. Now I couldn't even put into words how I felt about him. Not ones that made sense to others, anyway.

'I love you,' tumbled from my lips, and Baron's pupils dilated, his nostrils flaring.

'I love you,' he said. 'And I am beyond thrilled that you are mine. And mine alone. Now it's only fair we make it official.

Business

THE HOUSE—OR RATHER BEACH BUNGALOW—BARON took me to was located in Bora Bora.

When he'd told me we were going to one of the properties he owned, I wasn't expecting a resort, but then again, the man owned hotels and real estate all over the world, so I shouldn't have been surprised.

The sea surrounding the bungalow was the clearest of blues and the entire resort took my breath away. Before Baron, I hadn't owned a passport. There was nowhere to go, nobody to go with, and most importantly, no money to go away with.

My passport was in my new name, and I had stared at it multiple times while we were waiting for the plane to leave the runway. It was the beginning of my new chapter. A chapter I was able to write, no longer living in the background of somebody else's tale.

'Are you okay, my darling wife?' Baron's dark, seductive tone crept up behind me as he placed his body against mine. I was standing at the railing that surrounded the bungalow, looking out over the water, watching the sun as it set on the horizon.

His arms wrapped around my waist, and his warmth enveloped me, seeping into my pores. The air around us was humid, and my skin sheened with sweat, but Baron didn't seem to mind.

We'd only been on our honeymoon for a day, but already, I felt closer to him.

After we'd got to the resort from the plane, we'd both headed straight to bed to sleep. The excitement of the day, and then the long flights to get to our destination, meant we were both bone tired.

It also meant that we fell asleep instantly after a quick, chaste kiss. And I knew that wouldn't be the case for our second night in the bungalow.

I asked Baron to wait, and now, my time was up.

'Let's go to bed,' he whispered in my ear. 'I've been a patient man, but I can't wait any longer.'

'O-okay.'

I let him lead me into the bungalow, and to the bedroom, where he took me in his arms, and gently laid me down on the bed.

He didn't join me. He stayed standing, watching as I sat up, my legs hanging over the edge of the large bed. I tilted my head to watch his every move.

No part of me wanted to look away from him. Because I knew what came next. I knew that now that we were married, our marriage was hanging on a tenterhook if we didn't consummate it.

Baron was a gentleman through and through. He never pressured me before our wedding, and I wasn't going to give him the chance to now. Not that I thought he would, but still.

I couldn't mess up.

Because I didn't want to go back to my old life. Not after having a taste of something better.

'Are you sure?' Baron asked, his eyebrows furrowing together, his eyes warm. 'We don't have to, if you're not ready.'

'I want to.' I blinked up at him, hoping he didn't hear the waver in my voice. 'I'm just scared.'

'No need to be scared.' He leaned down to kiss my lips, and my stomach swooned. I knew he was the right person to cross over the precipice with. He made me feel special. Like I was the only woman on earth.

A man like Baron could have anybody he chose. Yet he wanted little old me.

'Will it hurt?' I whispered.

Every film and book told me it hurt. I'd watched porn before, but that was all fake, really, wasn't it?

Unless you went down the amateur route. But that always worried me. What if somebody was on there without their permission? At least with the fake shit you knew they consented to being there—to doing *that*.

'I'll be gentle,' he whispered back. 'I don't want to hurt you, princess. Not ever.'

I blinked away a tear that had formed in my eye, trying not to let my emotions overwhelm me. When I was with Baron, sometimes everything became too much. The whole world became a black pit, a hole, filled with something deadly. In a good way, mostly.

Like he was my drug.

My type of human.

The person I wanted to spend all my time with while sitting back and basking in their presence.

'You could never hurt me.'

I moved, so I was sitting on the edge of the bed, and he sat down beside me, finally moving from his spot standing in front of me. It felt awkward and stilted. As if the two of us had never spent time together in an intimate setting before we got married.

Even my mind was stalling.

'Are you sure about that?' he asked, brushing his lips against my neck.

A shiver passed through me, and my nipples peaked underneath my thin nightdress. It was something Baron had insisted on when I got my new wardrobe.

'A pretty sheer nightdress will look perfect on you, darling. It'll make me want to devour you nightly.'

There wasn't much I could say against that. Plus, I didn't want to.

Baron helped me to see me. *Really* see me. For the first time. Which I guess was becoming a bit of a theme between me and him. We'd experienced plenty of firsts, and my virginity would be another one.

'You'll only hurt me in a good way,' I replied. 'I feel certain of that.'

'All in good time.'

Baron began to trail kisses up and down my neck, behind my ear. Little bites. Short nips. Sharp teeth and an even sharper tongue.

'Lay back on the bed,' he said in between kisses and bites. 'I want you to be comfortable.'

I nodded and did as he said.

My mouth was dry, and I couldn't help gulping down air in a desperate attempt to keep myself from losing control.

'Breathe, princess.' His fingers felt smooth on my cheek, and I smiled up at him, even as he loomed over me. 'I've got you.'

'You promise?' The words scratched my throat, and a flood of anxiety washed me, as I wondered whether Baron would get mad at me asking something like that. Would find it offensive or disrespectful. His face gave no indication that he was affronted, though.

If anything, his features loosened more, and he gave me a small smile. One that instantly made me feel better. Less anxious and unsure.

'I promise.'

His kiss on my neck was soft, a gentle caress, and with each kiss he placed on my neck, then along my collarbone, a shiver travelled down my spine. My thighs clenched, and I could feel my wetness, and I worried again whether Baron was about to hurt me, even if he didn't intend to.

His hand curled under my knee, and my eyes fixed on his as he positioned my leg to the side. I sucked in a breath as he kneeled on the bed, slotting himself into the space between my parted thighs. Everything about him exuded power. Control. Lust. Love. I couldn't keep up with the different emotions as they flashed in his eyes, clear for me to see.

My skin prickled as his fingertips traced the length of my leg, stopping at the apex of my thigh. A tease. Tantalising and tempting.

Before my brain could catch up with the graze of his fingers on my skin, his body blanketed mine. It was as if he could feel my hesitation. Could feel my brain at war with itself. As if he knew I needed his body close to mine, but didn't know how to ask for it. Would never ask for it without a prompt or a sign from him first.

He gave me a sexy smile, picking up my hand and linking our fingers, entwining us, so he could place my hands above my head, one after the other.

His lips dropped to mine in the sweetest kiss, lingering for longer than maybe he even imagined.

I knew what came next. I might not have ever experienced it, but I could feel it in the way he moved over my body. The way his lips brushed my skin. The way his erection grew against my stomach. I knew with every fibre of my being that he was about to fuck me. And that I would welcome it. Welcome *him*.

Soft locks of his hair tickled my breasts as he reached down and freed himself from his boxers. Even though it wasn't the first time the two of us had been intimate, every time I saw his naked body, it felt like I was experiencing the rush of arousal for the first time. His large cock bobbed with his motion, and I licked my lips in anticipation. I had a strange relationship with sex—mentally at least—and I'd always told myself I would wait until marriage. Wait until I was with the one that mattered to me above all others.

Baron's hands dusted up my waist, and his thumbs brushed my ribs with the lightest touch, as his cock braced my entrance.

I felt my body recoil, bracing myself, preparing for the moment to come.

'Open your eyes, my princess,' he whispered, the soft sensuality in his voice causing my heart to beat faster with every second.

I snapped my eyes open, looking into his dark ones focused on me, all traces of the silver flecks gone. His hand soothed me as he palmed my stomach, sliding lower until it encased my pubis.

A gasp left my lips as his thumb teased over my clit in a sweeping motion. It wasn't gentle; it was meant to gain my attention. It was meant to distract me. Distract me from the rushing of thoughts and emotions—amongst other things.

On the second stroke, he slid into me, his cock meeting a harsh resistance.

His body hugged mine, his hand cupping my head and holding me to his chest.

Pain ripped through my core, and for the longest time, it didn't seem to ease up. I was sure it wouldn't. That I would be stuck, trapped by a terror I'd never experienced before, forever being torn from the inside.

'Breathe.'

I caught his lips as they hovered close, breathing him in just like he told me to. Losing myself in the scratch of his beard as it rubbed against my chin. In the candlelight, the blue tint that I'd noticed before became even more evident. It was a dark indigo that blended with his black hair perfectly. A warm glow flowed through me, the pain easing up, and I finally realised how dramatically I was acting.

After a minute, Baron rolled his hips, a carnal smile twisting against my lips as he sunk deeper.

Once again, my eyes scrunched up as I tried to adjust to his size. He was big, bigger than the average man, I was sure of it. *Of course he was.* Baron was more than the average man in everything else, so it only makes sense that the size of his erect member would be no different.

'Just a little more, princess,' he murmured, kissing me again. Tears leaked from my eyes, leaving a trail down my cheeks until they reached my lips. He kissed away the saltiness, licking his lips. 'Good girl. You're doing amazing.'

The rasp in his voice had my pussy dripping. I could feel myself coating his skin and it didn't embarrass me, not when his voice was like sex dipped in honey. Or at least I tried to not let it embarrass me. There were things that were easier to overcome, and my shame at wanting sex wasn't one of them.

He slipped his hand around my waist to rest on my arse before lifting my leg around his hip. This position had me taking him deeper, so close to the hilt it made his body shake. Made my eyes roll back in my head, and even though he couldn't see the effect he was having on them, it was as if he sensed it in our connection.

His need to go slow and treat me like a princess was oddly arousing, but he knew what I needed, and he would eventually let me have it. After all, Baron knew what I needed more than I ever did.

No matter how much it burned, I wanted to make it good for him. Needed him to know that he'd picked the perfect person to be his next bride.

I opened my eyes, wanting to see his reaction to any of my actions. Couldn't keep going without knowing how he was feeling.

I drew my hips back and then rolled them forward, holding back my wince as his jaw went slack. It filled me with an unknown pleasure to see his face shrouded in a joy I had never seen before.

Then I repeated the move, feeding his cock into me at a tortuously slow pace.

Just when I thought the pain was easing, he planted a hand on the pillow beside my head to steady himself. His hips rocked forward, finally giving us both what we needed. The full length of him seated inside me, filling me up, being choked by my tight channel.

My head burrowed deeper into the bed, giving his hot mouth perfect access to my neck. He knew that kisses on my neck turned me on. That it was a sensitive trigger for me.

His moans and my soft whimpers filled the room along with the smell of sex. A smell I wouldn't forget as it mingled in my mind with the memory of him. It was a potent and heady mix that was something beyond the norm.

His teeth sunk into my shoulder, and I clenched around him involuntarily. The bite was enough to pierce the skin, only a little, and Baron licked away the small bead of blood that rushed to the surface.

'That isn't the only drop of your blood I've drawn tonight,' he said against my ear, his breath chilling me as a full-body shiver ran through me.

'My blood is yours,' I whispered, the words coming before my thoughts caught up with them. But even once it registered in my mind, I knew that I meant every word deeply. Every part of my being was his. The outside and the inside; the flesh and the matter.

It sparked something inside of him. It drove him wild, his hips picking up the pace and driving me further into the bed.

It felt good. Tender, but in the most delicious way.

His hold on me grew tighter and tighter as we both neared our release. His hands went from my ribs to my hips, squeezing the flesh of my arse before he slammed back into me again.

The sound of our bodies slapping together was more erotic than I ever imaged it could be. It made me wetter than I'd ever been before, at home alone, reading literature or watching porn.

Heat spread through me, spearing me, making my stomach clench and my toes curl. Baron reached down and pushed his thumb past my lips. I took it into my mouth like he clearly wanted me to, then I sucked on it hard, nibbling and twisting my lips around the tip. I knew what he was thinking, and I was thinking it too. Both of us were linked. If I thought we were one before, then my belief was confirmed by the thread attaching us.

He removed his thumb with a pop and brought it down to my pussy, easing the slick pad around my clit in slow circles. Everything intensified, and when his thrusts became brutal, his control fraying by the second, I knew he was right there with me. That the two of us were about to combust together.

'Baron,' I moaned.

My hips bucked, and I tried to control my body as it began to shake. The thought of an orgasm was heavy and almost unbearable, but when it hit, the most euphoric feeling seeped into me. My body pulsed, my heart hammering away in my chest as sweat coated my body.

Our eyes locked. Baron's dark, almost black pupils were trapped in place by mine, as my breathing slowed down, my walls still pulsing around his dick.

Baron growled above me, his movements getting jerky as he pumped into me five more times before coming inside of me. The thought of his cum inside of me nearly pushed me to the peak, another orgasm sitting underneath the surface, just waiting to be unleashed.

But I couldn't.

It was Baron's show, and I was merely a player within it.

'You,' Baron whispered, his lips grazing along mine. 'Are more than I imagined you would be. You are mine. Forever. Don't forget that.'

The start of the sentence filled me with love. Made me feel every cliché that existed, all warm and fuzzy and sated.

The second part: foreboding.

Gateway

HENRICK MANSION WAS EVEN MORE IMPRESSIVE THAN I imagined it to be.

The car pulled up the mile long driveway, and the closer we got, the harder my stomach flipped. Baron was sitting beside me in the car, blending in with the dark leather interior, looking the epitome of cool, calm, and collected.

The cool leather underneath me did little to ground me. I refused to have the seat warmer turned on, because I'd quickly learned that it made me feel as if I'd peed myself, and the paranoia wasn't worth it.

At the end of the driveway, there was a circular fountain—because of course there was—and it was my first look at my new home.

The sheer size of it overwhelmed me. Even from the outside, I could tell that you would be able to fit my family's apartment in there at least one hundred times.

The exterior was limestone, and there was a dual staircase

leading up to the main entrance. Windows covered the entire front of the building, large imposing windows that overlooked the fountain. I wondered how many rooms there were in the building. From where I was standing, there was no way of knowing.

If I was being honest, the house was nowhere near as gothic and dreary as my imagination had cooked it up to be. I expected gargoyles and pointed arches. But they were more for cathedrals than stately homes. The one we'd married in was the height of gothic architecture.

The staff were all lined up in a row, awaiting our arrival. They must be freezing, standing out in the cold. There was an unnatural chill in the air for the time of year, and the weather forecast was even predicting snow.

'I'll introduce you to the staff,' Baron stated as the car pulled up outside the staircase. 'Then you'll be shown to your rooms.'

I startled, turning my head away from the house to look into Baron's eyes.

'*My* rooms?' My mind was jumbled and I wasn't sure what to think. I thought the two of us were going to have a shared room. The way most married couples did.

'Yes.' Baron looked down his nose at me. 'Is that a problem?'

'I just thought we'd be sharing rooms,' I said, my voice low. In the small space of the car, the air felt suffocating, and I fought the urge to grab the door handle and throw myself out of the slowing vehicle.

'And we will,' he replied. 'But you also have your own in case you ever have need for them.'

He gave no further explanation, and I nodded, not wanting to draw more attention to my muddled feelings. My fingers were playing with a frayed thread hanging from my coat, and I tried to sit tall. Straight back. Eyes looking ahead. The way a wife of a wealthy man should look when approaching their new manor.

The car stopped, and I took in a deep breath to ground myself.

The driver stepped out of the car and made his way to my door first, opening it and helping me to step out. Baron followed behind me, exiting through my door, and coming to stand up against me, his hand on the small on my back.

A warmth travelled through my body from the comfort of his palm—one that only he could provide.

The first member of staff to step forward to greet us was a shorter lady, older, with grey hair and a stern face. Her eyes were narrowed, as she closely scrutinised me from head to toe.

'Darling, this is Mrs Peters. She's the person that you'll go to for any house needs. She's in charge around here.'

'Pleasure to meet you, Mrs Peters.' I held out my hand for her to shake, and she looked down at it with pure disgust. As if she'd smelled something bad—and that something was *me*.

'And you, Mrs Henrick.'

Her entire tone was false. I continued smiling, bobbing my head at her acknowledgement, hoping that I was improving her first impression of me. It was odd to hear my new name. My married name.

Mrs Henrick.

It tasted like honey. Like a Christmas roast dinner with all the trappings.

Like all my dreams come true and then some.

'The others I'm sure you'll get to know in due time,' Baron said as we made our way down the line, nodding our heads at each of them in turn. I wondered if he knew their names—or their roles.

'It's a pleasure to meet you all,' I said, before we stepped into the large double doors that sat at the entrance of the mansion.

None of them moved, staying stony-faced, looking down at the ground. Their hands clasped together in front of their waists.

Suit yourselves.

'Come on, wife. I want to show you your new home.'

Baron's arm reached behind him for me, and I grabbed onto him like my own personal safety rope.

The entrance hall was spacious and airy. Minimalist, with barely any furniture, and there was only one mirror on the wall. The rest was dead space. The main feature of the hall was the large, bifurcated staircase.

It took my breath away.

All black and white, marble flooring, and a beautiful chandelier hanging in the centre. It was expensive, and decadent, and just so different from all I knew. My mother's sad apartment would fit into the entrance hall, and the entire cost of her place probably equalled the cost of one tile on the floor.

We didn't go up the stairs, though. We continued through the middle of the room, and at the end, turned to the right.

'Your rooms are down here.' He walked me down a corridor, and then we made a sharp right, heading back towards the front wall of the house.

He stopped at a large white door. The doorknob to enter resembled the large golden one from the animated classic *Alice in Wonderland*, and I wondered whose idea that had been. It seemed too fanciful for Baron. Full of whimsy and light.

With a gold key, Baron unlocked the door and pushed it wide open, affording me a view of my rooms for the first time.

They were massive, ginormous and every other word I could think of to describe really bloody big, and I couldn't believe that they were all mine. That I didn't have to share them with anybody else. That I could sleep alone while Baron was away on business without listening to the snoring and breathing of three other bodies.

The walls were a plain, bright white.

'You can decorate them however you wish, darling.' Arms came around my waist and pulled me back into a hard chest. He kissed my hair, breathed in my scent, and we both sighed.

Happiness was a feeling I couldn't describe well. It was like coming home. A joy with no description, but one you could feel in your bones all the same.

I was bored with describing everything as the first way, or the first thing, I'd felt or experienced, but my education was sorely lacking after all, so I didn't have much else in my vocabulary to describe it.

'Did Violet stay here?' I asked, the thought flying from my mind and out of my mouth.

Baron stiffened. The air leached out of the room, leaving me struggling to breathe. My stupid mouth. It wasn't often I spoke aloud, but trust that when I did, I'd put my foot in my mouth.

'She did not,' he replied with rigidity, anger radiating from him. I couldn't decide who he was angry at: me or the memory of Violet?

'I'm sorry.' My apology faded to a hushed stillness.

Baron didn't look at me.

'Now, I think it's time for me to show you to our bedroom.'

I nodded and followed behind him. Back to the hall. Up the stairs. And into the East Wing of the house.

It wasn't long before we were standing outside the room, and I let out a sigh of pure contentment when Baron lifted me into his arms and carried me over the threshold of our bedroom.

Our bedroom.

It was exactly how I always envisioned a master suite in a large mansion to look.

A large queen-size four-poster bed in the middle, with curtains and black satin sheets that drew the eye. The darker sheets matched the dark wood panelling within the room, and the whole room felt seductive because of it.

The sheets were cool underneath me, and I moved myself to the centre of the bed, unable to reach either side because of the sheer size.

'Remember when I asked you to read the *Story of O?*'

I propped myself up onto my elbows and assessed his captivated gaze. I always wanted to see him. *Truly* see him. Not the man he showed the world, but the man he showed *me* and me alone. Those other wives be damned.

Baron hadn't followed me to the bed. He was standing over by the fireplace, his face thoughtful. Above the fireplace was a large black framed mirror, tilted down so that I could see myself on the bed. There was also a mirror above the bed, on the ceiling itself, and the placement of it excited me. Tampering down those urges would be best, though. It wouldn't do me any good to become a wanton creature—my only thrill in life being the pursuit of pleasure and orgasms.

No. That wouldn't do.

'I remember.' My whisper carried to the fireplace. I looked into the flames. Saw the flickering of orange and red, heard the sizzle and crack of burning wood beneath, the shimmer illuminating the otherwise dull room. Baron stood there, half in shadow, devilishly handsome, and powerful. Impressive. The muscles that rippled underneath his white shirt caused my pulse to quicken. And the topic at hand.

I read the *Story of O,* just like he asked me—and I watched the 70s film on the laptop he'd given me, under the covers late at night with headphones in so my sister wouldn't be any the wiser.

It thrilled me. Excited me.

A part of me that I'd never dared to think of before was awakened.

'And you read it?'

'I did.'

'What did you think?' He stepped away from the fireplace. My eyes sought solace in something that wasn't him, or attempted to, but there was nothing to look at. No paintings or pictures lining the walls. No warmth aside from the fire raging. The only disturbance on the walls being the mirrors.

'About the writing, or…' I trailed off. He didn't mean the writing, and I knew it.

'About the story. Were there any parts that spoke to you? Sung to your soul?'

The bed dipped as Baron climbed on and made his way over to me, to hover over me on all fours. Baron's eyes locked on mine, the silver flecks swimming amongst the dark blue in time with the beating of my heart.

'N-no,' I lied. My heart clenched. My thighs did, too. Being married, you would think that I could open up fully. Tell him everything.

But whatever way I looked at it, we'd only known each other for just a little longer than three months, married or not. And I felt ashamed of my desires.

Which I knew was stupid. Because why would Baron have wanted me to read it if he didn't want some of it to 'sing to my soul'? He took me to that exhibition on our first date for a reason.

His lips pressed against mine with enthusiasm. The soft tickle of his beard was a comfort now, unlike when we first started dating.

'There is a part we could re-enact now,' he mumbled against my lips, kissing in between each word. 'But I only want you to agree if you're one hundred percent sure, okay?'

I nodded, wondering what on earth he could be about to ask of me. If another man entered the room, holding a collar and a chain, then I would have to bolt. New life be damned.

Since losing my virginity, Baron had opened something inside of me. But I wasn't at the point where I would be willing to head off to a chateau and learn how to be an orifice for men's pleasure.

The fire crackled in the fireplace and the room was heating up —but it had nothing to do with our close proximity.

'I want you to wear my mark.'

'Your mark?' I whispered. My mind flew through what he could be talking about. Hopefully, he meant a tattoo.

I'd never wanted a tattoo. Had never thought of anything that I would want on my body permanently. Plus, I couldn't afford one. And you constantly read horror stories about people ending up with crappy tattoos because they'd let a friend with a tattoo gun practise on them.

Although, in the book... Surely not.

I shook the thought away, laughing at my mind for running away like that.

But then my mind went to the flames...

'Yes,' he whispered back, his breath fanning my face. 'My name.'

Being intimate with somebody was strange. Before Baron, or BB, as I sometimes referred to it in my mind, I never thought much about what it would be like to open myself up to another person. To let them know everything about me. See everything I kept inside.

'Where?'

'Wherever you want. It can be hidden, something only you and I see. Or something more visible, on display whenever you choose.'

I mulled it over, tossing the idea around in my mind. Throwing it from one lobe to the other. The fleshier the area, the better, I assumed. But I also wanted something people could see. Wanted to shout out loud and clear that I was Baron's.

'Did the others have one?' I asked, a murmur of words, the question a highlight of my insecurities.

'No.' His tone was serious, and it was the only way he could have answered me that would make me happy. Anything else and I would refuse.

The flames of jealousy nipped at my feet, singed my hair, and burned beneath my skin. The flames were evident in my eyes. Like an overwhelming burn I couldn't control.

But I batted it away. They weren't here now. I was. And that was all that mattered.

And if they didn't have the mark, it meant that Baron had got the branding tool made specifically for *me*. So *I* could wear his name, branded into my flesh.

'Okay.' I craned my neck to place a kiss on his lips. Soft. Gentle. All my love and emotion in that simple touching of lips. Of souls.

'*Okay* as in... you'll do it?' His eyes were alight with hope. A beacon. Filled with excitement and lust. Sensual.

'I'm devoted to you.' The words were simple. True. My hand reached for his, grasped it in mine tightly, stroking his wedding ring with my thumb. 'I'm yours.'

'You're everything I hoped you would be and more.'

Baron moved off the bed, and now that my eyes weren't focused on his, I looked at the fireplace once more. With my eyes open—to both the situation and my surroundings—I saw the poker that was sitting in the flames, glowing brightly with a burnt orange and red hue.

The gravity of what Baron was asking of me hit me full force, punching me in the stomach and winding me within seconds.

'Where do you want it?' he asked.

'On my collarbone,' I told him, eager and intense. I didn't want him to convince me otherwise. For him, I was happy for it to hurt.

'Are you sure, princess?'

I nodded, moving off the bed, and falling to my knees on the dark wooden floor, bowing my head before him. It was what was expected of O at some point during her time at the chateau, and from my internet searches, I gathered it was something many submissive women did to please their master.

'Just do it,' I said breathlessly, my eyes still downcast. 'I'm ready.'

I clenched my eyes closed, not wanting to see his advance. Even though I hated surprises, I also knew that I couldn't see him coming. Couldn't watch him come closer with a red-hot iron in his hands, ready to burn my skin.

I couldn't block all my senses, though. His footsteps got closer, each step sounding like a crack of thunder travelling through my skull, reverberating around inside.

'This is going to hurt,' Baron warned in a harsh, raw voice.

Cool air entered my nose as I inhaled deeply, hoping that I would breathe through the pain.

But the moment the branding iron touched my skin, I fought the nausea that rushed into my stomach. My breathing went ragged, and I hissed out, the sound mixing with the sizzle of the tool on my flesh. The smell of burnt flesh was overwhelming.

My vision began to spot. The edges turned black and crept in further.

Then, the next thing I knew, I was back on the bed, with Baron hovering over me, placing a cool, damp cloth to my head, and looking at me with the biggest, most rare smile on his face.

'You look beautiful,' he said, his voice filled with awe.

My smile back was faint, but inside, I was the happiest I'd ever been. The sharp pain in my collarbone, the nausea swirling in my stomach, they all told me the same thing.

He was mine, and I was his.

The way it was meant to be.

Keys

Two weeks of living at Henrick mansion showed me how much I'd missed out on growing up. How much wealth could get you, and why people would do whatever they could to obtain it. Or keep it.

There were staff buzzing around at all times, there to wait on me hand and foot if I asked. All my meals were prepared for me, my clothes laundered, my bedding fluffed.

Everything I could've ever dreamed of was now my reality.

And I had Baron to thank for it all.

'Have I mentioned how much I love you?' I kissed his pec and squeezed him closer to me in our large bed, happy as always to wake up beside him.

'Once or twice,' he said with a smirk, brushing his fingers through my hair in a lazy fashion.

'Well, I do,' I whispered. 'You've given me my first ever safe space. I won't ever forget that. It means a lot to me.'

'And I intend to give you that safe space until the end of time.'

My lips turned up into an involuntary smile, even though Baron couldn't see my face. Even the way his voice said words made me squeal inside. Let alone the way the words themselves made me feel. Nobody had ever said words like that to me.

'I was thinking...' I looked up at his face, his long, dark eyelashes resting on his cheeks, and smiled. 'Maybe we could spend the weekend together, at home, alone.'

Nerves filled me. I didn't even know why I was so nervous. He was my husband, and I should be able to ask anything of him without fear or worry.

But he was a no-nonsense man, and I never knew when he would snap at me the way I'd seen him snap at his staff.

'Not this weekend, darling. I'll be going on a business trip, and I need you to stay home and keep the house running smoothly for me.'

'Can't Mrs Peters do that?' I asked, a little petulant, sticking out my bottom lip. Maybe if I pouted hard enough, he'd come around. Let me go with him. Or say fuck it to his business trip and stay home with me instead.

'She could,' he agreed. 'But I want you to learn, my dear. As the mistress of this manor, I want you to step up. Really take on the role you were meant for.'

His words amused him. The wolfish smile on his face caused my thighs to clench together. Everything about him exuded sex and power. Dominance. He was so assured in himself, so ready to take on the world and have them accept him for exactly who, and what, he was. I wished I was that confident. Wished I could enter a room and be all, 'this is me, like it or lump it', rather than entering and hoping the wall would devour me and I could go unnoticed.

'But what if they don't listen to me?' I frowned. I got the impression that the staff weren't impressed with having another mistress so soon after the disappearance of their previous one. 'They seem to think I'm some silly, naïve little girl.'

'If you have any problems with them, you can come straight to me. Or put them in their place, princess. They're not your equals. Remember that.'

I nodded. The feel of his heartbeat underneath my head grounded me.

'I've just never had that kind of power before.' And I wasn't lying to him, either. I'd never had much power in my life. Never had the chance to change anything, or anyone. The way people thought of me, the way they treated me, it had always been set in stone.

'Now, you do,' he said and placed a kiss on my forehead. 'And talking of power, I've got something for you before I go.'

'Yeah?'

He nodded in response.

His dark eyes focused on mine. There was a glint of something more in them. Amusement, maybe. Or malice.

I couldn't be sure.

A flash of silver caught my eye, as Baron held aloft a large circle ring that had more keys than I could count attached.

'I'll be leaving these in your safe hands,' he said, the keys jangling together with a soft clatter, sounding like wind chimes. 'While I'm away on business.'

'What are those?' I asked, confused.

'Keys,' he replied with a laugh. I laughed back, but the sound was false. 'A key to every lock in the house, to be precise.'

'And why are you handing them to me?'

'Because I want you to know that now that we're married, and you're the mistress of this house, that you have access to every-thing.' He paused. 'Well, everything except the West Wing, of course.'

Ever since Baron told me the West Wing was out of bounds, I'd tried to work it out of him in any way I could, but so far, he hadn't taken the bait. Obviously, I hadn't been able to get close to the area. I was either always with Baron, or some other member of staff was watching my every move. It was something that took some getting used to.

His fingers fumbled with the ring, and I moved my attention back to Baron once more. He began to rifle through each key, moving them around the ring one-by-one in a slow and meticulous way.

The moment a larger, antique looking key came into his fingers, he stopped, holding the key out to me. His gaze was focused on it.

'You must never use this key. The door it opens isn't for the likes of you, dear wife, and I'll know if you disobey.'

'And how will I know what door that particular key opens?'

'You'll know,' he said, darkly.

My mind rushed to the West Wing. Of course, the door that key opened had to be somewhere there.

Surely, he knew that by telling me not to, I would want to more than anything else.

And really, would he even know? How would he know?

I supposed there could be cameras dotted around that I wasn't aware of. Hidden in paintings on the wall or in flowerpots or the likes.

He would be gone soon enough. And then I could explore.

The day came for him to leave, and I was sad to see Baron off. But excited and apprehensive, too.

It would be the first time we were apart since our marriage started—since our entire relationship started, actually—and I wasn't sure of my identity without him. I understood that wasn't healthy, but I also didn't care.

In such a short period, Baron had become my world. He was the moon, the sun, and the stars, and all that other fluffy crap in between. Everything started and ended with him. He was the centre.

'I'll only be gone five days,' he whispered in my ear, his nose nuzzling against my hair, breathing in my scent. He told me when we married that I reminded him of a cold winter's day. The way the trees and leaves smelled when the frost hit, and the air was fresh and brisk. 'Then we can resume as if I never left.'

'You mean that?' I whispered, pressing up onto my tiptoes to place a chaste kiss behind his ear, a spot I recently learned was sensitive.

'Of course I do. And every night I'll video call you, so we can catch up about our days. Plus, then I'll be able to see your pretty face.'

I blushed.

Baron's words melted me in the best way, catching me off guard most of the time. He was the first person to call me pretty. Or beautiful. Or anything of the sort.

My mother used to tell me I was a nuisance, too plain to be of any use in her line of work, and that she wished I looked more like my younger sister.

Which I always found laughable, because even I could see that the two of us were the spitting image of each other—she was just three years younger.

'You're more handsome than I am pretty,' I said in a teasing tone. 'So who's the true winner here?'

'Still me,' he said, his lips tilted up into an easy smile, then he placed one last hard kiss on my pouty lips. 'It will always be me.'

The thought of the ring of keys he handed me flitted into my mind.

If I was being honest, they'd never *left* my mind. Ever since he first showed them to me, they had played on a constant loop, my imagination running wild with the possibility of what they could uncover. What secrets they were hiding.

Baron hadn't said anything else about them. He'd left them on the bedside table in our bedroom, and neither of us had touched them since. My eyes had gravitated in their direction a couple of times, but only when he wasn't looking or when I was alone.

'I'm going to miss you,' I told him truthfully. 'I love you.'

'And I you,' he replied, before he placed one last kiss on my lips.

Baron walked out of our room, and I waited ten minutes to listen to the sounds of him leaving the mansion. The tyres on the gravel driveway came, and I knew that he had left. My heart raced, and my nerves sung in my veins, pushing me to find out what he was hiding from me.

'Mrs Henrick,' a voice called out from the end of the corridor, causing me to pause on the spot. Baron had left on business three days ago, and I was still yet to find a way into the forbidden wing without being waylaid.

It wasn't the first time I'd been caught, but it was the first time I'd been caught by the head of the household. Mrs Peters and her stern face hadn't eased any in the brief time I'd known her.

Ever since I arrived here on Baron's arm, as his new bride, the old woman barely tolerated me. We hadn't met before I moved in here, although I'd spoken to her on the phone once when Baron was occupied, and I thought we were going to get along better after I'd married her master and became her boss—but clearly, I was delusional. The woman had disliked me on sight, and that dislike had only grown the longer we lived under the same roof.

'Oh, hello there, Mrs Peters,' I replied, keeping my tone bright and cheery. My smile was wide and welcoming, even if she didn't reciprocate. 'How can I help you?'

'It looks to me like *you're* the one who needs helping, dear.' Her smile was false, brittle, and it set my teeth on edge. 'Didn't Master Henrick tell you to keep away from the West Wing?'

'Yes,' I said through gritted teeth. 'How very Beauty and the Beast of him.'

I laughed, the sound fake even to my own ears, and Mrs Peters didn't join in. She merely looked at me, unimpressed, and saw through my innocence.

Of course, I wanted to enter the West Wing. I felt certain that Baron could've given that warning to anybody, and they would've instantly wanted to dart to the forbidden area.

There was a reason the saying *curiosity killed the cat* existed. A reason why it was never a good idea to tell children *not* to do something, because you could guarantee that telling them not to would ensure they did it with bells on.

'He doesn't like it when people disobey him.'

'I'm sure he doesn't,' I said, my tone dry. 'I was trying to find the library and got lost on the way. This house is mighty large for a girl like me.'

Her eyes narrowed. She didn't believe a word out of my mouth. But at the end of the day, she was an employee of my husband—and me—so there was only so much she could do to stop me.

It tickled me though that I'd compared Baron to the Beast, and then inadvertently made myself out to be Belle. Mrs Peters was a poor version for the teapot, though. There was nothing kind about her; nothing nurturing or caring.

'Let me show you the way,' she said, putting down the laundry basket in her arms outside a door on her right. 'Come on now, girl.'

My insides bristled at her disrespectful tone, and the way she called me *girl*. The moment Baron returned from his business trip, I needed to have a word with him. Tell him that woman wasn't welcome in our home anymore. Not if he wanted to keep me here.

Mrs Peters turned around, but not before cupping her hand to me and ushering me forwards to where she was standing. I rolled my eyes once her back was to me. It was a childish move, and probably would've proved everything she thought about me if she saw it —but that was why I waited until she turned around. I wasn't that dim.

My feet trudged behind her, unwilling, but aware that she reported back to my husband. He said he'd know if I entered the forbidden area. The hallway that beckoned me with its sweet song. Maybe he'd sent Mrs Peters to spy on me while he was away and that was how she'd come to find me there, on the very precipice of knowledge.

Or maybe she was just an intrusive, old so-and-so who couldn't keep their big, spider-veined nose out of my business.

'Dinner tonight will be served in the dining room,' she informed me, stopping up ahead to open the large wooden door of the entrance to the library. 'At seven p.m. sharp.'

'Thank you.' I stepped around her to enter the library. 'But I won't be needing dinner in the dining room to eat alone. Send my meal up to my suite.'

The smell of old books entered my nose, my mind wandering away from me, as the old bat behind me responded to my request —or demand—of eating dinner in my room.

Whether she liked it or not, I was now in charge of the household while Baron was away, and I wasn't going to be told by her what I could or couldn't do in my own home.

'As you wish, Mrs Henrick.' She lowered her head and swept away from the doorway, leaving me in silence.

The books felt cool to the touch, as I grazed my fingertips along their spines, taking in the titles on the old tomes, wondering who had placed them here.

Baron didn't strike me as a man who enjoyed reading old encyclopaedias or books about plants.

The room itself was spacious and sparsely furnished. Except for a table in the corner with an armchair and a reading lamp beside it, there wasn't really anything else in the room besides shelves and shelves of books. Both old and new.

I walked over to the table and placed the ring of keys down. The weight of them—both physically and spiritually—lifted when I did so.

Most of the books on the higher shelves were collecting dust and the bottom ones were only barely dust-free. I wondered who the room was originally decked out for. Which wife benefitted from the library before I came along.

Up ahead, there was a ladder resting up against the shelving, like those I'd seen in old-timey films, and I went up to it. The wood was rough under my palms, coarse, and I needed to be careful that I didn't get a splinter.

I'd never had a head for heights, and even being atop the ladder was causing my vertigo to kick in. I had every intention of making my way back down, already ready to welcome the solid oak flooring under my feet. But something stopped me.

I wasn't sure what.

Maybe a change in the air. A chill that travelled down my spine, uncalled for, but there, nonetheless.

The books on the top shelf weren't as dusty as the rest of their friends.

No.

They seemed recently disturbed. That would explain the ladder's position. The only explanation I could come up with was that Baron was the last person in here, up the ladder, and touching the books before me.

My fingertips traced the embossed lettering on the spines of the hardbacks, and I shivered. The titles weren't like any I was expecting. Not that I'd been expecting any in particular. Before that moment, I didn't even know that Baron had a fondness for books. The only time I saw him read was if he picked up The *Beurre Banner* and had a nose-through to see if we were mentioned.

The author of one of the books caught my attention.

Marquis de Sade.

The little I knew of him wasn't good and was enough to give me pause. He was a French philosopher, way back in the 1700s, who had a penchant for libertinism. The word sadist was derived from his fiction—books that included plenty of abuse of minors and other awful, unlawful acts.

Some titles were in French, and I had no idea what they were, but if they were up here sharing a shelf with the Marquis himself, then they were bound to be of a similar flavour.

I spotted the copy of *Story of O* that Baron had lent me, and beside it was a copy of the original French version.

A large thud came from somewhere in the house, startling me, and I had to grab onto the ladder quickly before I fell to the ground.

My heart rate was soaring. If my life had a score, then finding those books and my intrigue at what was inside the covers would have *In the Hall of the Mountain King* playing.

Mere minutes must have passed, but to me, it felt like a lifetime. Like so much had taken place within that short timeframe—something that had once again unlocked that yearning inside of me to find out what Baron was hiding.

What he wanted me so desperately to stay away from.

The next day, I would try again.

I had two more days until Baron returned from his trip, which gave me at least four or more tries at getting into the door unseen by any member of staff.

Maybe I needed to think of a distraction for them. Especially for that nosey witch, Mrs Peters.

I jumped to the floor, an extra spring in my step, my head feeling clearer than it had in days.

Yearn

BARON

Leaving her was one of the hardest things I'd ever done.

But it had to happen.

She needed to seek out that room on her own, without any nudging from me. Even if I nudged her by giving her the ring of keys in the first place. She wasn't the first I'd handed the keys to, but my god, I hoped she'd be the last. My princess had shown so much promise in the past three months, and I wanted to continue moulding her into the best wife for me.

Usually, I handed the keys over, and I wanted my wife to obey. To listen to me. To not open the door. But for *her*, everything was different.

The connection we'd formed. It was unlike any other I'd had. The other wives paled in comparison to my darling rosebud. My princess.

'I found her near the West Wing again, Sir,' Mrs Peters relayed through the line. Before I left, I asked her to keep an eye on my new bride. Watch her at all times—never giving her a moment to breathe alone.

After the first time, Mrs Peters called me. And has been calling me every time since. One day, it was the cleaners who found her. Next, it was the cook. And then now, Mrs Peters herself.

'What was she doing?' I asked, on the edge of my seat. Wanting to hear the words. Wanting to know that she was standing on the precipice.

'Lingering outside the hallway, Sir. I moved her on. I showed her to the library like you told me to.' I nodded, even though she couldn't see me through the phone.

'You've done a marvellous job as always, Mrs Peters. There will be a raise in your future.'

'Th-thank you,' she stuttered, quickly recovering. 'Just doing my job, Master.'

'Well, you've done it splendidly. Tomorrow, I'd like you to let her wander into the West Wing. Don't interrupt her. Let every member of staff know that she is to be left alone.'

'If you're sure,' she said, and I could hear the trepidation in her tone, could sense that she didn't understand my motives.

Mrs Peters knew the door was important to me. Knew that I would never let anybody enter it. But she didn't know why she wasn't allowed. And she certainly didn't know what the door was hiding.

It was my secret. And mine alone.

Until my bride discovered it, of course.

'I'm positive. That will be all.' I hung up on my housekeeper and paced the living area of the apartment I was staying in.

The business trip was a lie fabricated to give me an excuse to leave Henrick mansion. I didn't need an explanation to leave home, but we'd only been home from our honeymoon for two weeks, and I didn't want the staff gossiping about another failed marriage before it had even truly begun.

My phone still in my hand, I pulled it up and requested a video call.

She picked up within seconds. Had she been staring at her phone, just waiting for me to call?

It was our nightly routine, and I knew she looked forward to seeing my face. Hearing my voice.

The same way I looked forward to watching her blush creep up her neck, and the way her eyes widened when I smiled.

Her face came into view, and my nerves settled. She wasn't beautiful in the typical way. I saw what they said about her in the articles. The vicious comments they made on her appearance. Her lack of spirit. Good thing I ignored the tabloids like the plague.

'Hello, princess,' I drawled, watching the flush on her cheeks deepen with every second. 'Are you okay?'

She nodded, breathless, and bit her lip.

'I'm good, thank you. How are you? How's the trip?'

She was so eager to please. So eager to say the right thing and make me happy. It was one of the many things I loved about her. From the start, I knew she had the perfect hint of submission within her and the...

All in good time.

I couldn't let my mind run away just yet.

Certain events needed to take place before I could congratulate myself on finding the perfect mate for me.

'The trip's boring without you. I miss you so much. I wish I never had to leave.'

She smiled, soft and loving. I wanted to reach through the screen and touch her pink lips, trail my fingertips across her bare shoulders and into the hem of her sheer white nightgown.

'I miss you too,' she whispered. 'I can't wait to see you.'

Little did she know, she'd be seeing me the very next day if all went to plan. After my call with Mrs Peters, I knew she would try the door again tomorrow. And that nobody would stop her.

'It won't be long, sweetheart.'

'I love you,' she said, her eyes wide and pure. Her love for me shone through the phone and I relished it.

'I love you, too,' I replied. 'Speak later, okay?'

She nodded, and I hung up the call, my phone screen changing back to my screensaver. It was a picture of her that was taken on our wedding day. She looked stunning. All mine. The dress was beautiful, classy, and demure. White. Lace. With full length sleeves and a high neckline. The embodiment of the perfect, pure, virginal bride.

The thought of her finding the room fuelled me. Filled me with a fire unlike any wife that came before. They were all preparation for my true future.

But how was I to pass the time before I could leave to go home?

The bathroom called to me, and I made my way inside, ready to wash the day away. My new bride was so close to falling over the edge. So close to becoming everything I hoped she would be, and more. Born anew. Ready to take the reins in her own life.

The far end wall of the bathroom was occupied by my walk-in shower that had multiple heads, my favourite being a rainfall showerhead in the centre, and even just entering the room soothed my soul.

I'd worked hard for what I had.

Sort of.

When my parents died, I inherited a fortune. An empire, really. But in the seventeen years since I took charge of Henrick Hotels, the company had grown exponentially.

I stripped out of my suit, removing each item and folding them carefully, before placing them on the floor, taking care. Even having been born into wealth, I still appreciated everything I had. I'd seen enough shit in life to know that money could be lost in a matter of moments. Especially if the wrong person decided to out your *extra-curricular activities*.

I turned the shower on, and watched, mesmerised, as the droplets fell from the ceiling to the floor in a sheet, slowly heating up to the perfect temperature for me.

Once heated the way I liked, I stepped under the showerhead, ready to relax and have a moment to myself.

One where my mind could run rampant.

Could run rampant to a place where my wife was trussed up, ready and willing for me, allowing me to do whatever I wanted with her. Or, better yet, to a place where my wife was my equal.

The thought of her body, her eagerness to please, her obedience, was enough to send me—and my cock—into overdrive.

I placed my palm over my hardness, needing to relieve the tension the thought of her naked beneath me had created.

Before I had left for the trip, she had let me know with her mouth how much she would miss me. As I moved my hand up and down my shaft, slowly, I imagined it was her mouth. My mind flooded with the image of her from the night I left. Her plump lips gliding over my cock, her saliva glistening as she sucked the head before deep throating me with wide eyes.

My princess was perfect and had picked up on a lot of things quickly. I prided myself on knowing people. Knowing what was in their hearts and in their minds, no matter how they were presenting themselves. It was a skill you needed in order to run a multi-million-pound business.

And I sensed she would do anything to please me. *Anything.*

My arousal climbed at that thought. A willing subject who

would do anything for you was a dangerous thing. A heady mix. Easy to take for granted.

A grunt left my lips as I pressed my forehead against the dark, cold tiles, the images of my wife blinding my mind's eye as they flashed past at breakneck speed.

The way her eyes widened and her cheeks flushed on our first date when I took her to the erotic art exhibition. The way she responded to the forbidden images, and how her chest went red, her thoughts displayed on her face for all to see.

The moment her eyes glinted with pleasure when she agreed to wear my mark, branded into her skin, proud to be asked.

The way her face flooded with joy when I asked her to be my wife. To marry me, and live with me, *be mine*, forever.

She was a virgin when we met. Pure. Untouched. And forever, I would replay in my head the way it felt to break through the thin barrier within her. To see her blood coating my dick as I slowly thrusted inside her, opening her up for me. Only me.

My grip tightened to the point where it felt like I was choking my dick, and I moved my hand faster, the sensation slowly building. I closed my eyes, the thought of my wife's pale, smooth body lit up by the moonlight invading the senses.

Of all my wives, she was the one that turned me on the most. The one that I was in a constant state of lust around, even when she was doing something mundane like eating her cereal or brushing her long, dark hair.

Fuck.

I wanted her. Again.

I needed her to enter the room tomorrow. I couldn't wait any longer for it. She had to. There was no way we could move forward until she disobeyed me in that way. Although, if she didn't enter the room, then she was the most obedient, and that deserved a reward, too.

Once more, the picture of her lips wrapped around my cock entered my mind, wishing she was kneeling in front of me so I could fist my hand in her brown hair and throat fuck her until I came so far down her throat that she retched. The imagined sound of her whimpers and small gags pushed me over the edge.

My hand slammed against the cool tile, my face frowning with concentration as my cum exploded from me in a steady stream, splashing onto the bathroom wall. My mind pretended that the target was my princess's face. I loved the way she looked with a cum-covered face. Her eyelashes stuck together, her complexion a dark red, her lust shining out through her baby blues.

The moment of bliss didn't last long enough. If anything, it just prolonged my torment. She was at home, and I wasn't there, all because I wanted her to find my secret. I breathed out through my teeth, my whole body still on edge.

Washing my body, I allowed my mind to drift back to home. To where my heart was.

I just had to hope that everything was going to go to plan, and that I would go home to the best outcome. That I would go home to the dream life I'd envisioned ever since I concocted everything in my mind over fifteen years ago.

My dream was just beginning.

And I couldn't fucking wait.

Truth

ALL NIGHT I TOSSED AND TURNED, TRYING TO COME UP with a suitable solution to get Mrs Peters off my back and into the path of some poor, unsuspecting maid.

After I'd left the library, I snuck back to the West Wing undetected. For the most part, I was sorely disappointed. Nothing looked forbidden or any different from the East Wing, and it dawned on me that maybe Baron was playing a mean trick on me.

But then I saw it. At the far end of the house.

A door. At the very end of a corridor. One that looked... *different* from the others. It was a large black wooden door, with a brass antique lock and handle. The paint was starting to peel, and the moment my eyes locked on the door, a faint smell wafted into my nostrils. It wasn't a pleasant smell, but it was too faint to make out what it was. As of late, all smells were a nuisance to me, so it could be all in my head, anyway.

The door beckoned me. But in my hurry, I'd left the ring of keys in the library, and was unable to open it. I tried the handle, but it was locked. Plus, the moment I touched it, an electric shock travelled through my fingertips in warning.

I'd left in a hurry, with every intention of returning after dinner in my suite, but then I got distracted by Baron's evening call.

But with the morning came my resolution. No matter what happened, I would find a way to enter the West Wing once more and discover what was hidden.

I needed to get back to the door. The allure, the pull I felt, wasn't natural. That was the only way I could explain it. Justify it in my mind.

My gut churned. The want, the need, racing through my mind. Spiralling in front of me, like a rabbit hole, with no end. No bottom. And no white rabbit.

I'd always liked the story of *Alice in Wonderland*. It was a comfort thing.

When you read something at a young age and then it stayed with you through adolescence and into adulthood, it left a brand on your heart. One that nobody could scrub away.

They said Lewis Carroll was mad. Or they said something else that I wouldn't repeat. Way to go, humans, accusing a man long dead of something heinous all because he befriended a little girl named Alice.

People should be ashamed of themselves.

But then again, if it were true, it wasn't them who should be ashamed.

I shook my head, hoping it would shake away the tangent my mind had taken me on. No distractions would help me. Unless they were ones that told me how to get into the part of the house forbidden to me.

But wait.

Baron may own the house, and he may be the master, but I was his wife. And I had a say, too. Or at least I could see how far they'd let me go before they stamped their feet and stopped me.

The closet beckoned, and I went and found an outfit to throw on. My entire wardrobe was new. My old clothes were thrown out and burned for all I cared. They were of little value to me now that I was expected to attend balls and galas. I highly doubted my high street charity shop finds were going to wow anybody of Baron's calibre.

Putting on a day dress, I left the wood panelled closet and made my way out of my bedroom, making sure to grab the keys before I went from the side table I'd dropped them on when I returned after the library visit.

The heft of them wanted to weigh me down, both in strength and spirit.

Silent steps got me to the hallway, and in no time at all, I was standing in the same spot as the day before—and the day before that.

I was surprised that I wasn't accosted on my way there by a member of staff, but the house seemed silent. Nobody around whatsoever. I tried not to let my paranoia get the best of me, but it was definitely suspicious.

The circle of keys rattled in my shaking hand as I moved them away from the lock, then I pulled the door open, wondering what I would see on the other side.

There was a reason Baron didn't want me in here. There was a reason he'd made it a condition of the keys. Was it a test? A trick?

I wasn't sure.

But how was I to know just what was in store?

The staff had warned me away—or tried to, at least. But no matter what task they gave me, no matter what words they used to entice me elsewhere, my heart was still being tugged in the direction of the door.

The hallway that led to the door was plain. Nondescript. Cream walls, brown carpet.

Nothing to imply that there was anything unusual or suspicious about it.

Nothing except the large, wooden, old door at the far end.

But the hallway on the other side of the door told a completely different story.

I could barely see in front of my face, the darkness so never ending, so I searched for a light. My phone torch lit up the area, and I located a pull cord.

One janky old lightbulb burst on, pulsing to life. It hung in the very centre of the hallway—equidistant from the door I was standing at and the other door I could now see at the far end.

The brown damask wallpaper was peeling from both edges, and I wondered if it had always been a dark brown, or if it had turned that shade over the years. The dank and the dirt growing like a disease.

A chill travelled from the tips of my toes to the very top of my head. The very air I breathed had turned. Become something sour. Acrid. I couldn't put my finger on what the smell was, but I knew it wasn't right.

My hand covered my nose, as my stomach swirled, wanting to hurl the contents of my lunch onto the rust-coloured wooden floor. Was the floor naturally coloured that way, or was it from stains?

I paused before heading down the corridor.

A quick glance over my shoulder told me nobody was watching me. Mrs Peters hadn't appeared out of the blue to scold me, and none of the cleaning staff were there waiting for me to follow them on some pointless errand.

It was just me. Alone.

On the edge of something big.

My wedding band and my obscenely large engagement ring caught the light, sparkling away, innocent and clear.

By entering the passage, I would be going against my husband's wishes. His demands.

He made it clear that I wasn't to enter. That I would disappoint him if I did.

Baron didn't like being disobeyed.

The bruises on my hips could attest to that.

A faint scream carried along the hall and into my ears. The words unintelligible.

Was there somebody down there?

Of course not. That'd be ridiculous. I knew everybody who lived in the home. Baron had introduced me to them—each and every one was there to welcome us home from our honeymoon on our first night back.

They shook my hand and greeted me with wide eyes and even wider smiles.

Stop dallying. Get on with it.

One foot stepped forward, and then the other foot followed, until I'd stepped one foot slowly in front of the other all the way down the corridor. It may have only been a few dozen steps, but it felt like I'd walked for miles.

Maybe I had.

Not literally, of course. But spiritually.

With each step, the smell I'd caught a whiff of from the outside worsened. Like something rotten.

The door handle was cool to the touch, and there wasn't a lock. I pushed down the handle and pressed my way into the room. Slow. Tentative.

The darkness overwhelmed me. I could barely see in front of my face, but there was another sense that was working just fine.

My stomach turned.

I gagged—a nuisance that had arrived a week prior—and swallowed down the acidic watery saliva that filled my mouth in a quick rush.

The putrid smell was stronger here, and I had to stop myself from letting loose the vomit rising within me. The smell was familiar, even if I'd never smelled it that concentrated before.

It was the smell of waste. Human decay. Decomposing flesh.

Pushing through the smell, I stepped even further into the room, scanning the walls for a light switch of some kind. A pull cord. A lantern. *Anything.* Any light that would help me see through the pitch-black nothingness that stood before me.

'Help!' a muffled voice called.

The noise startled me, and in my shock, I dropped the ring of keys. It landed with a splash, a sound that turned my stomach even more, but I couldn't tell what liquid the keys had landed in. The room was so dark, I could barely see in front of my face.

What kind of place had I stumbled across? How could such a room exist in my own home without my knowing?

My fingers trailed across the stone wall, and I held my breath. I couldn't even tell how big the new room I was standing in was. The voice that called to me came from somewhere nearby, that much I was certain of.

'Over here!' the muffled voice yelled to me, and I tried to follow the sound, but I couldn't see anything.

'Where are you?' I called out, trying to keep my voice low enough that if anybody was in the West Wing, they wouldn't hear me. But then again, I doubted anybody could hear in here.

It was probably soundproofed at the least.

As fast as I could, I took a deep breath in through my mouth, not wanting the smell to reach me again.

'The floor.'

'Is there a light?' I asked, hoping that there was.

'The way you came. You must've missed the candle holder.'

The candle holder?

I retraced my steps, back to the door I'd entered through, hoping that nobody would be there waiting for me.

It was still empty. Cold. Dark. A candle holder sat on a side table I'd missed before in my eagerness to reach the door at the end. It was as if I'd stepped into an old-fashioned tale, with a candlestick holder and an antique key that led to Hell.

There was a lighter beside it, taking away from that old-fashioned feeling, and I lit the candle, hoping it would be enough to guide my way. Or at least help me enough to find the light switch.

The room hadn't changed when I stepped back inside. But I had.

My fear of discovery was higher now. Now I knew just what was at stake. What Baron was hiding from me—from everybody. No sane man kept a woman prisoner in a locked room in a forbidden area of their home.

I cast my mind back to the library. To the books on the shelves. Those written by Marquis de Sade and the others like him. A quick online search had told me more about them and their ideas.

My collarbone burned. The way it did when a strong wave of emotion towards Baron overtook me. Sometimes it was love. Sometimes anger. But never hate.

Even at that moment, on the edge of something terrible, I couldn't hate him. Not really. Because he was the man who saved me.

'Hello?' the voice called.

My feet moved back inside, the candle showing me more of what the dark was hiding. And the dark could hide a lot.

The dark could hide the very essence of who you were.

It was the light people feared the most.

'I'm coming,' I said, my voice low.

The flickering flame of the candle reflected off the metal bars placed in the centre of the room. I looked down to see the cage. And the girl within it. The one who had called for help.

She looked dreadful.

I crouched down so that the two of us were at eye level. I couldn't make out many of her features, even in the candlelight, but I could tell she was around my age.

She had the look of youth about her.

The look of somebody who shouldn't have seen the things she had. Shouldn't have experienced the true horrors of the world we all occupy.

'Are you okay?'

'No,' she whispered, tears falling down her cheeks in thick streams. 'I just want to go home.'

'How long have you been here?'

'I don't know. A year or so?' She gripped the bars. Her thin, pointy fingers looked unnatural, and her face was nothing more than skin covering bone. 'He won't ever tell me.'

'Who won't?' I asked. I knew the answer, though. But I wanted to hear it from her. From the girl kept captive in a cage. Only she could confirm my worst suspicions.

'Master,' she said, her voice a low hush. 'He won't let us call him anything else.'

'Us?' I looked around, squinting my eyes, looking for other cages. For other people. But I couldn't see anything.

'Sorry.' Her eyes were glassy, and she looked past me, to a scene I couldn't see. 'It's just me now. No more us.'

I nodded, my movements slow so as not to startle her.

'But there was somebody else here with you?'

'Yes. But she's gone now.' Her head moved in the direction of the furthest corner. I wasn't sure what possessed me, but I needed to look in that corner. Like a compulsion of sorts. Now that I'd seen inside the room, I had to witness all aspects of the depravity to truly believe what I was seeing. Because who would believe me? If I fled the mansion and went to the police—the press—who would believe me? Baron's little, young, poor, naïve wife. That was how those people viewed me. As nothing more than a status symbol. A trophy wife for an older man to have on his arm while attending galas and premieres and the sorts.

The sight that waited for me in the corner was one I shouldn't have sought out.

The body of a woman lay there. Discarded. Uncared for. A rag doll in death, her rotting corpse excreting odours and liquids I never thought I would come across in my lifetime.

If I wanted to work in a morgue, I would have.

I stumbled away from the corner. Away from the dark-haired woman who was so neglected in death that she was thrown into a darkened corner of a hidden dungeon.

The next time I gagged, I couldn't hold back the vomit that rushed up my throat. It tasted acidic. Burnt. Vile.

'Who was she?' I gasped, hobbling back to the girl in the cage. Crouching down again, I put my hands over hers on the bars, placing the candlestick holder down on the floor beside me.

She was like ice.

Frozen.

'Emmy.' Her bottom lip wobbled, the tears still making their way down her face. 'That's what I called her.'

'Emmy,' I whispered to myself. Rolling the name off my tongue. Trying to place it. My mind swirled.

I was back in my bedroom with my sister. Back before I'd even gone on my first date with Baron. Our conversation filtered into my mind.

. . .

'And the fifth?'

'Emmeline Sanders. Nobody knows what happened to her.'

'What do you mean, nobody knows?'

'She's presumed dead... she went missing around the same time that Baron moved into what is now called Henrick mansion.'

Could Emmeline, missing wife number five, be the Emmy the girl spoke of?

'When did she die?' I whispered. The body must have been there a while if the smell was anything to go by, but the fact she wasn't skin and bone yet told me it was relatively recent.

'A couple of weeks ago,' she replied, her tone a low hush.

My stomach flipped at her sentence. The woman, *Emmy*, had died around the same time I moved into the mansion. Was that a coincidence?

It wasn't like me to ask myself such a stupid question. As a rule, I didn't believe in coincidences. But then again, there was always an exception to a rule, right?

'Does Baron know?'

She nodded, her dark, stringy hair falling in front of her face, reminding me of a horror movie spectre.

'He was the one who placed her body in the corner.'

I gagged. Vomit threatened to rush up my throat and coat the blood-stained stones.

'I've got to go.' The words rushed out, and I knew I needed to leave as fast as possible. There was no way of knowing how long I'd been in the chamber, but I could guarantee that Mrs Peters would be looking for me sometime soon. Plus, Baron would be calling me at some point in the evening to talk, and I needed to have myself together for that. Needed to be cool, calm, and collected, even though I felt like my insides were melting.

'Y-you can't leave me here,' she stuttered urgently, shaking her head, horror distorting her features. 'He'll kill me.'

Her bony hand grabbed my arm through the bars, and I flinched at her touch.

'I'll come back,' I said, brushing my hand away from hers. I didn't want to analyse my gut reaction of repulsion. Was I repulsed by her? Or by the situation? Maybe because of my own feelings?

My vision went black around the edges, slowly growing inward as the pain pulsing through my skull increased. I just knew that in ten minutes' time I would be in excruciating agony because of it, and I didn't want to crash here. Not in the dirty space, breathing in the foul-smelling air that clung to every surface.

'You promise?' Her hand tried to grab mine again, but I shuffled my feet backwards so she couldn't touch me.

'I promise. I will return.'

I stood up, brushing my hands down my thighs and knees to rid my clothes of the filth I felt certain had seeped into every crease. A layer of grime covered my skin, and I needed to get away from here and into the shower so I could scrub every inch of my body until it was red raw.

Bending down to grab the candle holder, I took one last look into the girl's eyes and nodded at her. Sealing my promise to return.

There was no way I could live in the house and not. Having the knowledge of the room, and not acting on it, or doing anything about it, didn't sit right with me. I had no idea how I would get around Baron, but the man was a busy and successful businessman. There would be more trips. More time away from me.

Before I could flee, I needed to locate the ring of keys I'd dropped when I entered. I knew they were somewhere near the door and had landed in a puddle of something I probably didn't want to see, but I couldn't leave here without them.

Baron would want them back.

Would demand me to hand them over.

And I couldn't disappoint him.

I found them a couple hundred yards into the room, lying in a puddle of what looked like blood.

I grabbed them. Then fled.

As quick as my feet would carry me.

Home

The gravel of the driveway could be heard throughout the front of the house. The stones being squashed under the tyres, the drag of the pebbles, filled my veins with dread.

Those noises could only mean one thing: Baron was home from his business trip. *Early.*

When I spoke to him on the phone the night before, he hadn't mentioned that he was cutting his trip short. He was meant to be gone for another two days, at least.

I rushed around my room, hastily tidying up the whirlwind of clothing that had occurred ever since I found *that.* Since I'd entered the chamber, I'd packed and unpacked my clothing multiple times, unsure whether I should stay. Whether I even *wanted* to stay.

I loved Baron. The way he looked at me. Worshipped me. How strong he was in private and how powerful he was in public. The way he rose above the whispers, ignoring those who wanted to talk poorly about him because of his past.

And, ultimately, the way he'd saved me. Saved me from my dull life with no prospects. With no chance of anything better coming my way.

He saved me from the whole eat, sleep, work, die routine.

The front door opened, and heavy footsteps could be heard from the hall just as I placed my last dress back in the closet. I breathed a sigh of relief that he wouldn't know my turmoil. Wouldn't know that I'd been planning an escape from him. Because I wasn't sure how he would react if he knew.

After all, the man was keeping a girl trapped in a secret chamber in his home.

I also wasn't sure if I truly wanted to escape him. At first, when I fled the chamber, my mind was focused on getting out. Anyway. Anyhow.

There was no prenup agreement, but we hadn't been married for long. It would be an easy annulment for a man like Baron.

But what if he didn't agree?

What if I ended up like those who came before me? Drowned in a swimming pool, or worse, locked up in a hospital after suffering from a mental break. And that was the story the press told. I had a feeling the truth was even more grim.

'Honey,' he called, his steps getting closer. Each one sounding like a gong that counted down the moments until my time was up. 'I'm home!'

'In here!' I called back, even though he knew where to find me.

The door to my room swung open to reveal him standing on the other side, a small smirk spreading across his face. Like he knew a secret. Like he knew what I'd done.

I swallowed.

'How was your trip, darling?' I rushed to him and took his coat from his outstretched hand.

'Filled with business,' he replied, the smirk still firm on his face.

His amusement was growing. 'Honestly, it was dull. I wish I'd stayed home with you.'

'It was pretty dull around here, too,' I said with a laugh. The sound of it was false to my ears, and if I could hear the fakeness, then no doubt Baron could as well.

'And what did you get up to while I was gone?'

I walked into his closet and hung up his coat on the rack. The task was a quick one, but I dragged it out. Not wanting to go back into the open and stare into his assessing eyes.

'Oh...' I trailed off, glad I wasn't facing him. 'Nothing much. Mrs Peters showed me the library.'

'And what did you think?'

'I wondered what wife it was for.' I closed my mouth in horror at what I'd let slip out. Dread at the reaction I would get. 'I didn't mean that.'

To my relief, Baron chuckled.

'I think you meant every word.' His voice was at my back. I hadn't heard him come closer, as his footsteps usually gave away his position, but clearly, he'd learned how to walk stealthily while away on business. I wondered what else he had learned.

Lips grazed my neck, the softness of them making me weak. Baron knew the spots that turned me into a puddle. Melted me to the core.

'Let's go to bed,' he murmured on my skin, heat rising with every kiss placed on my neck and my shoulder. 'Greet me as a wife should.'

My laugh was awkward. Uncertain.

'It's a little early for that, isn't it?' I asked, taking a peek down at the large—and expensive—watch on my left wrist. It was another one of Baron's wedding presents to me. They seemed to be never ending and slightly overwhelming. 'Aren't you tired from travelling? Hungry? If you'd like, I can call the kitchens and request some dinner.'

He grabbed my shoulders and turned me to face him. The wolfish grin on his face told me he saw through my machinations. Could sense that I was stalling, biding my time.

'The only dinner I require...'—he leaned forward, clouding my space—'is you.'

Baron's cologne overtook my senses, and I breathed in his bergamot and vanilla scent. Alongside his words, it worked as an aphrodisiac, making me want the same thing he did.

I hoped that maybe if I obeyed and gave him what he wanted, then he wouldn't ask about the bundle of keys. About the forbidden wing and the door not to be touched.

Or, if he did ask about the keys, then he would be in a sated enough mood to not be angry with me. Because deep down, my heart knew that he was going to be angry with me.

His temper was like a flickering flame. Something that burned strong, and then waned with the next gust of wind, until the oxygen once again breathed new life into it. Ebbing and flowing.

No end in sight.

I was lucky that his anger and frustration had never been turned on me.

'I guess I could oblige,' I whispered, licking my bottom lip the way I knew he liked. His reaction didn't disappoint. His pupils dilated as his nostrils flared.

On silent toes, I swayed my way over to the bed, exaggerating the movement of my hips, knowing he was watching me. Transfixed. Unable to tear his gaze away.

'Come get me,' I called over my shoulder. I hoped my eyes conveyed the right amount of submission and need. Two of his favourite things.

He stalked behind me, but I didn't look back. Didn't look

behind me to see his darkened gaze and upturned lips. I didn't need to. It was a face I knew well, even having just been married for two weeks.

I got to the bed and climbed up, positioning myself in the centre, lying face down on my stomach. Baron liked it best when I faced down.

'Easier to tie your wrists, my dear.'

Not that he tied my wrists every time we had sex. That was just for the weekends.

And apparently, I was also allowing it on days when he returned home from important business trips, and I'd lied through my teeth mere minutes before and was trying to distract the heck out of him.

Normal circumstances.

Or at least they were becoming normal in our marriage.

'Raise your ass in the air for me, baby,' he whispered in my ear as his weight pressed down on the mattress. My stomach fluttered, and I obeyed.

There was something thrilling about handing over my trust to him. Something dark and forbidden, in a way I'd never experienced. Invigorating. Born anew.

Baron gripped my hands together behind my back and wrapped his tie around them tightly, but not too tight that I couldn't escape if I wanted to.

That was part of the fun.

The trust was there, and he knew I wasn't going to move, regardless of how tight my hands were fastened.

It was merely a part of the charade. The act. The play we were performing in together.

And at that moment, the act had never been more real. And more serious.

I knew about the girl. Knew about the secret room. And I

knew Baron was into things more messed up than wanting to tie up his new bride and love her senselessly.

'I want you to stay in that position while I fuck your perfect pussy,' he said in a low tone, brushing his fingers down my spine. He lifted the skirt of my dress above my hips, keeping it there with his left fist, as his right hand unzipped his trousers.

I knew this was going to be fast. With Baron having been gone for a few days, we were both craving one another in the most primal of ways.

My face pressed up against the sheets meant that I couldn't see what Baron was doing. I had to rely on my other senses, and that always upped the ante for me. Made me more excited.

He hadn't even touched me with his cock yet and my clit was throbbing in time with my pulse. Even though I was using sex as a distraction, I still wanted him. Still wanted his big dick stuffed inside me until I saw stars.

'You ready for me, baby?'

'Yesss,' I hissed, as he entered me, not even waiting for the answer to his question.

I felt violated. Deliciously so. And I was already close to coming, and he'd barely started thrusting yet.

His hands gripped my hips, his fingers digging in hard enough to leave bruises. Or maybe they were only making the bruises already there stay around for longer.

Baron began to move in earnest, ploughing inside of me, and I thrusted backwards with each pound of his hips to meet him. There was something so delectable about the way our bodies met, the sound they made as they connected, and I could feel my wetness soaking him, dripping down my thighs and onto the mattress.

'I've missed you so much,' Baron said between thrusts. He leaned forward, and placed kisses on my back, his hands still planted on my hips, and I shivered when the air hit the saliva his kisses left on my skin.

'I've missed you too,' I said, breathless.

Too quick, I felt my walls clench around him, and I knew I was close to coming. I couldn't help it. The animalistic grunts that were leaving Baron's lips heightened everything.

'I'm going to come,' he said, and I couldn't hold myself back any longer. The thought of his cum inside me, swimming to reach my cervix, had me pulsating around him. Moans left my lips and even after they'd escaped, my mouth stayed open in a soundless cry.

With one last pump, Baron came inside me, whispering curse words into the air.

'Fuck,' I whispered, both because of the feelings that were still sticking to my skin and the fact that I would have to come clean soon.

Baron pulled out of me, and I collapsed onto the bed, lying on my front. My breathing was ragged, and I needed a moment. He came up and lay down beside me, on his back, and our hands found one another on the mattress, entwining.

We lay in silence, the two of us breathing heavily as we came back down to earth. I hoped that my seduction attempt had waylaid him, even for a moment, but I underestimated Baron. Or overestimated my wiles. I didn't want to analyse either.

'Darling,' he said, his tone low, alluring. 'There's somewhere in the house we need to visit.'

'There i-is?' I stuttered, sweat coming to the surface of my skin, seeping into my hairline. 'Where's that, dear?'

His abrupt movement caused me to jolt on the mattress as he turned onto his side to face me. I did the same, following his lead, so the two of us were looking into each other's eyes—unable to hide.

'The West Wing.'

I blinked, schooling my features into something that looked the epitome of cool, calm, and collected. Even if my heart rate was climbing and my skin was heating up.

'The West Wing?' I repeated. 'But I'm not allowed to go there.'

'I know,' he said with a devilish smirk. 'So I'm giving you the chance to.'

Saliva rushed to my mouth, and I swallowed it down, dampening the fear overtaking my body. Because I was scared, no matter how much I'd tried to convince myself otherwise. Baron did scare me. But not in the way he should.

A smarter person would have found that chamber, attempted to free the girl held captive, and then attempted to flee the house. We may not have succeeded, but at least we would have tried.

It said a lot about me that trying to free her from the cage didn't enter my mind. Not as a first or even tenth thought. It shamed me.

'What's made you change your mind?' I asked, the waiver in my tone giving away the cool demeanour I hoped to portray as a lie.

'My love for you,' he said simply, with a shrug of the shoulder that wasn't trapped up against the bed. 'You're my wife now, and I want us to share *everything*.'

The words sounded like a threat. Dark. Deadly. Menacing.

'Everything?'

'Yes. Put on your nightgown, wife.'

'Shouldn't we wait? The house will be asleep now.'

'It's our house and they work for us, remember?' he said, the sternness in his eyes hitting me full force. 'Plus. There's no time like the present.'

'If you insist.'

'I do.'

Slowly, with tentative steps, I made my way to the wardrobe chest of drawers and pulled out my nightgown.

'Oh, and darling?' Baron called, having not moved from his spot on the bed.

'Yes?'

'Don't forget the keys.'

I took a deep breath, closing my eyes against the pain threatening to split my head open. How could I forget the keys? They were seared into my brain, the image of what they unlocked burned into the back of my retinas, promising to stay with me until the end of time.

'I won't,' I called back, then whispered to myself, 'I shan't ever.'

Ultimatum

I followed behind him.

The house was deathly silent, with nobody in any of the corridors. Not a soul in sight.

Usually, the house was filled with people and noise, everybody working hard to prepare for the next day.

Maybe Baron had warned them all away. Told them to stay in their rooms no matter what they heard.

Did they not know the house of horrors in which they lived in? Or did they willingly partake in it, by knowing what took place, but turning a blind eye, anyway?

Baron's footsteps were heavy, filled with purpose.

I was barely breathing in case he turned around and struck me. Not that I expected him to, not that he'd ever raised a hand to me before, but now it felt like everything was out of sorts.

The moment he stopped in front of the door to that darkened hallway and asked me to hand over the key, my fate would be sealed.

Ever since I dropped the key in the pool of blood, I hadn't been able to wash away the remnants. The blood had stained the key so thoroughly that nothing I did saved it. For hours I'd scoured, bleached, scrubbed at the key. A real modern-day Cinderella.

If anything, the stain got worse the more I scrubbed. It got deeper. A darker scarlet than it was to begin with. I began to wonder whether the key was cursed. It looked old enough to have seen more than I could imagine, and the door it belonged to definitely hadn't been a new feature in the house. As if the house was built *around* it.

Baron stopped ahead of me. In front of *the* door. The one that had filled my dreams and called to my soul. Had seduced me to disobey my new husband—my salvation.

He coughed, grabbing my attention away from the black door handle.

'I heard from Mrs Peters that she found you here yesterday.' His eyes became narrow slits, judgemental, perusing me. Was he looking for weakness? Did he expect me to lie?

I knew Mrs Peters was going to pass on what she saw. Would tell him she escorted me away from the forbidden and into the library. Was that why he'd come home early? Because he knew I was close to breaking my resolve?

Seemed a silly reason to cut short a business trip, but Baron acted rashly at times. Since having learned his secret, I wasn't sure whether I knew much about the *real* Baron Henrick at all.

'Yes,' I said, noting the waiver in my voice, knowing he would too. 'Before she showed me the library.'

'Ah, yes.' He nodded his head, his finger aimlessly rubbing his beard. 'And is that where you spent today?'

I paused, sensing the trap. Whatever I did—whatever I said—would be wrong. The key would tell the truth, even if my lips did not.

'No,' I murmured, keeping my gaze on the floor. 'Not today.'

He perused me thoughtfully, his expression giving nothing away.

'Whatever you did, I'm sure you spent your time wisely.'

Man, he infuriated me in the exact same breath that he aroused me. The way he stood, the sheer way his body moved, was filled with a cocksureness that only money could buy.

'Now,' he said, running his hands up and down his thighs, 'hand me the keys.'

Should I stall for time? Should I tell him I left them back in the room?

No, of course not. I wasn't a liar. Plus, the dress I was wearing was little more than a transparent slip with pockets. He could already see the ring of keys there.

Had probably heard the jangle of them when I picked them up before we left our suite.

My fingers shook as I reached into the pocket of my nightgown. I clasped the keys and pulled them out, careful not to look into the very depths of Baron's eyes—his soul.

'Here you g-go,' I stammered, handing them over, still unable to make eye contact. The situation was fraught with nervous energy, the walls seeming to close in and surround us too closely. Pressing in on all sides, as the ceiling lowered until I was as small, and as crouched, as the girl within the cage.

Would Baron give me more insight once he saw the bloodstained key? Would he tell me what she was doing there? Or would he trap me there alongside her and give me my own personal prison?

His fingers grazed my hand as he took the keys, the magnetism that was always present between us still going strong.

I held my breath.

His eyes travelled down to the keys as he inspected each one in turn. He was prolonging my torture. We both knew it.

The key he cared about the most was the large antique one—too different from the others to ever be mistaken—and I wondered how long he could drag it out.

My collarbone ached. His mark on me was as permanent and powerful as ever. After the events of the day, it took on a different meaning. I was his. To obey. To fall in line.

Forever.

One by one, he looked at each key, and I was becoming rather lightheaded. If I held my breath much longer, there wouldn't be anybody to unleash his fury on.

'Ah.' His tone was soft. Low. Barely audible.

Slowly, he removed the key from the ring and set the others aside. He had no use for them. They'd served their purpose.

He held it aloft, gazing at it, his expression neutral.

'Can you tell me what's wrong?' he asked, still staring at the key.

I opened my mouth. Tried to get my vocal cords on board to say something. *Anything.* But they'd seized up. That, or they couldn't find the words to say. Not the right words. Not ones that would help me out of the mess I'd stumbled into willingly.

Nobody had forced me to use the key.

If it was a test, then I failed.

The rusted patch on the key was a sure-fire sign of my guilt.

'Darling,' he bit out, moving his gaze to me. When I didn't look up to meet it, his fingers gripped the bottom of my chin and tilted my head, so we were eye-to-eye. No escape.

His eyes were cold, dark, bottomless pits. Completely altered from any other time I'd gazed into them. Something harsh and hurting, but also, was that relief I saw?

Surely not.

But then I glimpsed it again. A small spark. A twinkle of something more than what he wanted to show me.

Enough to make me doubt everything. His intentions. His ire. All of it.

I stayed still, not moving, barely breathing, unsure how to respond. How does one act in a situation like that?

'Yes,' I whispered. My skin prickled with heat. Our awareness of one another was ever present, biding its time under the surface.

'Did you use this key?' he asked, deathly quiet.

I nodded as my bottom lip wobbled.

I couldn't lie. Not when the evidence was in front of both of our faces.

'With words, princess.'

'Yes,' I responded, shame rising in my cheeks. 'I did.'

'And did you see what you wanted to? Learn anything new?' he growled. 'Was it worth it, to disobey me?'

A tightness came around my wrist. Baron's vice-like grip pinched as he pulled me closer, the key still held aloft in his other hand.

'Please,' he whispered in my ear. 'Do the honours.'

He pushed me back and forced the key into my open palm before manhandling me until I was standing in front of the door.

Baron was pressed up against my back, his breath fanning my neck. Heavy. His hard body was a formidable wall behind me. Solid. Unmoving. No part of him yielded to me; no softening towards me in gesture or tone.

'Open the door, *wife*.'

With shaking hands, much like the one other time I'd opened the door, I inserted the key into the hole. The sound of metal clanking together was all I could focus on. Slow seconds crept past as each tumble of the lock opened.

My hands were still trembling when I turned the handle and pushed open the door into the dark, dingy hallway.

It looked no different to how it was when I fled.

I pulled the cord for the light, and the singular lightbulb hanging in the centre of the corridor flickered on. A slight buzz of electricity filtered through the space, and I stepped over the threshold into the hall.

'Keep going,' Baron whispered. 'I won't bite.'

The words were at odds with the tone.

Time passed slowly, even though I made my way to the other door as fast as I could. Without any nudging from Baron, I opened the second door, once again entering the filthy room.

Baron's hands landed on my waist, using them to guide me to the centre of the room. The darkness made it hard to see anything, but I knew what lay underneath the pitch black in front of my retinas. He tugged at me, and I stumbled.

I twirled one hundred and eighty degrees, so the two of us were facing each other. I tried to hold my nose. Tried to fight off the stench that wanted to reach its way into my very core. The rotting corpse in the corner, and the smell of human waste that lingered around the cage, swirled together to create the foulest odour I'd ever known.

'So you entered my play area,' he stated, all-knowing, his features hard to make out in the lighting. As my eyes adjusted, the more I could see of him. Of the dungeon we were standing in. 'Specifically, when I told you not to.'

I trembled under his touch. A whimper passed through my lips involuntarily, and a chill made its way through my entire body. Every bone feeling the terror of my situation, looking for a way out.

But there was none.

I was trapped. Like the girl in the cage. Like the dead body in the corner, who would never see another day outside of the chamber.

'You have a choice here, darling.' Baron's deep rumble broke the silence. 'One I'll only offer once.'

He reached out and brushed a strand of my limp brown hair behind my ear before placing his hand on my arm. Firm. Solid. His warmth reached me through my thin nightgown, and instantly I broke out in a sweat.

'What is it?' I asked, breathless. My nerves pulsed away under my skin, and it felt as if my heart was going to beat out of my chest. It was beating that hard. That fast. Everything that had happened over the last three months culminated in that moment. In the question—*the choice*—that Baron had for me.

My dear husband. The man I wanted more than anything in the world was more sadistic than I'd ever given him credit for. Had ever thought possible.

'Are you sure you're ready? Because once you give your answer, you cannot change it. You'll be tied to it, forever.'

My knees buckled underneath me, but Baron's strong grip on my arm held me upright.

I'd only been a wife for three weeks. Such a short amount of time. And to learn the man you married is wholly changed from the man standing before you was a hard and bitter pill to swallow.

'Ask me,' I choked out, gazing into his cold, empty eyes. There was no silver in them. Not when he was focused. Or turned on. Or angry.

No, they were the blackest of nights. They were filled with tar, trapping me in their toxic substance, ensuring I couldn't get away. Free myself from the torment.

'I'm offering you an ultimatum. A chance never given to any of the others.'

I nodded. He meant his other wives. The ones who came

before. I wondered how many of them were scared when they found out the truth. Were they terrified? Did they find the chamber on their own, or did they have a nudge? A member of staff who wanted them gone, perhaps?

It did no good to think that way.

'I'm ready.'

'I'll free our *guest*, if you wish to take her place. Or, you can stay here with me forever. Unharmed. And continue by my side. An equal partner. In all things.'

His grip on my arm tightened, but his eyes softened. The depth of his want for me—his need for me—was apparent. But would he tire of me the way he had the other six? Was I just another one in a long line of deceased spouses?

Baron had the money, after all. The resources. People would forever cover up his crimes if he asked them to. If he paid them enough. Bribed them enough. Blackmailed them enough.

'Take her place in the c-cage?' I asked, my bottom lip wobbling, every emotion hitting at once and overwhelming me. The cage would only heighten my claustrophobia, and my anxiety wouldn't be able to take it.

What was a girl to do?

On the one hand, I could take that girl's place and let her free. I had no idea how long she'd been trapped in there, but if her body was anything to go by, it had been some time since she'd had a decent meal.

On the other hand, I could keep my position here by Baron's side, warm, fed, and happy. The only thing I would have to do is help him in all things. Whatever that meant. Although I felt pretty certain it included the abuse of an innocent in a cage.

Neither of us looked at the girl in question. The girl whose life now hung in the balance—her freedom sitting in the palm of my hand, waiting with bated breath for my decision. She hadn't said a word, or made any kind of noise or movement at all. Too scared of what Baron would do if she did, or so I assumed. I hadn't spoken to her about any of that earlier. The thought never crossed my mind.

'Yes,' he answered, his stern eyes taking me in. 'And what a pretty cage dweller you'd be.'

He laughed, but there wasn't any humour in the action. Even while laughing macabrely, the man was the most handsome I'd ever seen. The most alluring specimen. And, best of all, all mine.

'Or,' he continued, 'you can help me. The choice is yours, princess.'

Some wise dead bard once wrote, "To be, or not to be, that is the question." And in a sense, Baron was asking me the same one. To live and be free, as somebody's jailor. Or to lose my freedom—my life—to be held captive. Never to breathe the outside air again.

I answered the only way I could.

'I'll help you. I love you, Baron. I'll do anything for you.'

'And so you shall.'

PART
TWO

THAT SNIVELLING LITTLE BITCH.

Her bones protruded out of her skin, and I could see every single rib; every single one. Her shoulder blades. Her hip bones. All of it.

And the sight filled me with so much joy, I thought I'd burst from the happiness of it all.

Because she deserved it. Every laceration. Every bruise. Every sore.

All of it.

I recognised her. I'd recognised her the first time I entered this godforsaken chamber, and I knew the moment I laid eyes on her that I wanted her to suffer for her sins. Suffer for the sins of her sister. For everybody she'd harmed.

And little did I know at the time, but Baron handed me the solution on a silver platter.

When he asked me whether I wanted to join him or take her

place, I thought about it. Of course I did. Any sane person would. But it wasn't a particularly difficult decision.

Why would I give up my comfort? My life for *her*? Even if she had been an unknown random to me, I felt certain I would've chosen the same.

My whole life, I wanted to hurt people. Wanted to see them suffer for their shitty actions. For the things they did, knowing it hurt others but still choosing to do it, anyway. No care for anybody but themselves. Selfish and self-absorbed. Rotten to the fucking core.

First, it was my mother, and her sickness, that seeped into everything. Every crack of the wallpaper. Every word she uttered a lie.

It was frowned upon to want your mother dead. But there were many times in my childhood when that exact thought flittered through my mind.

Her actions. Her choices. They were all fundamental in making me the way I was. In warping my brain.

Then came my brothers. Not that I'd wanted to hurt them often, but there were times when I wanted them out of the picture. If there weren't that many of us to feed, then maybe we wouldn't have been so goddamn hungry all the time.

And lastly, my sister. That stupid, good-for-fuck-all know-it-all brat that seemed to judge *me*, when really, she needed to take a look in the mirror.

I knew my flaws. I saw my jagged edges and the things wrong with me. Wrong with my brain.

They couldn't see themselves the way others did. Couldn't see through the bullshit they ladled thickly onto themselves every single day.

'You've come b-back for me,' she stuttered, her face pressed up against the bars, tears tracking down her face. 'I knew you would.'

'Shut your pathetic mouth,' I snapped. 'I'm not here for *you*.'

'You're not?' she whispered, blinking at me. Her doe-eyes were creepy and looking out of place, and too large on her emaciated face.

'Why would I be?' I raised an eyebrow at her. 'I'm sure that whatever you did, *Emily,* to put you in that cage was bad enough to warrant your punishment.'

'I didn't,' she said, moving her face away from the bars now that she knew I wasn't here to spring her from the joint. She shuffled so her back was up against the bars on the other side. Not like she had much space to move around in. 'He took me after I bumped into him behind the local supermarket. I didn't know who he was.'

'Likely story,' I spat. I ignored the fact I didn't know who he was when I first met him, either. Even if meeting him was my plan all along by applying to work at one of his properties. 'Your sister was married to the man!'

The girl trapped in the cage was none other than Emily Brown.

She was the younger sister of Baron's sixth wife, Violet Brown, and a total bitch. We'd gone to school together back at Hollowdale, but she disappeared after her sister married. Something about a boarding school up north. Clearly, the boarding school wasn't as north—or as much of a school—as we were all told.

Her sister, Violet, was a bully. She was five years older than us and was one of the most popular girls in school. Anything she said happened, and if she didn't like the look of you, you'd know about it. One time, she pretended to be interested in my oldest brother for a prank.

She was a vile piece of work.

When the papers started to write about how she'd gone missing, I felt relief. In life, bad people should get what they deserve, and good people should prosper. That was never what happened, but it was how it should be.

So when she went missing, it was as if the universe was righting a wrong. Only a small, insignificant one, sure, but one that meant something to me. And to the other students of Hollowdale High.

'He took me *before* he married Violet! Why else would she marry him?' she shouted, distressed. I had no sympathy. No pity.

My foot began to tap on the ground, implying she needed to hurry her story the fuck along. I wasn't going to stand here all night. I wanted to be upstairs, waiting, when Baron got home from work.

He'd told me I could enter the room without him. But I couldn't do anything to harm her without his permission. Only talk to her.

'Because he's one of the richest people in the country,' I told her. 'Or because he's the most handsome man she'd ever laid eyes on?'

There were a lot more items on the list, but I stopped there. The bitch looking up at me from her rightful spot on the ground didn't deserve to know all the things I loved about my husband. Didn't need an insight into my inner workings.

'Violet never cared for that!'

'No?' I crouched down, staring through the bars into her green eyes, enjoying the thrill I experienced when she recoiled further. Moved further back in her cage. Shivered at my very presence.

A sick urge to hurt her rushed through my veins, like a hit of a drug. Or so I imagined. I'd never tried drugs. It was one of the reasons Baron loved me. I was pure. Sheltered. Not ruined like the piece of trash splayed out before me, with only her off-white underwear to keep her warm.

'N-no.'

'Well, she definitely cared about a person's wealth when she humiliated my brother!' My tone was scathing. How could she make such a bald-faced lie with no remorse? Even being held captive couldn't stop her lies. 'She humiliated him because of our situation. And you think that's okay, do you?'

'Well,' she said, brushing her hair back behind her ear. An old move of hers I recognised from our school days. She wanted to cut deep. 'Your *situation* has clearly changed now. Let me guess, you slept your way here just like your mother.'

'Leave my mother out of this,' I warned. Baron may have told me I couldn't hurt her, but if he knew the words spewing out of her mouth, he would make an exception. I was sure of it.

He loved me. He wanted me to be happy.

'So you're not sleeping with a rich man for money, hm?' She quirked an eyebrow at me, and I lashed out. She was off limits, but her bowl of water wasn't. Neither was the bucket in the corner that she was forced to use as a toilet while locked away. The stench of the room wasn't as bad as the last time I came in here, but it still turned my stomach. It was revolting, the mess she was in. It just made me happier.

'Oops,' I taunted, my smile wide. The cat who got the cream, the canary, and the cheese. 'Sorry about the spill.'

'You did that on purpose.'

'There's nobody but me here to hear you.'

'He won't be happy.'

'You don't know shit,' I told her with a laugh. 'You think you know my darling husband better than me?'

'I've known him longer,' she said.

What an insufferable little bitch. Her words rang through the spacious room, echoing off the stone walls and reverberating back to where we were. They were true words, but my chances of survival were a lot higher from out here than they were if I was in there. She would never break free from the chains of her imprisonment—both literally and figuratively.

I stood, not wanting to be near her for a second more, otherwise I wasn't sure I'd be able to contain my anger. It would be too easy to reach through the bar and grab her hair. Pull it and rip out a massive chunk, hoping she'd bleed during the process.

'If you're not going to be polite, worm, then I'm not going to stick around here and listen to you.' I kicked her water bowl again, the metal sound hurting my ears, but doing it anyway. I wanted to make sure all the water was missing—dehydration would look good on her.

'You won't get away with this.'

'Get away with what?' I asked, looking around me. Mocking her. Acting the villain. 'Because to me, it looks like we already have.'

Without another glance in her direction, I turned and walked to the door. To my salvation.

Because on the other side of the door was my new life, my freedom, my Baron. And I wasn't going to let anything come between me and what I wanted.

What I deserved.

'Evening, my queen,' Baron greeted, pulling me into a hug as he grazed his lips on my hair. 'Had a good day?'

Ever since I'd agreed to stay here with him, by his side, he'd upgraded my nickname.

"Only a queen would've made the choice you made. I'm proud of you, darling. You've impressed me more than I ever expected."

'It's been okay,' I told him, placing my hands around his waist and pulling him closer to me. 'I went to visit *her*.'

'You did?' he asked, pushing me away enough to look at my face. 'And?'

'And she's a brat,' I spat. 'I got mad.'

'What did you do?' His tone bordered on angry, but it wasn't there yet. He probably wanted to know what I did first, before letting his displeasure known.

'Nothing major,' I told him, brushing away his worry. 'I only kicked over her bowls. She spoke ill about my mother.'

'Hmm...'

'She also told me something interesting about *you*,' I emphasised, looking up into his eyes, gauging his mood before I continued.

'She did?' He stepped away from me and moved around to the other side of the counter. 'What did she say?'

'She said that Violet only married you because you'd already taken her.' I watched his face — watched for any slight change in his features. But none came. His stare stayed set on my face, unimpressed and cold. Stern eyes.

I pushed him further. My need to know the truth outweighed the smart choice.

'Was that *her* ultimatum?' I asked, derision in my tone. 'Did every wife get one?'

Before my conversation with the brat, I thought I'd been the only one to be given such an ultimatum from Baron. He'd told me so. The first wife he wanted to keep by his side. But when she told me that Violet married him because he had her, I wondered how he'd coerced his other wives.

I guess some would say he coerced me. But I didn't believe that.

Everything was my choice.

'Now, now, sweetheart.' He placated, placing his hands splayed out on top of the marble kitchen counter. 'You're the only one I gave such a delicious option to. I may have given the others alternatives, but none of them was ever given the chance to rule at my side.'

I breathed out. The harshly expelled air was hot and felt like it would explode my lungs if I kept it inside any longer.

'Hmph,' I sounded, even though his words were like a balm. Cool water. Dripping onto my head and travelling through my veins, reaching every nerve ending. 'I don't like thinking that you cared for them.'

Had he cared for them?

I thought back to our conversation about his wives. It had happened so long ago, and at the time, I wasn't as invested in him. Hadn't yet met the *real* him. The one he hid from everybody except those few closest to him.

'They meant nothing to me,' he said, staring across the room, his tone flat. 'They mean nothing to me.'

I shrugged.

I wanted him to keep talking. Keep saying the words I longed to hear. Keep telling me that I was the only one he wanted. The last wife. The final wife.

'That isn't what I asked.' My voice was pointed. He knew that wasn't what I wanted to know. He'd avoided my question about Violet—inadvertently—by answering whether the others were given ultimatums.

'Violet's options were nowhere near the same as yours, darling. I held her sister in the room, yes, but as you can see, marrying me didn't relieve her sister of her prison.'

That was true. Emily was still imprisoned, a captive, yet her sister was divorced and missing.

Baron's motivations were difficult to understand at the best of times. He was a closed-off specimen who only let others see what he wanted them to see. I needed to remember that. Needed to remember that he could be only letting me see what he thought I needed to, and nothing more.

'I want to know them all.' His blue and silver eyes pierced the distance between us. 'Tonight at dinner. You *will* tell me everything.'

'Fine, my queen. I shall tell you everything,' he conceded, with a tilt of the head. 'All in good time. But from then on, you will earn anything you seek first. We may be equals in most things, but nobody demands anything of me.'

I bit my tongue.

Nodded.

And left him at the kitchen counter to head back to my parlour. The bastard. *Earn anything I seek.*

I growled in frustration as I went, raging my way through the house. Knocking vases to the floor and anything else that was in my path. The fucking staff could clean up my mess for all I cared. The same question repeated in my mind. Over and over.

Hadn't I earned everything already?

I was sitting at one end of the table, while Baron was sitting at the other, our gazes colliding in a mixture of fury and passion.

'Where shall I start?' he asked, placing his knife and fork down on his plate, the clang of cutlery filling the spacious dining room.

It seemed silly to me for us to have our meals here when it was just the two of us, but Baron insisted on it. Said it wouldn't be proper if we ate elsewhere. Guess it was another one of those rich people things that I was yet to understand. Back home, we were lucky if we even had a decent meal, so where we were wasn't exactly a priority. Plus, we didn't have a dining table to sit at in the first place. It would've taken up too much space, and we needed all the space we could get.

'At the beginning, I suppose,' I replied, mimicking his action and placing my own silverware down. But then I picked up my glass, needing to do *something* with my hands.

'I can still take you over my knee,' he stated, his voice low and sensuous. I bristled under his gaze, not wanting to give him the satisfaction of knowing he'd appealed to me. My act was probably as transparent as the wine glass I was holding. 'But something tells me you'd like that.'

'This doesn't sound like story time to me.' I ignored the thrill of desire that shot through me at the image he painted.

'All in good time.'

'I've been patient enough,' I snapped, slamming my glass down on the table, the motion so hard it shattered. A shard of glass embedded itself in my pointer finger, and I stared at it, transfixed. I watched as the blood pooled on the surface of my skin and slowly made its way from the small wound and down to the palm of my hand.

A staff member rushed into the room. I assumed they'd heard the smash of glass and came to aid us. Baron waved them away with a gesture, and a rush of love for him ran through my veins. The power he exuded—even from one hand wave—was enough to make me weak.

'Elena was my first wife,' Baron said, and I glanced over at him. His body hadn't moved. But his eyes... they were stuck on the blood trailing down my hand to my wrist, following its path. 'We met in school when we were fourteen, acting like we were forty. The two of us clicked straight away, and I thought she'd be my forever partner.'

I raised my eyebrows, pissed that he was starting the story there, at a place I already knew. He'd told me all about Elena back before we married. Or at least he'd fobbed me off, trying to convince me that he'd told me everything.

'But we were young and dumb, as the papers would say.' He coughed, finally moving his eyes from my blood to my eyes. 'And they did say it. Often. The *Beurre Banner* has been following my family for years, and I was fair game from a young age. My marriage really appealed to them. That was when the trouble started.'

'What trouble?' I asked. If he was irritated by my interruption, he didn't show it.

'Elena liked the spotlight. She loved having her face plastered in all the gossip rags and she loved playing up, always wanting to be the centre of attention. It sickened me. As somebody that values their privacy above all things, I couldn't have that.

'As I told you before, my dear Elena drowned. But what I didn't tell you was *how* she drowned.'

'And there's a distinction, is there?' I smiled, picking out the small pieces of glass that were still in my finger.

'There's always a distinction.' His smile was wider, and I could tell he relished in telling the next part of the story. It was something he was proud of. Or at least it was something that made him happy.

'Go on.'

'One night, the two of us were enjoying drinks on the outdoor patio after coming home from a gala Edward held up at Hawthorn Academy. This was back before I bought and moved into this mansion.'

'I forget that you haven't always lived here.' The chamber hidden in the West Wing looked like it had been an old part of the house, untouched. It seemed ludicrous to me that the chamber was owned by anybody other than Baron. But it must've been.

'Elena accused me of cheating on her. Said I had a new woman lined up, and that once she found out who it was, she'd kill her.'

'And was there another woman?'

'No,' he said, then corrected himself. 'Well, not exactly. Not yet, anyway.'

There were times when Baron and his vague statements pissed

me off. It made me want to scream. To shout at him: *Just say it! Just tell me what I want to know!*'

'She needled me all evening, pushing me to tell her who could hold my attention that was better than her. Prettier than her. Sexier than her. She believed that she had no rival. That there could never be another rival for my affections.' As he told the story, his face turned red, a twitch in his eyebrow evident to me even from my place at the opposite side of the table. 'So, I came up with the idea to offer her an ultimatum.'

'And is that when your obsession with ultimatums began?'

'I wouldn't call it an obsession.' He chuckled, a glint in his eye. 'But yes, that was when I turned it into a game of sorts. How far could you push somebody out of their comfort zone? How much control could you have over another? Without them pushing out against it. Fighting you.'

'You enjoy the power it affords you.'

'Amongst other things,' he murmured, straightening up in his chair. The way the chandelier light hit his features made me squirm. He really was so fucking beautiful. From his long eyelashes to his beard, with its glorious tint of blue, all of it made my stomach flutter.

'What did you ask her?'

'I told her she could quit the jealousy, have my children, and stay quiet about any extra-marital relationships I partook in. *Or* she could divorce me and get nothing. She'd signed a prenuptial agreement and was entitled to absolutely fuck all. She'd be unable to sell her story to the papers because of the NDA.' He laughed. 'As you can imagine, that didn't go down well with her.'

'What part?' I was certain I knew. Elena sounded like some of the girls I knew from school. Or, should I say, knew of. Not like I was friends with any of them. I didn't have any friends. They were overrated.

The last one I had was now locked up in a cage in the depths of my house. Funny how life works sometimes, isn't it?

'All of it,' Baron said, bringing me out of my smug thoughts. 'She started swearing at me, trying to hit me, slap me, scratch me. Anything she could to get me to change my mind. As if her lashing out at me would do that.'

He scoffed.

'So what happened next? Did she ever answer your question?'

'I snapped,' he replied simply. 'Her hitting me was her answer, and clearly, neither option worked for her. So, I lured her into the pool house. Smashed her skull against the tile, then threw her into the pool, watching as the blood drained from her head into the water. It clouded with red, and I knew the moment my anger left me that I needed to get ahead of the situation. I rang the chief of police, who at that time was a lower ranked officer, and told him to get to the mansion fast.'

'And he helped you cover it up? Got it changed to an accidental death?'

He nodded and took a sip of his whiskey.

'Accidental death by drowning, yes. And from that day, he was by my side, helping me with anything I needed.'

'And let me guess, you helped him rise up the ranks?'

'Mhm,' he confirmed. 'And he's been helpful, to say the least.'

'I bet.' I met the man he was talking about at our wedding. He was a short, dumpy man and looked exactly the way I would've expected him to look. Why was it that the policemen and politicians I'd met since marrying Baron all matched the stereotype I had in my mind?

'Find that amusing, do you?'

'You know I do,' I said with a laugh. 'Let's just hope he continues to be as helpful to *us* as he has been to you.'

My wording made my intention clear. We were a partnership,

and I wasn't to be overlooked. And I most certainly wasn't going to have my death covered up by some shoddy chief of police who was so crooked they could be paid off to lie on death certificates. Or at least convince the people who did to do so.

'That's all for tonight,' he told me, and I growled.

The bastard had barely told me anything.

All he'd done was graze the surface. Sprinkled me some sugar as a sweetener before refusing to tell me more.

'You promised you'd tell me *everything*,' I whined, then closed my mouth and bit my tongue. I may get away with a lot of shit now, but there was no way Baron was going to allow me to disrespect him like that.

'And I will. I thought we could make it our little game,' he said, causing my ears to perk up. *A game?* I liked the sound of that.

'What kind of game?'

'Each night, I'll tell you a new tale.'

'A tale?'

'A *true* tale about the next wife.'

'So, you're telling me that in one week's time, I'll have everything? I'll *know* everything?'

'Everything there is to know and more. It will all be yours to do with what you will. You just have to promise me one thing?'

I mulled it over in my mind. I wondered what he wanted me to promise. He must know that whatever he wanted, I would oblige. I wanted to promise him the world.

After all, I'd already promised him myself.

'What's the promise?'

'I want you to promise me that once I've finished telling you these stories, you'll stay. No matter what.'

'I've already promised to stay with you no matter what,' I said with a smile. 'Didn't me choosing to stay with you instead of freeing an innocent girl and living in her cage tell you that?'

'That was a choice, wasn't it?' he asked with a smirk and we both laughed. Because he was right, but he was also very wrong.

It had been a choice. One I made of my own free will. And one I would choose again and again if I had to. And Baron may believe that he'd cornered me, but really, I'd chosen him before he ever offered me that ultimatum. I knew the rumours. I knew the tales that whispered through the trees; knew the way people talked about him around the town. And yet I jumped in anyway with both feet. Or maybe even headfirst.

'Either way,' I replied. 'I'm sticking by you, Baron. You're mine. And I'm yours. Forever.'

'Forever.' He raised his glass, and I raised mine. We couldn't clink our glasses together across the table because of the distance between us, but we made the motion anyway, and took a sip.

Blood filled my mouth.

The cracked glass at the rim of my cup had cut into my lip— the sharp sting of it awakening my need for vengeance. And my need for knowledge.

I could wait Baron out and give him what he wanted.

I'd become rather good at it as of late.

X-Rated

Baron

I stroked my dick in slow, measured movements, watching her writhe around on the satin sheets of our large bed as she pleasured herself.

It was one of my favourite views, watching her... unravel. Become her true self. The person she was destined to be when with me. I often wondered if there was a higher being. After my previous wives, I doubted. I still doubted. But watching my queen like this told me that she was put in my path for a greater reason than the distraction I initially thought her to be.

Her fingers slid in and out of her wet pussy, glistening as she whimpered, her bottom lip quivering with each new sensation.

Beethoven's *Moonlight Sonata* played through the speakers, encasing the room in its rich, dark tones. The music had two purposes. Firstly, it set the scene. There was nothing better than listening to an orchestra of sound while you fucked—while you held such power and control over another human being.

Ever since the day I met her and she told me of her love for classical music, I knew I wanted to use it with her in the bedroom.

'Does that feel good?' I asked, my lip curling up with excitement.

She nodded her head, her eyes turning a shade darker. They were usually bright, but when she was turned on, you could tell it from her pupils.

'On your knees,' I demanded, pointing to the ground. 'On the floor.'

I walked around the bed, stripping off my clothes and folding them neatly, before discarding them on a chair by the window. She positioned herself eagerly on her knees the way I knew she would. The way she knew I liked her.

Stepping up to her, I wound her ponytail around my fist, drawing her head back until my thighs brushed her tits.

'Good girl,' I said, encouraging her. 'Now take my cock all the way.'

With my hand on the back of her head, I eased her forward, sinking inch by inch into her mouth until I hit the back of her throat. The first time, she couldn't take me fully inside her throat, but as time went on, she'd perfected the act of giving head the way I enjoyed most.

I raised a brow, and she shifted her position, knowing exactly what I wanted. What I needed. She lowered her torso, tipping back her head, and my cock shifted further down her throat, making her retch.

'Again.'

Her head bobbed, and her eyes went wider.

'Yes,' I hissed, sliding my hands into hair, loosening the hair tie so her strands fell in a sheet around her shoulders. I grasped the sides of her head and held her still.

She swallowed around me, making my cock grow, and her eyes watered. I loved the sight of tears in her eyes, whether they were from happiness, exertion, or anger.

Before I could thrust again, she slid my cock free, placing it in her small hand, working it with vigour.

The glint in her eye had my back straightening. It was filled with sass and sauce. I watched as she licked her bottom lip before sucking the tip of my cock back into her mouth.

'Fuck,' I groaned, loving the feel of her wet mouth around me.

She lifted my erection up, fisting the base as she slowly licked down the underside, not stopping until she was sucking on my balls.

'God, queen. You feel amazing.'

She hummed, acknowledging my praise, but not breaking her concentration from the task at hand.

The sound vibrated against me, making my toes curl into the carpet as she lapped and sucked at my sack.

My arms slid down and around her, to pick her up and throw her onto the bed.

'Enough,' I commanded, the one word stopping her in an instant. She obeyed beautifully. 'Or I won't be able to fuck you.'

'I wouldn't have minded if you couldn't.'

'Wouldn't you? Why, my love? What have you got cooking up in that brilliant mind of yours?'

She smirked, rolling onto her stomach and rising onto all fours, her dripping pussy and arse in the air for the taking. Her head turned on the mattress, smooth against the silk sheets, to face me.

'I want your tongue in my arse,' she told me, her voice barely audible over the Beethoven piece still playing through the speakers. It was a quiet admission. Something she felt embarrassed about. It always amused me when something embarrassed her. She was so confident most of the time, especially with me, and it was nice to see that my girl could still have insecure moments, no matter how willing she had become.

'Do you, now?' I smoothed my palms up her calves, then to her thighs until I had her cheeks in my hands.

I spread her wide, then gathered up all the saliva in my mouth.

'Beg me for it.'

'Please, Baron,' she begged, her breath coming out in short, little pants. 'Fuck my arse.'

My spit fell in a string, running from the top of her arse crack down to her puckered hole.

'I want to feel your hot tongue inside of me, making me come for you over and over. I want to be the wife you want. Your dream.'

'You are my dream. You're everything to me.'

My finger followed the trail of spit, massaging it into her tight little hole before I pushed inside. She gasped, and I knew she was adjusting to the pressure. Since our honeymoon, I had suggested she use butt plugs to stretch herself wide enough to take me. The fact she'd suggested I fuck her arse told me she thought she was ready. Had prepared enough.

I considered using lube, knowing that would be the right thing to do. No matter how much she'd prepared for me, she was still an anal virgin. I weighed up the decision a second longer, before I decided not to. Her wetness would be enough, alongside my spit. I'd never known a woman to get as wet as she did. All you had to do was pinch a nipple between your fingers and kiss her neck with pressure and tongue and then she'd be dripping wet.

'Yes,' I hissed. 'Good girl.'

I worked my finger into her, stretching her open before I added another. I used the juice from her pussy to coat her more, slowly working my fingers in and out, until I could add a third. Her hips trembled as I removed my finger and spit on her again, this time fisting my cock and rubbing the head through her folds and up to her arse.

'Beg.'

'Baron,' she pleaded, her voice muffled as she lay face down on the sheets. 'Please. I beg you. Fuck me.'

I forced my tip inside.

'Is that all you've got?' I asked, wanting to hear her whispered pleas. There was nothing more pleasing to the ear than my wife begging for my cock while on all fours in the bed that we shared.

'Fuck me. Fuck me hard.' I could hear her desperation. Could feel it in every twitch of her body, every breath she took. 'Make me come with you buried deep in my arse.'

'Good girl,' I praised. 'You're doing so well. I'm proud of you, my love.'

She moaned, my words speaking to her on a more profound level.

I pushed forward, watching as my cock disappeared inch by tortuous inch.

'Fuck!'

She held firm on her hands and knees, and I decided to help her by taking some pressure off her arms. My cock went to the hilt, and I reached forward with my hand.

I wrapped my palm around her neck, lifting her arms off the bed and taking her upper body weight until she hit my chest.

The movement had her sitting on my cock, her back flush up against my chest. The scorching heat of her skin was burning me.

'Ride me, my queen.'

She worked her hips up and down as soft whimpers fell from her lips. Her body rolled forward, and my hand clenched on her neck, holding her in place.

I slipped my other hand around her front and rubbed along

her wet folds, waiting until she moved up for me to gain access to finger her pussy. She worked her ass down harder onto me, and I had to close my eyes to try to control my need for release. If I didn't know any better, I would assume she was lying about being a virgin. Maybe she was being coy when telling me of her preparations.

I pushed her forward with my chest and tightened my hold on her, listening as she struggled to suck in a breath. I rolled my hips into her, pulling her back to my chest only to repeat the move seconds later, just as she caught a deep, ragged breath.

'Squeeze me tighter,' she whispered, her voice hoarse. I held her neck so tight it would bruise.

When her pussy contracted around my fingers, I glided them out at the same time. Then I slid my cock out, removing my hand from around her throat to flip her over. I lifted her hips and slipped right into her pussy. The change shocked her, and I watched as her eyes widened with surprise and lust. Her inner walls tightened around me at the invasion and my cock was wrapped in a vice-like grip. It was like coming home.

I fit perfectly inside her, and even though we were back in the missionary position, it didn't feel any less sordid. The moment I moved my palm between us to flatten my thumb on her clit, she began to convulse. Her body shook, and I covered her throat again with my free hand to finish her off.

My hips bucked into her, her face reddening to a beautiful hue. I eased up on my hold, but not my thrusts. I nailed her to the bed, the sound of our bodies slapping together overriding the music. Every sound, every thrust, was pure perfection. I may have wanted to marry her for my own nefarious reasons, but the more I got to know her, *truly* know her, I knew that some higher being made her to my specifications.

She came hard, and I fought to hold off from my own release, not wanting it to be over just yet.

I pulled out of her and shuffled my knees up her body until I was kneeled over her chest. Pushing her tits together, I slid my cock between them and chased my own orgasm.

I fucked her tits, watching her face intently as she came down from her high. Her breathing was just as ragged as my own. The flush on her cheeks a perfect pink, and my handprint was a blazing scarlet on her neck. Alongside my mark on her collarbone, there was no way of denying she was mine.

'You're perfect.'

I came in a rush all over her tits, throat, and chin.

The way my cum glistened on her face was a beautiful sight. It marked her as mine. Marked her as the one. The final one.

The *only* one.

She licked her bottom lip, and her pupils flared when she tasted the salt on her tongue. My wife loved the taste of my cum almost as much as I loved the way she came undone underneath me.

'I love you,' I said, placing a kiss on her plump lips, tasting myself.

'I love you. More than you know.'

Once sated, we both lay on the sheets, staring up at the ceiling. Bathed in our own sweat and juices, smiling to the heavens.

'Have you ever had sex with her?' she whispered. So low I barely heard her.

'With who?' The question was purposefully obtuse. Of course, I knew who she was referring to. Lovely prisoner number one. The *only* one these days.

Pity.

'You know who,' she spat, sitting up to stare me down. The fire in her eyes was deadly. The banshee that lived within on the cusp.

Living on the surface of her skin, ready to devour me whole. *'Emily.'*

'No.' My arm ran up hers, trailing my fingertips until they rested on her cum-stained skin. Her face was beautiful.

Plain, sure.

But true beauty lay within. And hers shone brightest in the dark.

'Why don't I believe you?'

'I don't know, my queen. But I'm more than willing to show you.'

'Show me how you're *not* having sex with her?' she spat. 'Explain how that one works. Enlighten me.'

'Just come with me,' I grumbled, knowing I needed to get her out of the bedroom, out of her current mindset, and into a better one. She always did better with focus. With something to fixate her mind on.

'Let me get dressed,' she said. 'Anything in particular?'

'Wear whatever you want. Go naked for all I care.'

'You wish.' Her smile returned to her face. 'Are we going to the chamber?'

I nodded and watched as my baby's eyes lit up, and her entire demeanour changed. As if I'd given her a gift. And maybe I had.

The gift of being her true, authentic self. One who didn't need to hide. Who didn't have to act a certain way because that was what society expected—nay, *demanded*—of her.

Most people would most likely have been surprised at the switch in her personality, her seemingly sweet and naïve self replaced by a jealous, vindictive, and very manipulative bitch. But I wasn't.

I hadn't expected it to happen as fast as it had, but I had hoped it would. Ever since I first lay eyes on her in the coffee shop, I saw behind the shy, retiring girl in front of me. Saw down to her very core, and observed what she was attempting to hide.

'Any family?' I asked, a smile on my face. I loved knowing something others didn't, and the fact that this naïve girl in front of me had no clue who I truly was fed my soul.

'I have two older brothers, but they left a couple of years ago. Then one younger sister.'

'And you're happy to leave your sister.'

'Not happy, no,' she replied, her honesty shining for all to see. 'But this job will help her. Help my entire family. Working for Mr Henrick could be the change my family needs.'

It was the perfect chance to let her in on the secret. To let her know who I was.

I took a breath, looking into her eyes once more.

'Please,' I said, with a large grin taking over my face. 'Call me Baron.'

'B-baron?' she stuttered, her eyes widening, the picture of innocence. But I saw a flicker of something she wanted to hide. It was a look I'd seen in the mirror before on my own face, when I was on the phone and an opportunity landed in my lap. One I welcomed.

I smiled at her, recognising a part of myself in her. Something I'd never seen in another person.

'Pleasure to meet you, Sir.'

The moment the word Sir *left her lips, I knew that my plan was a good one. That somehow, seeing her job application on the top of the pile that day was fate.*

'I'm ready to go,' she said, pulling me out of the memory.

I looked over at her and took in the outfit she'd decided to put on. It was entirely black, and she looked unreal, the top a leather style corset that fit her every curve. A necklace sat between her breasts, a gorgeous pendant that she'd got herself for our engagement party, and I smiled at her.

Was there anything more beautiful than somebody coming into their own?

I didn't think so.

Most people would assume that having had six previous wives, I knew a thing or two about marriage, and what it was like to share your life with somebody else. And to a certain extent, I did. But what people didn't tell you was that no matter what happened, if you and your spouse weren't aligned, then nothing would go right in the long run.

Even in Emmy, I hadn't found the perfect match for me.

I had thought that I wanted—no, needed—a girl or woman to submit to me at all times. One who had no opinion. One who wanted to always be degraded and treated poorly.

How very wrong I was.

'Tonight I want the tale of Livvy,' my wife demanded the moment the staff left the room.

I knew she would be eager to learn. Eager to know the truth of it all. And really, wasn't that why I suggested telling her about a wife each night in the first place? Because I wanted her to have all the facts. Know my past, and understand her future.

She wasn't like Emmeline, that much was clear.

'The tale of Livvy has quite a ring to it,' I responded, wanting to make her laugh. Or at least see a small smile raise up at the corners of her mouth. But I got nothing. No reaction.

Except for the narrowing of her piercing blue eyes, partially obscured by her brunette bangs that hung low enough to cover her forehead.

'So, you remember what I told you last night about Elena?' She nodded. 'Well, I told you she died after the gala at Hawthorn. It was at that very gala that I met wife number two, Olivia. Everybody called her Livvy, though.'

My queen nodded her head, acknowledging me now that she was getting the story she wanted. Her mood swings were always unpredictable, but you could always guarantee her co-operation if she believed she was about to get her way.

'She worked at the school as a teacher, or at least she'd just started working there, and was attending the gala as one of Hawthorn's guests. Nervous and shy the whole evening. It appealed to me. Livvy was so different from Elena, who had spent the entire evening drinking herself silly and making a fool of herself in front of everybody.'

In my mind, I saw Livvy at the gala, awkward in her own skin. Her red hair was in perfect contrast with the emerald green satin dress she wore.

The old anger I felt towards Elena bubbled up again.

'So what happened next?'

'After Elena died, I bumped into Livvy again at a charity evening. It was a cause that helped children in need, and she was extremely passionate about it all. Loved being a teacher.'

'How old were you?'

'Young,' I said with a laugh. 'I was twenty when we got married. If she hadn't fallen pregnant, I doubt we would have got married so fast.'

'Moving fast seems to be your M.O.' The smirk covering her face held contempt. Anger.

Was my queen jealous? Probably. She was the type to compare

herself to others. Already she was worrying about whether or not Livvy had given me something she hadn't.

'Livvy wanted to be a mum more than anything else. She loved teaching children, but really, she wanted to teach her own. And I was more than happy to oblige.'

'You?' she scoffed. 'A father? Puh-lease.'

'You find that repulsive, darling?'

'No. But I find it hard to imagine. What with your obsession of keeping women in cages.'

'A mere hobby,' I said with a wave of my hand.

The large clock on the wall struck eight, and the staff entered the room like a well-oiled machine. The shuffle of plates and the refilling of glasses filled the air. My wife and I stayed silent throughout the commotion, staring into one another's eyes. Staring into each other's souls.

She kept her features deceptively composed, but inside there was a storm waging a war in her mind. There always was. Hiding in plain sight. Visible to those who looked close enough, but invisible to those who passed her by.

My pretty little monster had claws that she hid until you got too near.

'So,' she continued the moment the door closed behind the staff. 'Livvy *was* pregnant, then. The rumour mill says she died in childbirth. Let me guess, that one was true?'

'Ah,' I replied, amused. 'Not quite.'

'Okay...' She swirled her wine around in the glass, her eyes fixated on the small whirlpool she was creating. 'How did she die?'

'You can't force me to skip ahead to feed your curiosity.' I tutted, wagging my finger at her with amusement. 'The tale will be told in good time, my love.'

'Well fucking get on with it, then.'

'Livvy fell pregnant around six months after we started dating.

She had a traditional family, and she herself held traditional views of family life. So we got married to appease the masses.'

'Where were you living? I remember the papers from when you moved here. They weren't from that long ago.'

'We lived in the next town over. You know Lakeland I assume?' She nodded. 'I had a mansion there. Nowhere near as grand or picturesque as this one. Plus, the location wasn't a great fit for me.'

'And why was that?'

'There were no trees. No privacy,' I said simply. 'We're out of the way here. The woods act as a barrier between us and the town. A mile long stretch of road, too. It makes all the difference when you want to hide certain... activities.'

'Did that house have a chamber, too?'

'Of sorts. There was a locked room at the back of the house that acted as a playroom, but I hadn't fully committed to keeping anybody captive then. It was just an idea I toyed with in my mind.'

Not only was I waiting for the perfect prison, but I was also waiting for the perfect prisoner. To go against the law like that—and the very laws of nature—you had to feel attached to the subject. Attached to the situation.

Plus, at twenty years old, I still wasn't sure of my path.

I'd been wealthy my whole life. Had never wanted for anything. Everything was just handed to me on a platter, ready for the taking.

I needed to forge my own way in the world. Create my own empire.

'After you and Livvy married, what happened?'

'Nothing much. We lived a boring, mundane life of marital bliss. The two of us gave money to charity, and we helped the children we could. And I was fucking miserable.'

'Sounds like a problem you made for yourself.'

'And I'm sure that brings you joy.' I took a swig of my whiskey, amused that my little spitfire was enjoying hearing about my mental anguish. 'Livvy wanted to change the playroom into a nurs-ery. I let her because it was the easier option. The location in the house made sense, and it was the safest room in the house, with all the locks already installed.'

'So you became a boring father-to-be. Come on, Baron. There has to be something exciting about this story soon. I'm dying just listening to it, let alone living it.'

'I'm getting there. I'll spare you the gruesome details. They're not the kind you relish in.' I took a deep breath. It wasn't often I allowed myself to remember that time. It was the lowest point of my life, and I hated any reminder of it. 'Livvy went into labour early, in the nursery. Our baby was stillborn. Livvy was beside herself with grief, never once leaving the chamber.'

'So she didn't die?'

'She did. Just not in childbirth.'

'Fucking hell, Baron. Do I have to tell you to hurry again? It shouldn't be that hard to tell me how some ex-wife of yours died fifteen years ago!'

'Livvy wouldn't stop crying. After a month, she still hadn't come out of the room, and I knew it was time to offer her an ulti-matum. I couldn't have my wife shrivel away to nothing while I stood by and watched.'

'What were her options?'

'She could either follow our child into death. *Or* she could have more children and stay in the room forever. Never allowed out.'

My wife's jealousy reared its head once more. She straightened in her seat, her tall, slender neck drawing my eye.

'And she chose death.'

'She did.'

'And you did it?'

'I did.'

'How?'

'That's enough story for today.'

'I say it isn't!' she shouted, slamming her glass down on the table. 'You don't get to give me half-truths, Baron. That wasn't a part of the deal.'

'Sweetheart,' I said, placating her. 'I made the deal.'

My queen stood abruptly. The table shook with the motion, and I raised an eyebrow at her. She wanted to make a scene. Would most likely throw some things around. Show her anger towards me in a way that didn't harm me.

Because she would never hurt me. Could never hurt me. Not physically.

No. The only way she could harm me was by leaving. And although she stomped out of the room, most likely to her own rooms away from me, I knew she wasn't leaving forever.

She'd be back.

After all, she still had four more wives to hear about.

DYNAMICS

When I first met Baron, he was merely my ticket.

My ticket to a better life. A way out of the miserable, poor, shit life I'd somehow been handed by the powers that be. Obviously, at first, I thought a job with him would serve as a way out, but then at my interview, when he introduced himself, I saw a bigger picture.

But I didn't realise that he would be my salvation, too.

Because I loved him. Truly loved him. And the more time we spent together, the more the feeling grew deep within me. It wasn't just lust anymore. Or a power exchange.

As time passed, the two of us were slowly becoming equals.

In everything.

Had he pissed me off the night before when he wouldn't tell me the true end of Livvy's story? Of course. But I knew he had his reasons. He was prolonging it for some reason or another.

And I would let him.

Not like I had anything better to do.

'I was twenty-two when I met Lilliana,' he said, his eyes dark and hooded. Lost in the past. 'And she was twenty-one. A law student at a university in the city, about to graduate.'

He looked at me, but my face gave him nothing. Not like I was about to smile about his tale, especially not when it was about an ex-wife.

'She was fun to begin with,' he continued. 'And she came from a wealthy family like me, so she never acted the way Elena did.'

'Baron,' I said, cutting him off. 'I've got a question.'

'And what question is that, my queen? Not like you to politely mention anything. Usually, you just interrupt and ask what you want, no holds barred.'

'Well, maybe I'm trying to turn over a new leaf.' I bit my bottom lip, my eyes glowing at him—or at least I thought they were. 'Be the good wife you deserve.'

'Ah, but my darling,' he mused, his tone as low as sin. 'I've never wanted a good wife.'

'Thank fuck for that,' I said with an amused chuckle. Sometimes, I felt like two people with two different personalities.

Was I the weak, quiet, innocent that met Baron and agreed to marry him? Or was I the bitch that enjoyed harming Emily and being tied up in bed?

I had one answer for that.

Why couldn't I be both?

'What did you want to know?' Baron asked, placing his elbows on the table and clutching them underneath his chin.

'I want to know if you loved any of them.'

'Loved any of them?' he repeated, unclenching his hands to run one of them through his dark, ruffled hair. 'Why, my queen, are you feeling a little jealous? A little worried that you aren't the only one to have caught my eye?'

'Oh, shut up, you prick,' I said through laughter. 'Just answer the question.'

'No,' he said matter-of-factly, rubbing his chin. 'No, I never loved any of them. I may have thought I did once'—he looked off into the distance, his face passive—'but the moment I met you, I knew I was wrong. I've never loved anybody before you. Not even family.'

'Now you're just trying to flatter me.' I raised my wineglass to my lips and took a small sip. I needed to keep my hands busy, and drinking wine seemed like a good plan to me.

'Is it working?' He waggled his eyebrows at me, and his uncharacteristic goofiness caught me off guard. I snorted with laughter, some of my wine escaping out of my nose.

'Definitely,' I replied. 'But it doesn't mean that you can get out of telling me about Lilliana.'

'Fine,' he conceded. 'But it was you who interrupted *me*, remember?'

'Get on with it.'

'Where was I?' He took a sip of his drink, and I watched fixated as his Adam's apple bobbed with the motion. 'Oh, right? As I was saying, she was a breath of fresh air, honestly. Nowhere near as attention-seeking as Elena, and nowhere near as maternal as Livvy.

'I still lived in Lakeland, and the room that Livvy died in had become my own personal playroom once more. It was then that I got the idea of pulling a Bluebeard inspired test.'

'Bluebeard test?' I asked, confused. I had no fucking clue what he was talking about. Baron was intelligent, and well-learned, and sometimes his knowledge made me feel so stupid and insignificant.

'An old tale.'

'Let me guess,' I said, raising an eyebrow in his direction. 'French?'

'Of course.' He smiled, an irresistibly devastating grin that set off a blaze of desire in my stomach that radiated throughout the rest of my body. Warming me up from the inside.

Baron was handsome, and he knew it, but the thing about him that I found the most attractive was his sheer confidence. The way he held himself, the way he took what he wanted and exceeded in his business endeavours. All of it, combined with his wolfish smile, made me want to fuck him every day for the rest of my life.

'To see if his wife obeyed him, he gave her a key to a forbidden room.'

'Well, this sounds familiar. And let me guess... she disobeys.'

'Of course. As did the wives that came before her, or so it's implied.'

'And you decided to hand the key to Lilliana?'

'Yes.' His eyes widened, a faint smile playing on his lips. 'We'd been married for a couple of months, and frankly, I was bored. The moment we married, she became an entirely new person—and not in a good way like you did, my dear.'

'What do you mean?'

'Looking back, I now know she was depressed. But at the time, I only saw her sadness as an excuse. She never wanted to leave the house. Never wanted to have sex. Never wanted to do much of anything, and honestly, it pissed me off. I felt cheated.' His hands clenched into fists on the table, his knuckles turning white. 'The whole time we dated, she was always game for a laugh. Always wanted to go places and see new things. Explore the world.'

I nodded my head, feeling a pang of sympathy for Lilliana. It must have been hard for her, and with Baron not understanding what she was going through, she would've felt so alone and trapped. Back when I lived with my mum, there were times when I felt alone and trapped. Unloved. And it was a slippery slope. I was lucky that I met Baron at the right time. Even if it was a time I engineered by specifically applying to work for him to try and catch his attention.

'Giving her the key was a risk,' he said, continuing his story.

'She studied law and her father was in the police force. But I had to. It became a compulsion, an obsession, a sickness that I couldn't control. Every waking moment, I thought of putting my plan into action. Every night, I dreamt of what would happen. How she would react.'

His eyes were glazed over. Fully trapped in the past. Seeing things I would never see.

Other than Violet, I didn't even know what any of his previous wives looked like. The articles I'd read online didn't include their pictures. Which is why our wedding pictures were such a big deal to The *Beurre Banner.* Baron had never allowed it before me.

I wondered how much money and power that took. The media didn't just listen to anybody. Everybody knew that the tabloids and other media outlets were a drain on society. Vultures, the whole lot of them.

'So, I made up a trip I had to take. Left her home alone. Told her not to enter the room. You know the drill,' he said, an amused glint in his dark eyes. He was enjoying telling me, as if I was a partner in crime as well as his partner in life.

'The room that used to be the nursery? The one Livvy died in?' He nodded.

'I left her in the house with the staff there to keep an eye on her. They were to report her every move to me. Obviously, I hoped she'd take the bait, but because she was the first, I wasn't sure how any of it would go.'

'By staff, do you mean Mrs Peters?' I scoffed. Even before he answered me, I knew she was who he meant.

'Yes,' he confirmed. *Or course it was.* 'She's worked for my family for years, ever since I was a boy. I'd trust her with my life.'

'Does she know?' I'd been wondering how much the old woman knew ever since she found me the day she showed me the library.

'She does,' he said, his tone solemn. 'That's how I know I would trust her with my life. She knows the good and the bad. You should give her some slack, my queen.'

'She's the one who hates me,' I hissed, irritated that he was turning it around on me. 'From the first day you brought me home, the woman has barely tolerated me. Giving me evil glances whenever we cross paths. Disrespecting me in my own home.'

'Maybe at first she didn't like you,' Baron admitted. 'But that was before she knew how you would react. She knew I would give you the keys. Maybe she couldn't see through your act the way I could.'

'Hm.' I pondered his words, mulling them over in my mind, tossing them around in the frying basket I called my brain. 'You could be right. But wait... How *did* you see through my act?'

Baron laughed. A low, throaty sound that made my thighs clench together underneath the table. My collarbone burned the way it always did when his actions turned me the fuck on.

'Darling. I can spot a manipulator a mile away. I'm one myself, after all. And I could see the signs in you during our very first meeting. The way your eyes flared the moment I announced my name, and the speed at which you changed your facial expression after the fact told me more than you wanted me to see.'

His words penetrated my skull, and I nodded, understanding what he meant. There were times where I saw the same in him.

It was funny to me that the two of us were both trying to manipulate the other, gauge the other's intentions, and to play one another all while slowly falling in love.

And it was love.

Maybe not in the traditional sense. Not quite yet. But we were on track for a forever kind of love. I knew it, and so did Baron.

'So you were trying to manipulate me into becoming your wife.

And I was trying to manipulate you to make me your wife. Seems like we were both destined to achieve our goals.'

'Seems like we were,' he agreed, his smile still firmly planted on his face and his eyes flared. 'Back to Lilliana. And stop distracting me.'

'Yes, Sir.'

The word unlocked something between us. It hung in the air, a sweetener, a treat we could both taste, and I breathed in deeply through my nose in an attempt to stop myself from launching out of my chair and onto his lap.

'Get on with it, and then we can go to bed,' I told him, my voice dripping with lust. I wanted him. But I wanted the end of the story more.

'Your wish is my command.' His voice was equally filled with lust, and one of his hands disappeared under the table. He shuffled, and I smiled, my teeth on show.

'Having a hard time?' I asked. Gleeful and oh so fucking amused.

'For now.' He adjusted himself before returning his hand back to where I could see it. 'As I'm sure you've already guessed, Lilliana used the key. Once inside the room, she found Livvy's corpse hanging from a hook in the centre of the room. I had her preserved, and usually she was kept in a glass coffin elsewhere in the house, but to scare Lilliana, I had Mrs Peters move her.'

'I was meant to ask you, actually, about how you were able to keep your dead wives' bodies.'

'All in good time, my dear. Let's finish this story. I want you naked and underneath me as soon as possible.'

My wetness dampened my knickers, and I nodded, ready to get this over with.

'The moment she found Livvy, she freaked out. Screamed and screamed for hours on end. Mrs Peters had watched her enter the room, and it was two hours before a shell-shocked Lilliana walked out of there. Mrs Peters said she resembled a ghost. Her tanned skin paler that she'd ever seen it before, and she kept mumbling to herself.'

'Then what happened?'

'Somehow, she managed to give the staff the slip. She fled the house and headed straight for the police station. Before she studied law at university, she ran track at high school—long distance. She ran all the way from the house to the station, never once stopping. On arrival, she told her dad what she'd seen. I was already on my way back into Lakeland when Mrs Peters rang to tell me what had happened.'

'Was Lilliana still at the police station when you returned?'

'She was,' he said, his tone solemn. 'Lucky for me, Mrs Peters had already sorted for Livvy's body to be moved back to her coffin, so by the time Lilliana and her dad—and the rest of the Lakeland police force—showed up, things were back to normal.'

'And she looked stupid?' I asked, a smirk on my face.

'Very,' he replied, his smirk matching mine. 'Her dad looked pretty poor too in front of his team, and they lost a lot of respect for him. They searched the property, and they found Livvy, but having her body was all above board. I planned to bury her on my property, after all.'

'You did?' Disbelief laced my tone, and I raised an eyebrow at him. It should probably repulse me a little that he just kept dead bodies lying around, whether he intended to bury them or not, but it didn't.

'I did. Just not *that* property.'

'How did you know you'd end up here, though? I remember you told me the moment this place went up for sale you knew it was yours. Why?'

'Because of the secret room, of course. I knew the son of the previous owner briefly for a time, and he told me about the hidden room at the end of the hallway that his father used for his *activities.* A year later, the son passed away from an overdose. A week after that, the previous owner died suddenly after a dinner party. He was poisoned.'

'By you?' I asked dryly. I didn't believe in coincidence, after all, and the story Baron told sounded far from coincidental.

'Maybe,' he admitted and took a sip of his drink. 'Either way, the house became mine and I could finally lay Livvy to rest with the respect she deserved.'

'With the same respect you showed her in life, I assume.'

'Naturally.'

I took a sip of my wine and rang the bell I'd placed beside me on the table. It was one of my grand ideas. It pissed me off when the staff interrupted our conversations to bring in food, or refill our glasses, and the introduction of a bell was the best way to summon them when I wanted them to appear.

Mrs Peters tried to put a stop to it, of course, but Baron had agreed with me and fought in my corner. He made the right decision, because if he hadn't, I may have considered stabbing him in his sleep.

Or branding *his* collarbone. I could always find a way to convince him. I felt certain of that.

My fingertips aimlessly ran across the raised skin while we waited for the staff to bring in our dessert before we continued.

The moment our tiramisu was in front of us, Baron went on as if we were never disturbed.

'Once Lilliana's dad left, she ran from me, but I'd anticipated that move, and had locked all exits so she couldn't slip out again. Of all the places she could run to, she chose to run to the room. I found her pacing in the centre, up and down, back and forth, muttering to herself.'

'What was she saying?'

'Most of it was incoherent. One sentence stuck on repeat, though, was, "I'm going to die here. I will never be free. She will never let me be free." The moment she saw me, all hell broke loose.'

I was lost in Baron's story, wondering what came next, when my phone buzzed in my pocket. It was always a weird sensation when my phone buzzed, because it wasn't something I was used to. Nobody ever really contacted me. It helped that I didn't have any friends, and it wasn't like my mum was messaging me asking me how I was. The only time I had heard from her since we returned from our honeymoon was when she pleaded for money. A plea I ignored.

Baron stopped his train of thought and widened his eyes at me in question. I shrugged, then pulled my phone from my pocket.

It was a text message from my sister—a pretty bare text message. It included a link, and one line that read, *Be careful.*

I rolled my eyes at that and clicked the link, wondering what on earth she wanted me to look at. Baron was still silent at his end of the table, waiting for me to tell him to start talking again.

'Text from my sister,' I told him, and he nodded his head.

The page loaded, and the content surprised me a little. When I saw the message, I thought it was going to be another article about Baron or Violet or something like that. But it wasn't. It was a weather report that stated snow was on its way to Beurre.

'Looks like we're about to get snowed in.' My sister knew I didn't like snow much, and I guess she knew that we lived secluded in the woods and that snow could trap us for a bit. I held up my phone to show him, as if he'd be able to read my small phone screen from across the large table. 'Weather report.'

He nodded and responded, 'Yes, Mrs Peters told me. She's already sorted for staff to salt the driveway.'

I let out a small growl at the mention of Mrs Peters. The

woman rubbed me the wrong way. It was as simple as that. She acted like a mother figure to Baron, and I assumed that was why he let her get away with so much shit.

'Sorry,' I apologised, but didn't know what I was apologising for. 'You were saying that all hell broke loose?'

'Right,' he said, accepting the apology for whatever he believed it was for. 'Lilliana lost her way very fast. Within a day, I knew our marriage wasn't going to work. I didn't need another broken wife. I was only twenty-two with plenty of time to find the right person for me.'

'So what did you offer her?'

'Her ultimatum was simple. Either she ended her life, *or* I ended it for her. And I'm sure you know what one she chose.'

'She killed herself, didn't she? I remember my sister telling me that she committed suicide.'

'She did,' he said, solemn. 'My third wife in five years, dead. Gone from this world. Because of me.'

'Not exactly a great track record.' My words came fast, and I smiled at how fast I'd replied, wanting to make him feel better. It was rare Baron showed human emotions that weren't lust, love, or anger.

His face cracked into a wide smile that split his face. The two of us laughed and joy filled me. I loved making him feel good. Loved making him laugh. It was one of those things I would never get enough of. And the thing was, I wasn't even really joking.

After all. A great track record was a bit of a fucking understatement.

'I'M SO SORRY, MASTER,' EMILY WHIMPERED, HER LARGE eyes as round as orbs, staring up at Baron with an apology written in them. She was kneeling before us, her knees bruised by the stone-cold flooring. 'I won't do it again.'

'Make sure that you don't,' Baron replied, his treacle voice making my knees weaken. There was something about his authoritative voice that killed me inside.

The hope on Emily's face sickened me. Her relationship with Baron—if you could call it that—sickened me. Twisted my insides until they were nothing more than a helix of hate.

She may be his captive, but they shared something I hadn't been a part of.

She had to go.

When she least expected it, I would end her life. But not before torturing her first. No, I wasn't going to ruin my fun prematurely.

I just needed Baron to stay away.

He couldn't have her.

He was mine.

She'd spoken back to Baron, as if she had a right to. And it made me bristle with anger. Who the fuck did she think she was? She was in no position here to be calling the shots.

'You won't do it again,' I seethed. 'Or you'll have me to answer to. Stand up!'

On shaking limbs, she stood before us, her head tilted down, and her eyes once again on the floor. Her bones protruding from her skin made me smile. Every angle, every pointed joint, filled me with joy.

I hadn't always hated Emily Brown.

Back when we were younger, the two of us were best friends. It all started one day at age five on the playground at primary school. Everybody wanted to play Mums and Dads, yet the two of us wanted to play Dodgeball instead. A beautiful friendship was born that day.

One that didn't last.

As time passed by, we grew apart. But truly, it was when we both started Hollowdale High that broke us for good. My older brothers both went there, and so did her older sister. They'd told us stories of what to expect of the classes, the teachers and things like that. But none of them had mentioned how horrid kids in high school were.

The bullying. The shoving. The name-calling.

The downright vicious attitudes of pre-pubescent teenagers and the even worse ones of the older kids.

Within no time, it became clear that my mother's profession was common knowledge around the school, and that I wouldn't be able to go anywhere without hearing them talk smack about her. And the most frustrating part? I agreed with them most of the time. But it wasn't socially acceptable to talk about your whore mother in public without people paying attention. I didn't want any services to get involved and take us away. Yes, our home life was rotten to its very core, seeping pus from the inside out, but it could've been so much worse if we were removed from it.

During the first week, it became apparent that Emily was befriending the popular kids. Her sister was one of the Rebels—a ragtag group of students who ran the school—and that gave her a level of clout that I couldn't compete with. I wasn't included in their plans because I was too poor to go shopping with them, or to the cinema, or to the local coffee shop for food every day after school.

She stopped talking to me.

Stopped catching my eye in the hallway, and messaging me at night.

After a month, we were enemies. And I had nobody left.

I was standing in the chamber, watching Baron tie Emily to a ring on the wall, but my head wasn't fully present.

The time Baron brought me in here before flashed through my mind.

I grumbled as I followed Baron into the chamber.

I was pissed that the two of us had just finished celebrating our love and one another's bodies, yet now here I was, back with Emily Brown, so Baron could somehow prove that he wasn't fucking her.

How he planned to prove that I had no idea.

'Emily,' Baron called as we entered. She shuffled on her knees to the front of her cage, and I laughed at her eagerness to please him. 'My wife's taking over today, okay?'

She nodded, and I stood still, unsure what he meant by that.

We'd both been here before, and so far, Baron had introduced me to a couple of torture methods he found fun. Or we'd ask her to complete an impossible task, and when she failed, we would whip her, or we made her kneel on the painfully hard floor while we ate rich food in front of her. Baron had told me that not all torture needed to be sexual in nature, and so far, he'd proved that. But for some reason, my paranoia got the best of me, and I asked Baron if he had sex with her.

I'd never had a prisoner before—obviously—and I wasn't exactly sure of the etiquette. Was there something I was meant to do?

All I knew was that I wanted to slice her skin with paper cut thin slashes, just to see her covered in crimson, but not enough that she'd bleed out.

She wouldn't be as much fun dead.

'Do your worst,' Baron whispered in my ear, before leading me to the table in the corner laden with instruments of torture.

My reaction to the table always surprised me. It was as if my skin became a magnet, and all I wanted to do was hold each of them in my hand in turn and learn how they worked.

While Baron let her out of her cage, I perused the table, running a game plan through my head as I did so.

But then a thought came to mind.

Sometimes, the best torture had no tools.

'Come over here,' I demanded, pointing at Emily. Her underwear hung off her body, and the dirt clinging to her skin made me cringe. I wondered if she ever washed. But then I shook the thought away. It wasn't for me to care about.

Emily stood in the spot I pointed to.

'Do you know what the jetliner position is, Emily?' I asked, raising an eyebrow at her, looking for a flicker of recognition on her face. It didn't come. She shook her head, her greasy, limp hair hanging in strands around her face, swinging with the motion, and it made me smile. Back when we were friends, Emily had always prided herself on her appearance. Always wore designer clothes, had *her hair styled in a salon, and her nails always had acrylics affixed to them.*

'No, Mistress,' she replied, and I paused. There was something so delicious about being called Mistress. *I loved it. Love wasn't even a strong enough word for it.*

'Sometimes it's referred to as the captain's chair,' I told her. 'Here, I'll demonstrate.'

I walked over to the wall and moved myself into the chair position, my back flat against the wall. I slid down until my thighs were parallel with the ground, holding myself up against the wall. After a moment, I had to stand, unable to hold the position for longer than thirty seconds.

Which was how I knew it was perfect.

'I want you to hold that position for ten minutes, and if you can't, then I'll whip you with the cat-o'-nine-tails. That sound fair?'

'Yes, Mistress,' she whispered. And I almost laughed in her face. We both knew none of it was fair. And we both knew she would be lucky if she could hold the position for longer than a minute.

Like a good little prisoner, Emily walked to the wall and got into position.

And like I predicted, she lasted thirty seconds before her weakened body failed her.

I smiled with glee.

'Oh, Emily,' I taunted. 'That wasn't very good. I'm feeling generous. Try once more.'

So she did. And once more, she fell.

'Well, that just won't do,' I told her. 'Face the wall.'

I didn't need to watch her to know that she obeyed my demand. She wasn't stupid. She knew that it would be worse for her if she didn't follow our orders.

I went to the table and grabbed the cat-o'-nine-tails, enjoying the heft of it in my hand. It was black leather, and it looked a lot prettier than it should for an instrument that could cause so much damage.

'Now,' I said, stalking over to Emily's back. 'I want you to count.'

'...good girl,' Baron whispered, and I tore myself from the memory of her back as I struck her with the cat. Even now, her back still showed signs of what I did, and I relished in it. I ran my tongue across my top teeth as I surveyed the two of them.

I hated it, but I also loved it.

Basically, I couldn't decide. And it pissed me off.

'That's enough for today,' Baron asserted, and I nodded. I wanted out of there. I was too in my head to be of any use.

'I want to talk to her,' I said, an idea popping into my head. 'You leave, and I'll lock her up.'

'If you're sure?'

I nodded and mumbled, 'Of course.'

Baron handed me the keys and left the room. The moment he was gone, I spun on my heel to face Emily. She was looking at me, frightened, yet also dumbfounded.

'What do you want?' she asked, accusation in her tone.

'Do you want out?' I asked her, looking her directly in the eyes.

She narrowed her eyes on my face, and I could see the question written all over her. She was wondering how sincere I was being.

'What d-do you mean?' she stuttered.

'I mean. If there was ever an opportunity to get out of here, would you take it?'

'Are you offering to help me?'

'Just answer the fucking question,' I said, stomping my foot on the ground. Why did she have to make it so hard? Either she said yes or no. There wasn't exactly much else she could do.

'I don't know,' she whispered. I scoffed at her response, but I wasn't surprised. Not really. I wouldn't believe me either.

Fuck, even I didn't know if I believed me, and I was the one saying it.

'Have a think, and get back to me.'

'Veronique was my fourth wife.'

I nodded and continued eating the meal in front of me. Baron had stuck to his promise, and I knew I needed to stick to mine. Besides, there wasn't anything he'd told me thus far that made me want to run away from him.

Not really.

He didn't think much of me if he believed I would run away because his first wife was an attention seeking whore and his second couldn't cope with the loss of her child. Oh, and his third offed herself. Not like he killed her—not really.

He just told her to do it, or he'd do it for her.

She still had a choice.

'How did you meet her?'

'She was an aspiring actress and model, and I met her at one of the hotels I own. Something about a film premiere she was attending being held at the cinema opposite. She was slightly famous, and I knew I was taking another risk by courting her. You would've thought I learned from my previous mistake, but I was still pretty young and foolish.'

'How young?'

'Twenty-five.' He rubbed his hand across his chin, deep in thought. 'It was a whirlwind marriage. Something secret, which naturally, meant that everybody knew about it. She needed to boost her profile, and I was happy to oblige. Lilliana's death was ruled a suicide, and if people thought me remarrying within two weeks was suspicious, then they kept those opinions to themselves.'

'Let's be honest, babe,' I said, a smile on my face. 'It's definitely fucking suspicious.'

'Completely,' he agreed, his dark eyes alight with his amusement. It hit me at that moment how much I was genuinely falling for him more and more. It may have started out as a means to an end, but really, Baron got me. And I got him. We were two peas in a very tainted pod. And our new routine of him telling me his past over dinner was something I loved and would miss when it ended. In the car on our first ever date, he'd told me that I couldn't ask about his past. It amazed me how much could change in such a short period of time.

'She's alive, isn't she?' I asked, recalling what my sister told me.

'Then there's the fourth wife. Even less information about her and their time together. The only thing I could find was an article about her admittance to a rehab facility after she suffered from a mental break.'

'She is,' Baron confirmed. 'There isn't much to tell you about our brief time together, honestly.'

'How long were you married?'

'Only six months. The signs were there early on.'

'What kind of signs?'

'Most of the time she would lose her train of thought mid-sentence. Or her eyes would glaze over, and she would dissociate from her surroundings. I knew it was pushy of me to hand her the key and have her find the room, but my mind wasn't in the right place back then, either. The thrill of putting my plan into motion with Lilliana overrode the disappointment at the way it all ended.'

'And you did the same thing?'

He nodded.

'I told her I was going away on business. The room was prepared, now with both Lilliana and Livvy inside–'

'Wait,' I interrupted him. 'Surely, Lilliana's dad put up a fuss about you just keeping her body in a glass cage? He knew you had Livvy's body, still above ground, so wouldn't he have wanted a proper funeral for his daughter.'

'I assume that is what he would've wanted,' Baron concurred, his top lip curling up at the edge in a sadistic smirk. 'But he wasn't alive to know.'

'He died?' I ran my fingertip around the rim of my glass absent-mindedly, staring at Baron as my forehead wrinkled. 'Did you do that, too?'

He chuckled, and asked, 'Do you always think the worst of me?'

'No,' I replied with a small giggle. 'I always think the best of you, which would probably be the worst for everybody else.'

'You really are one of a kind, aren't you?' The love and lust in his eyes couldn't be ignored. I hadn't asked him what he thought of me from the start, but I knew that soon we needed to have that conversation. What had made him pick me? What had he seen in me that others didn't have?

'I try.' I shrugged my shoulders, with a coy smile.

'I didn't kill him,' he said, going back to the topic at hand. 'His wife died a few years before, and Lilliana was his only child. He left a note. Said that he had nothing to live for anymore.'

'And you believed him?'

'No reason to think otherwise. Seemed a pretty open and shut case. His note referred to the death of his darling daughter.'

'Fair enough. Guess I'm just the suspicious type.'

'Sometimes, wife, an accidental—or otherwise—death is exactly as it appears. I'd even go as far as saying that's the case at least eighty percent of the time.'

'You have no way of knowing that statistic is anywhere near to being accurate.' I laughed. 'Bet if my sister was here, she'd know.'

'Your sister's quite intelligent, isn't she?'

'She likes to think she is, yeah,' I spat, my old anger towards her rising. It was rare I thought about her and didn't get mad. 'She definitely likes to act that way.'

'You never talk much about your family,' he pointed out, and I bristled at the accusation. As if Baron Henrick could judge *me* about how little I opened up. The man barely told me shit about his life. I didn't even know his parents' names. All I knew was that they were long dead, leaving him his hotel empire at the age of eighteen.

'Hark who's talking!'

'Fine. I'll finish my story and we can spend the evening however you want. Does that suit you, my queen?'

'It does.' My mind ran through all the possibilities. It wasn't often that Baron handed the reins over to me, but when he did, I always made sure my choice was worthwhile.

'So... I gave her the keys. Left on business. You know the drill.' I nodded. 'Veronique's eyes didn't light up the way Lilliana's did.'

'Did mine?' I cut him off and he growled, slowly getting worked up that I was constantly stopping him mid-flow. I wasn't sure what had got into me, but I had questions. 'When you told me about the door I couldn't unlock?'

'Oh yeah. Yours burned the brightest. That was how I knew.'

'Knew what?'

'That you were the one for me.'

I flushed, and I knew my cheeks were burning. There were

times when Baron caught me unawares and made my heart soar. Made me realise that he saw me. The real me. The me that everybody else either ignored or pretended didn't exist because acknowledging it meant living with it.

'So, did you think that Veronique wouldn't go for it? That you'd come back to her having not unlocked it, the whole charade for nothing?'

'It wouldn't have been for *nothing*, though. I would've found out if she was the type to obey.'

'But she wasn't. Otherwise, I doubt we'd be sitting here having this conversation.'

'I have a funny feeling that no matter what happened, we would still somehow be having a conversation now. Maybe not this exact one. But fate meant we would meet. I feel certain of that.'

'You're very sure.'

'Don't you feel it, too? The magnetism that draws us together. The thread that connects us no matter where we are. Or what we're doing.'

He was showing me a vulnerability, and I had two options: sink or swim.

I could admit that I feel it. That I could always feel it, even from the start. Or I could lie and tell him I felt nothing of the sort. Protect myself in case everything went wrong.

But then I remembered that there was a little-known third option to that conundrum. One that many people didn't consider or think about.

I could float.

'Most days I do.' It was all I was willing to admit. Being vulnerable was hard for me, and even though I knew Baron wouldn't throw it back in my face, you could never be too cautious.

'That's a start.' He studied me thoughtfully. 'Either way, no, Veronique didn't obey. It took her a couple of days before she unlocked the room, and the moment she did, Mrs Peters called. It took me a day to get home, and when I did, she was in the room waiting for me.'

'She didn't leave it?'

'She did. Mrs Peters said she left the room around ten minutes after entering it, then went back to bed, and that was that. But she must have gone back when nobody was looking because I definitely found her in there.'

His eyes looked haunted, and his tone was sombre. He was no longer joking around with me.

'What was she doing when you entered?'

'She was sitting in the centre of the room, in between the bodies of Livvy and Lilliana on the floor. Her legs crossed. Her nightgown pooled around her, reminding me of a small child. She was covered head to toe in blood, just screaming. Incoherent words tumbling out in between the screams. I couldn't even see where the blood was coming from. Not at first.'

'Then?'

'Then I saw her wrists. I couldn't see what she'd used to cut them, but the cuts were jagged and rough. I removed her from the room and called an ambulance immediately. They took her off, and she never spoke again.'

'And she's still alive? Where is she?'

'A facility I pay for.' He looked down at the table, not meeting my eyes. Something like shame washed over his face.

'Because you care, or so you know if she speaks?' Sue me for being a little sceptical about his intentions.

'Both.' His one-word answer told me all I needed to know.

I nodded at that. It made sense to me. Even though he didn't outright say it, I could tell Veronique weighed on his mind more than any of his other wives did. The fact he was still paying for her treatment told me more than his words had.

'And you got a divorce?'

'After she'd settled into her new home, I wrote to her and asked for a divorce. She signed the relevant papers, and it all went away.'

'So, the tale of Veronique is a sad one. Why didn't you kill her?'

My question was blunt, and it sounded completely heartless, but I wanted to know. It wouldn't be above Baron to have done it. To make her—and her problem—go away. Or if he'd let her bleed out, he wouldn't have been to blame.

'She was too famous. We may not have had much press, but if my second wife in the space of a year died from suicide, I would've faced questions. People would have turned to me and my lifestyle. I didn't want that.'

'I understand.'

'I'm going to go to the pool,' he stated, abruptly standing from his chair, his face agitated. 'I'll see you later.'

With that, he left the room.

And left me boiling with a rage I couldn't explain. How dare he leave me sat here alone, all because of the ghost of a woman who wasn't even fucking dead.

The dickhead.

I wouldn't let him get away with treating me like that. Not without the appropriate grovelling. I was all that mattered in his life.

Not them.

Never them.

THE DAY AFTER TELLING ME ABOUT VERONIQUE, BARON was apologetic from the moment I awoke.

I had chosen to sleep in my bedroom, away from him, and it was the first time we hadn't slept beside one another since we married. Except for the time he left me, of course.

At some point, he snuck in, getting in beside me and moulding our bodies together. As if he couldn't bear to stay away from me for too long. Couldn't cope without our skin touching and our hearts connecting in the dark. I didn't acknowledge him. Just went back to sleep. Served him right for upsetting me. From walking away from me. *He left me*, not the other way around, and he needed to remember that.

When I woke up, he was already awake, lying beside me, studying my face.

'Darling,' he whispered against my neck before placing a soft kiss there. 'I am so unequivocally sorry. I was stuck in my own head, and I knew I couldn't be around you. I couldn't let her ruin us.'

'Then why did you walk away from me?' I spat. 'By doing that, you *almost* let her ruin us.'

'I wasn't thinking clearly,' he replied, placing another kiss on my skin, before trailing his tongue down to my collarbone. To his name, indented in my skin. 'You make me the happiest I've ever been. Don't ever confuse my past with how I feel about you in the present.'

'You could've fooled me.' I turned on my side to face him, the sprinkling of dark hair that covered his chest catching my eye. It made him look so manly, and adult, and I was so happy that I'd never slept with anybody my own age. I could imagine that the boys my age were all childish and too immature to be worthy of my time.

'Baby,' he said, and my stomach fluttered. Butterflies made a home in my gut, and they weren't going anywhere fast. 'You know how much you mean to me. Fuck, queen, it feels stupid to even try to voice what you mean to me. It's as if words can't begin to explain the way my heart beats whenever you're around.'

It wasn't often I was at a loss for words, but somehow, Baron had managed it. How did you top that? How did you continue to act like a stuck-up bitch after somebody had opened up to you in that way?

The answer was, you couldn't. Not without being totally heinous.

I moved the duvet off my body and left the warmth of the bed. Baron's eyes tracked my every movement, confused, wondering what I was up to.

Without words, I shed my clothes, wanting to offer him my nakedness. If I couldn't give him words, then my body was the next best thing. And even though the morning had started with him needing to grovel to *me*, I wanted to give him something in return.

He was my world.

My life.

And I wanted him to be secure in that, no matter how hormonal I acted.

I stood at the end of the bed, waiting for Baron's next move. He removed the duvet from his side of the bed, then came to stand before me.

His hands travelled up and down my body, grazing my nipples on their path before they settled on my hips.

'Are you sure?' he asked, his eyes looking into mine. I hoped he saw what I wanted to convey. That I needed him the way he needed me. That we were the start and end of each other's life.

'I want you,' I told him plainly. 'Where would you like me, Sir?'

'Go kneel in the centre of the bed, facing me.'

I nodded, moving to obey the moment the sentence left his lips.

Baron savoured the moment.

His queen kneeled before him, his brand on show, ready and willing to be what he needed me to be.

'You are exquisite.'

I bowed my head, looking down at the bed, wondering what move he would make next.

'Lay down,' he demanded.

I obeyed.

My back touched the mattress within moments, and I stayed still. The soft, cool caress of the black satin sheets was luxurious against my bare backside, and I loved the way Baron was looking at me.

Baron loved obedience. *My* obedience.

He took a step forward, and his hand grasped my right ankle, causing a hissed breath to escape my mouth, unbidden. With deft fingers, he tied my ankle to the bedpost using a taut rope. If I moved too much, I would be in agony, the rope burning into my skin. Exactly how he wanted me to be. Exactly the way we both liked it.

He did the same with my left ankle, and still I stayed in the same position, not moving an inch, splayed out for him to see.

My eyes caught sight of myself in the mirror above our bed and I was surprised by the rush of excitement that ran through my veins at seeing myself that way.

Like the sweetest of nectars.

As if I was transformed.

Four months ago, I had no real knowledge of what married life would be like. What a relationship would even look like for me. Barely out of school and out of work, I wasn't looking for it. But like most things in life, it found me anyway. *He* found me.

Since I discovered the chamber, I'd wondered if it was more than him simply finding me. Whatever way you looked at it, he had somehow been the person at the coffee shop to interview me. That wasn't a coincidence. It couldn't be. I wouldn't allow it to be.

Baron removed his clothes, placing them carefully on the sofa, and I smiled at his action. He always folded his clothes, and it amused me. There was something so insane about it. So unusual and controlled.

His erect dick bobbed against his stomach, and I swallowed at the sight of it. My tongue darted out to lick my bottom lip, wishing I could taste the salty pre-cum I knew would be gathering on his head.

I was leaning up on my elbows to see him, but when his eyes locked with mine, I knew to lie down.

Sometimes, his eyes told me more than his words ever could.

He came to rest between my thighs, his dick lined up where I wanted him most. He held his cock and rubbed himself up and down my entrance, coating himself in my juices, and with every brush of my clit, my heartbeat climbed erratically.

Without a word, he ploughed into me, the one thrust seating him fully inside of me. I gasped. The feeling in my stomach when he did that made my brain malfunction. I had no words to describe it except for *fuck me, that feels amazing.*

As I wriggled beneath his thrusts, writhing on the sheets, sweat clinging to my skin, the ropes around my ankles burned in the most delicious of ways.

'Fuck,' I whispered, my eyes rolling to the back of my head.

Baron was relentless, thrusting hard, his dick constantly hitting that part inside of me that made me see stars. The elusive G-spot that most men—and women—believed was impossible to find.

'You like that, my queen?' His voice was a low rasp. The way he called me *queen* was pure perfection, the word filled with a certain reverence.

Instead of responding with words, I gripped his dark hair, threading my fingers within, forcing his head down to mine.

Our foreheads pressed together to the point of pain, and I relished in it. Loved the sharp, acute feeling that pain caused.

His face blurred in my vision, but I knew that if I could see it, his eyes would be as dark as the sheets beneath our entwined bodies.

My inner walls tightened, gripping him as I searched for the high only he could give. The rush that invaded my body overtook my senses whenever he was deep inside of me, joined as one.

'You're beautiful,' he whispered, his lips brushing against mine. The fanning of his breath on my face made me shiver. In the darkness of the bedroom, I could barely see him, but I knew what his next move would be.

He moved his thumb to my clit, his thrusts coming harder and faster, until we both came in a euphoric moment of togetherness. I knew that it was a rare thing for a couple to come together, but for me and Baron, there was no problem. It was as if our bodies were truly one.

And I hoped that they always would be.

I would do anything within my power to make it so.

'Tonight, I want to tell you about Emmeline,' Baron told me, and I nodded, taking a bite of the pasta dish the cook had prepared for us. One of my favourite things about being insanely rich was the staff we had at our beck and call. A chef to cater to my every craving—and I'd been having a lot of those as of late. Mrs Peters to handle the running of the household. My personal assistant, Ruby, who didn't do much except talk to me when Baron was too busy with work to occupy my mind.

I swallowed my pasta and took a small sip of the glass of water in front of me.

'Okay,' I said when he didn't continue speaking. The previous couple of nights, he'd dived into telling his tale the second dinner was finished, with no prompting from me. But for some reason, he wanted to get it off his chest early.

'But not here,' he said.

'Where then?'

'The room.'

'But *she's* there,' I spat, pissed that he wanted to tell me about his ex-wife in front of our prisoner. Why the fuck did she get to hear the story, too?

She was nothing. She meant nothing. Yet here he was, giving her the chance to listen to his silky voice and bask in his presence. My skin blistered with anger towards her *and* him.

'I want her to hear the story,' he said, simply, raising his eyebrows at me. 'Got a problem with that, darling?'

'You know I fucking do.' I picked up my glass and threw it at his head, my anger hitting a new peak. One it hadn't reached before. Not with Baron, at least. The two of us were passionate, and we both had strong feelings and emotions, but I'd never thrown anything at him. If a long table didn't separate us, then I would've probably reached across and wrapped my fingers around his throat and squeezed, ever so slightly.

'How many times do I have to tell your jealous arse that she means nothing to me?'

'Maybe another ten times if you insist that we go spend time with her in a friendly manner. We go there to hurt her. Not to tell her a fucking story. Want to take a book down there for her to enjoy while we're at it?'

I knew my anger was irrational. That I shouldn't be getting so worked up by Emily Brown. But I couldn't help myself. Ever since we were younger, I had compared myself to her. Compared my life to hers. Our personalities. *Everything.*

And now I was feeling a compulsion to compare my husband's treatment of me with his treatment of her. It wasn't logical. Especially as she was being kept nearly naked in a cage with a shit bucket and I had the run of the house. Everything at my fingertips.

'Want to dampen down that green-eyed monster, hm?' Amusement laced his voice, and it was obvious he was humouring me. Or finding humour *because* of me. 'You've got nothing to worry about, and deep down, you know that.'

'Fine!' I slumped down in my chair, dropping my cutlery onto my plate with a loud clunk. Whenever I felt sad, or threatened, or just downright pissed, I turned into a child. As if my brain couldn't deal with all the adult emotions that swirled around inside it, and in order to come to terms with it, I regressed mentally. Throwing a tantrum rather than facing my problems.

'Darling,' he said, ignoring my petty shit. 'There's a good reason I want to tell the story down there. And believe me, it may be a story Emily wants to know, but it isn't going to make her happy.'

'You promise?'

'I do. I wouldn't lie to you about something like this.' His eyes were wide and genuine, but even though I could see that on his face, my gut still churned with anguish. Pain.

'You better fucking not. If I find out you're lying to me, Baron Henrick, then you'll live to regret it.'

'Why would I lie to you?' The savage smile on his face was at odds with how he wanted me to feel, but fuck it. If I ever found out that he lied to me, I'd kill him.

'Let's go get this shit show on the road,' I told him, willing to forgo my meal to get my answers. Baron didn't shift in his chair or get ready to stand. No. His only movement was to bring his fork to his lips and eat whatever nasty meal the cook had prepared for us.

Yes, I was aware I called it delicious beforehand, but all of them had royally fucked me off and my childish tendencies knew no bounds.

'Finish your meal.'

'I don't want to,' I grumbled, petulant to the end. 'I don't like it.'

'You were scooping it up like your fork was a shovel,' he pointed out, his face stern. He didn't have time for my antics, that much was clear. 'Eat. The. Food.'

Feeling thoroughly scolded, I picked up my fork and ate my dinner, the whole time imagining a gruesome death for Baron in my head.

I imagined poking his eyes out with my fork. Using my knife to stab or slice him, watching with morbid fascination as the blood pooled on the surface; at first a dark red that turned a paler shade the more it made contact with the air.

Maybe I could use the candle burning in the centre of the table to pour wax in his mouth, or burn his skin, putting the flame out using his flesh.

My morbid thoughts continued throughout the rest of the meal, and they kept me happy. Or at least happy enough to wait until the end of dinner to go to the room. The place that still called to me, even though I knew what was inside.

If anything, now that I was in on the secret, it beckoned me more.

Baron finally finished, and the plates were cleared away.

'Now we may go,' he asserted. They were the first words spoken to me since he forced me to eat my food, and I gave him a Cheshire Cat grin.

I stood from my chair, as he did the same, and I went to his side. He grabbed my hand and held it firmly, pulling me with him as the two of us made our way through the house to where our prisoner was trapped.

'Emily!' I called, making my way down the hallway with the cracked wallpaper. I'd asked Baron why he left it looking so decrepit, and he told me it was to get into character. Leaving the bright white clean surfaces of the manor and entering a dark, dingy underworld that only he got to experience. 'Emily!'

My voice got louder the closer we got, and I relished in the fear she was undoubtedly feeling at our approach. It was why I called her name, after all. Just arriving without an announcement was no fun.

Although I did it once. Moved like stealth in silence and made her shit herself when my voice came from behind her cage in the dark. She didn't actually shit herself, but wouldn't it have been funny if she had?

Baron's low chuckle travelled through the hall, and I knew that would only make her more nervous. She hated it when we came alone, but she despised it when we came together.

Couldn't blame her, either.

We entered the room, one in front of the other. Baron switched the bulb on, so the room was awash with that synthetic glow of a single bulb hanging from a cable that swung slightly with any movement, causing the light to move too.

'What are you doing here?' she whimpered, cowering in the corner, her back pressed up against the metal bars. It was rare for her to talk back when Baron was here. She respected him a lot more than she would ever respect me. I'd probably feel the same way if it was Baron that had snatched me from my life and locked me up. The glint of fear in her eyes came swiftly at her mistake. 'M-master.'

'It's time for a story,' Baron responded. Out of the corner of my eye, I saw Emily sit up a little straighter, interested in what was going to come next. Little bitch. I hated the way she revered *my* husband, even though he was keeping her captive.

I supposed it was some kind of Stockholm Syndrome type situation—even I could understand that.

'What type of story, Sir?' She'd lost so much weight that her eyes bugged out of her skull, and at first, it was something that amused me about her. But now it fucked me off. It reminded me of those paintings. The ones that dude said he painted, but really, it was his wife doing it all under duress. I hated the way it gave her a look of vulnerability.

'The one you've been asking for.' Now there was no way I could deny that she was sitting up straighter. She wanted the story —Baron had told me as much—and a deep-rooted anger ignited within me that he was giving her something she wanted. 'The story of Emmeline.'

'Thank you,' she whispered. 'You're a generous master.'

Generous master? I scoffed. Did she want to be even more pathetic?

'Fucking get on with it, then,' I demanded, wanting to interrupt the sycophantic behaviour I was witnessing before me. 'Don't want to be down here with the trash for too long.'

Baron gave me a stern scowl, but didn't comment on my petty attitude. The way the light hit him, the way his features darkened, made me wish that the two of us were upstairs in our room. There was something about my husband that spoke to me on a deeper level. I couldn't explain it, wouldn't be able to explain it, even if you tortured me.

'I met Emmeline when I was twenty-seven,' he started, and I realised that I was going to have to stand for the entire story. Not like I was about to sit on the floor with Emily. I crossed my arms across my chest, fighting the impulse to tap my foot on the floor. 'She was twenty-one, broke, and had little family to help her.'

I hated the way his tone changed. The way it had softened.

Had the fucker not learned his lesson the previous evening when he told me about Veronique? Did the events of the morning mean *nothing* to him? He grovelled. He told me how I was his world. The only one who had elicited such a response in him emotionally.

I told him before that if he lied, I would kill him.

He was walking on a very thin line.

'...happy for crumbs.'

I shook my head, clearing away my jealous and somewhat murderous thoughts. If I kept disappearing into my head, I would miss the story. Would miss the bits I actually gave a shit about. And I couldn't have that. Fuck only knew what Baron meant about crumbs.

'What do you mean?' Emily asked, crossing her legs and listening to every word from Baron's lips with intent.

'Did we give you permission to speak?' I sneered at her. Not like she needed to know that she'd asked something I wanted an answer to. Emily looked up from her spot on the floor, surrounded by her own filth, and I smiled at her. A vicious, vindictive smile that showed all my teeth.

'She was one of those lost souls,' Baron continued on, ignoring my scolding. 'Had no family, no friends, lived in a shelter for home-less women, and lived a life unlike one I'd ever come across before. Growing up wealthy meant she was the first real poverty case I saw, and it struck a chord with me.'

'What did?' I asked, bitterness leaking into the air like bile does to a liver.

'The helplessness. The fact she had nobody to call her own and was willing to do *anything* to change her situation.' He shrugged before running his hand through his hair, deep in thought.

The hair on the back of my neck bristled at his tone. At the offhand way he was telling us about Emmeline's situation, espe-cially as it didn't sound much different from my own a short few months prior to marrying Baron. Did he think that little of me? Was I somebody that intrigued him because I would do *anything* for him?

'Let me guess,' I interrupted again, already bored and ready for the story to be over. It made me feel a certain way, a way I didn't *want* to feel, and it was best I nipped it in the bud sooner rather than later. 'You saved her from that, asked her to marry you, and then you gave her the keys.'

'Not quite,' Baron replied, his lips turning into an amused smirk. 'But nice to know you think you've got me sussed.'

'Then what happened?' I asked, still feigning boredom, even though I was a little more interested after learning he hadn't followed his usual M.O.

'This house went up for sale. I told you that I knew the son of the owner'—he gestured around us, breathing in deeply—'and that I knew about this room. So I made sure to snap it up quickly. When I told Emmeline about it, she seemed eager. We toured the house, and she fell in love.'

'With the library?' I whispered, my gut telling me I was correct in my assumption.

He nodded, and said, 'It was her favourite room in the house. She loved it at first sight. We married, moved into the manor, and were happy for a time.'

Baron began to pace, up and down in front of the cage, lost in his memories, as if me and Emily didn't exist to him. He needed to tell the tale, and he knew he had a captive audience.

'The usual itch began to feed me. Control me. I obsessed constantly over ways to get what I wanted. A way to have an alive wife for a change. So, I told her I was going on business, like I'd done previously, but this time, I tweaked the plan.'

'Tweaked it?'

'I never left the manor. Waited at the end of the drive and snuck back in when Emmy was in the chamber. She found this cage.' He kicked the bars of the cage Emily was crouched in before continuing. 'She found the bodies. The usual. But before she could leave, I entered the room too. Grabbed her arms and bound them behind her back. Shoved her into the cage before she could escape me. Locked her up and left her there for the night.'

'Why?' I asked, following along with the story in a detached fashion. If I didn't, there was no way of knowing how I would respond.

'I wanted to see what her reaction would be. After the time we'd spent together, I got the vibe that she'd be down for something a little... peculiar. And I was right.'

'Of course you were,' I said, a scoff leaving my throat. 'You seem to be able to read everybody.'

'In a way,' he agreed. 'The next morning, I made my way into this chamber. Emmy was in the position I'd left her in, her hands still bound behind her back, and her eyes were frantic. Words tumbled out of her mouth. "I'll do anything you ask of me, Baron. I want to be everything for you. I don't want to end up like *them*." She pointed at the bodies that were still in the room, her face twisting into something beautiful. "Tell me what I can do. Tell me, and I'll do it. Please don't do this to me."'

Baron coughed, still pacing, running his hand through his hair.

'So, I gave her an ultimatum. I told her she could stay in the chamber forever and be the perfect prisoner, *or* she could help me find the perfect prisoner.'

He laughed, his eyes seeing something neither me nor Emily could see. She glanced up at me, seeking my eyes, but I wouldn't give in to it. We weren't allies. Not in anything. Plus, she knew Emmy, and that only made me hate her more.

'As you can guess, she chose to become my prisoner. She stayed in the chamber and became what I asked of her. Emmy became the perfect prisoner. And for seven years, we were as happy as we could be. The world thought she'd disappeared, and nobody was looking for her in her own home.'

I hated the way he called her Emmy. Hated the fact she was a wife with a nickname. The special one. The *chosen* one. The wife he kept alive for seven fucking years, unknown to anybody.

'But then everything changed,' he said abruptly, his tone darkening. 'The routine we established burned with one wish.'

'What happened?' I asked, trying to envision Emmeline in my mind, but struggling to, seeing as I'd never seen a picture of her. Baron didn't exactly give me great descriptions of them. 'What changed?

'Emmy wanted a child.'

 his stance, holding his hands together in front of his hips. 'So, I knew that I wanted to give her one.'

'A child?' My disgust hit me thick and fast. He *wanted* to give *Emmy* a child? The thought made me sick, the nausea that lived in my stomach ever since moving to the manor reaching a peak. I fought it, not wanting to lose my dinner so soon after having it.

'Not a baby,' Baron clarified. 'No, she wanted a teenage child. After six years of acting as a prisoner, she didn't want to do it anymore. She wanted to change her ultimatum answer. Wanted to help me find the perfect prisoner. Which is where *you* came in.'

He stopped his pacing, standing in front of the cage, and looking down at Emily's emaciated figure.

I wondered if Baron would class her as the perfect prisoner. Had he and Emmy trained her to their specifications? How did you even train the perfect prisoner?

Emmy would have been having sex with him, surely? As his

wife, and captive, she would've done anything for him. Hadn't she made that clear from the moment she met him?

Baron continued, talking to us both with his next sentence.

'Unknown to Emmy, enough time had passed that I was able to have her declared legally dead. After seven years, you can do that with no issue, body or not. It meant, if I wanted, I could look for my next wife. And I wanted to. Emmeline may have been what I needed when I met her, but in the seven years that passed, we lost our spark. *She* lost her spark.'

I began to shift from foot to foot, pissed that I was still standing listening to Baron's drivel. Irritated that I couldn't sit down, but also irritated that I knew I couldn't leave, no matter how much I wanted to.

'But I wanted to give her one last chance,' Baron said. 'It wasn't fair of me to discard her with no compassion after all she'd given me. Her last chance was the idea of a new prisoner. A daughter for her to talk to. Train. Somebody to spend time with while I went away on business. So I cast my attention to finding a teenager that she would fall in love with.'

'And somehow, you decided to kidnap me?' Emily asked, ignoring my glare, her tone hushed. 'How? Why?'

'I guess I should backtrack a little,' my husband responded, resuming his pacing. I glanced around the room, trying to occupy my brain with something other than my anger at the situation I'd found myself in. 'Emmy asked for a new girl, and I wanted to make her happy, so the two of us sat down and discussed what she wanted.'

'Clearly, she wanted someone fucking boring and ugly,' I piped up, unable to stop myself.

Baron ignored me, continuing like I never spoke.

'Emmy wanted a blonde teenager with bright eyes. A wide smile that lit up a room. Somebody defiant that would need to be broken before they were of use to her. Somebody she would enjoy having around. Could tell her stories of the world Emmy chose to leave seven years before.'

'And how did you decide on *her*?' My arms were still tightly crossed in front of my chest, and the tapping of my foot was increasing in speed with every second he dragged on his bullshit tale.

Jesus, did Baron want to piss me off for the entire evening? He'd told me that the story would bring Emily misery, but so far, it just sounded to me like he was gassing her up. And I didn't subscribe to that. No part of me wanted her to feel good about herself in any way.

'I was passing Hollowdale High one day, and I spotted somebody who fit Emmy's description. Was a perfect fit. Looked to be around the right age. And I knew I needed to get her somehow.

'So, I stalked the girl. Watched her patterns. Noticed her friends, family, her routine. Everything. Then I would go home and tell Emmy all about her and the two of us would talk of the future.'

'Well, I'm happy for the two of you, truly,' I drawled. 'But I'm also bored as fuck, so if we could get a move on, I'd appreciate it.'

I stamped my foot, no longer able to control my outward anger towards Baron. He was taking me for a ride, and I wasn't going to stand for it. Emily could continue to listen to his shit if she wanted —not that she had a choice—but I wouldn't be.

'Emily can tell the rest,' Baron stated. He stopped pacing in front of me and turned to face me fully for the first time during the conversation. His eyebrow raised, and I knew he was wondering if that was enough to get me to stay. He knew me better than I knew myself, so of course he knew I was thinking about walking out.

'I can?' she stuttered, then a light filled her eyes. She saw an opportunity. 'Master, may I have permission to get out of the cage and stretch my legs?'

It shocked me that my eyes didn't roll out of the back of my sockets and down my throat with how hard they rolled at her question. My nostrils flared, and I clenched my jaw tightly to stop myself from snapping at her.

What shocked me further was Baron bending down to unlock her cage door with the keys he kept in his back pocket at all times. He was going to let her out without even asking me first if I agreed.

Had I entered an alternate universe?

'If I let you out,' he told her, 'then you must stay within the circle drawn on the ground.'

'I promise,' she whispered, fluttering her eyelashes up at my husband. 'I won't misbehave, Sir.'

Baron nodded, accepting her statement as fact, and continued unlocking the door. Emily stepped out with tentative steps, her hand in Baron's, her knees shaking with the action, and I saw red. Bet she didn't even need the support. Bet she was just making it all up so he would have to help her.

Bitch.

'You're a good girl, Emily.'

I gagged at the charade. Sickened to the bone.

Emily stood in front of us, stretching out each limb in turn, before returning to a statue.

'Thank you, Sir.' She took a deep breath, and her ribs pushed against her skin as she did so, all gross and pointed. Her eyes darted to me, and a flash of embarrassment flickered in them. 'It was a normal day, nothing different from usual. I woke up, went to school, and nothing was off about any of it. It was only when I was walking home from school that day that things felt wrong.'

She swallowed, and I wondered if she was choosing her words

carefully. Or maybe she was just dehydrated from having too little water over the last few days.

Since finding her, I made sure she had even less than she'd become accustomed to. Didn't want her to think she was liked, or that her life was going to improve now that I knew of her existence.

'Wrong how?'

'I can't explain how I knew,' she replied, her eyes lost in her memory. 'But it was like I could feel eyes on the back of my neck. The hairs there all rose to attention, and every couple of steps, I looked over my shoulder to check there wasn't anybody walking behind me.

'I walked through the town centre, and there were enough people there that I just put my worries down to me being paranoid. It was when I turned onto the corner of Hawthorn Hills that the air changed. A car pulled up alongside me, and before I could look to my right, I was bundled into the car by an unknown figure.'

'Baron?' I asked, hating that he knew she came from the rich side of town. Well, of course he did, he married her sister. But even before that, he knew she was wealthy. My old insecurity of what he must have thought showing up to my family's apartment when he picked me up for our first date trickled through me. Fuck Emily for making me feel insecure. For bringing up old wounds.

She nodded, still looking at me instead of Baron.

'Bundled me into his car. Took me to the mansion. Dragged me kicking and screaming into this room, and introduced me to my new *mother*, Emmy.'

For a moment, I placed myself in Emily's shoes. Imagined how it would've been to be taken from the streets and thrust into a chamber by a handsome yet evil man, who was telling me the woman inside was to be my new mother. I flicked through my mind to figure out when I remembered Emily disappearing. A year ago, at least. If I didn't hate her so much, I might even feel a little sorry for her. But I did, so I didn't.

'He left us alone together to get to know one another. She kept telling me that she was going to move back into the house after training me up. Was adamant she'd be leaving her prison and that if I was good and followed her instructions, maybe one day, I would be free too. After six months, she changed her tune. She knew she would never be free. And then, Master came home one night and told us he was getting married.'

'Did you know he was marrying your sister?' I asked, unable to stop myself. I needed to know. Had Baron picked Violet because he had Emily? Or was it a happy surprise?

'Not at first,' she admitted. 'But I knew after a time. And there was nothing I could do about it. Emmeline was still hopeful that she would return to her life above, but she didn't connect the dots the way I did. If Master was marrying again, then Emmeline Henrick was dead.'

I tore my gaze from Emily to look at Baron. He was standing straight, an amused smile on his face, enjoyment at the story clear as day. Maybe he'd never heard her version of events, never given her the chance to tell of her torment.

Emily opened her mouth, but Baron cut her off before she could talk further.

'That's enough for tonight,' he said, his deep voice covering my body in chills. 'The rest of the story isn't yours to tell.'

He turned to me, opening his arms wide, and I walked straight into them, happy to breathe him in. He smelled of Baron, a scent that aroused me and excited me more than any other.

'Let me lock her up,' I told him in a soft, melodic whisper. 'I want to talk to her.'

'If you want, my love.' He placed a hard kiss on my forehead before inhaling my hair. 'I'll see you in our room in half an hour?'

'I won't be that long.' I pulled away from his hug. 'Leave the keys.'

He put his hand into his back pocket and took out the key for her lock to hand to me. He placed it in my palm, and I turned it around, feeling every groove. Every smooth curve. It was the key to her freedom—literally—and I loved having it in my hand.

Baron left, leaving me there with Emily, giving us some space, and my heart filled with even more love for him. He accepted what I needed whenever I needed it.

'Did you think any more about what I told you?' I asked once I heard the door at the end of the hallway slam closed behind Baron.

'A bit hard to think while trapped in a cage,' she bit out. Her left eye was swollen shut, and she winced with every small movement she made closer to the edge of her prison.

'Doesn't look like you're trapped in a cage right now,' I pointed out. 'And anyway, your body is trapped, not your fucking mind.'

I spat on the ground, and it landed close to her feet.

'Are you really that stupid that you can't think?' I added when she didn't reply. I wanted to push her to do something stupid. Wanted her to make a rash decision she'd regret.

'I can think perfectly fine,' she replied. 'But I need assurances from you.'

'What kind of assurances?'

'That I won't die.' Her voice was matter-of-fact. Detached from the topic at hand.

'There's no guaranteeing that.' I looked at her square-on, assessing her. 'And what would it matter if you did? Not like you have much of a life here.'

'Just promise me. Or I won't do it.'

'Baron will never believe you if you choose to tell him. Just so you're aware.' Not that I thought she'd tell him, but still. She needed to know who held all the power. And it wasn't her. 'I'm going to leave it in your hands. Do what you want.'

I stood up, brushing my skirt with my hands. I hated the dirt on the floor. I was just lucky that the smell didn't faze me anymore. If you experienced something long enough, then it became the new normal.

'Why?' she whispered. I shrugged and turned my back on her, then walked out.

I didn't need to tell her shit.

'She's gone.'

Baron stood a foot away from me, wringing his hands in front of his chest, staring with wide eyes. It was the morning after he'd taken me to the chamber to tell me about Emmeline, and I was still a little bitter about the fact that he cared about one of his wives enough to keep them alive for *eight* years.

'What do you mean, she's gone?' I roared.

'Her cage is empty,' he said, his tone barely above a whisper. Deadly. 'Are you sure you didn't leave it unlocked?'

'Of course I didn't fucking leave it unlocked,' I replied, my voice no longer a roar, but a low, venomous sneer. 'Do I look that stupid to you?'

'No.' He took a small step towards me, his hands outstretched to pull me into a hug, doing his best to placate me. 'Of course not.'

'Well, don't accuse me of such stupid things, then.' I let him pull me closer, but I didn't reciprocate the affection. My feelings were still hurt by his accusation, and it would take a little time for me to overlook his foolishness. 'Where do you think she could've got to? Surely, she can't have left Henrick manor.'

'None of the staff have seen her.'

'Oh?' I raised an eyebrow, tilting my head up to look him in the eye. I usually loved the way he loomed over me, tall and strong, but at that moment it just made me angrier with him. 'And how did you explain that to them? *"Mrs Peters, have any of your staff happened to see a teenage girl running through the halls? No, not my wife. A different one."* Yes, I'm sure that went down a treat.'

'The staff know what's best for them,' he replied, not worried in the slightest. 'They get paid to do their job and to turn a blind eye to anything out of the ordinary.'

'Like teenage girls running through the halls?' I smiled.

'Something like that,' he responded, smiling back.

But our smiles could only last so long. Because if she wasn't in the mansion, then that meant she'd headed out into the grounds. Maybe even gone into the woods, looking for a sister she would never find.

'She can't have got too far,' I mused. 'I saw her only a few hours ago.'

'Let's hope not. This would be a big cover up if she managed to get herself far enough away to alert the police of her presence. I'd have to pay a lot of people off. Bribe a few officials.'

'Like that would bother you.'

'It wouldn't,' he admitted with ease. 'But it'd be a fucking pain, to say the least.'

I nodded, agreeing with him. I didn't really know what bribing an official entailed, but I could guess that it wasn't as simple as handing over a small cheque. People that found themselves in power, in the big, important positions, were rarely fine and upstanding members of society. Most people in power—or perceived power, at least—were hungry to keep that position in any way that they could. Including taking large amounts of money from a man as wealthy as my husband.

'Well, then we go search for her.' I rubbed his forearms, finally softening towards him enough to want to touch him. To soothe. 'The woods are empty now, aren't they? They've stopped searching for Violet?'

'The police have, yeah. But there are still some voluntary groups out looking for her. Fucking idiots,' he spat. 'That woman had no real friends. She was vile and deserved everything that happened to her. Yet all these people are still seeking her out, wanting to find her alive and well. It makes me sick.'

'I know, baby. But there's nothing we can do about her image, is there? All we can do is downplay anything that comes our way. We need to focus on Emily now. She's the one that could ruin us.'

'I'd never let her ruin you,' he vowed, gripping my chin with his pointer finger and thumb in a vice-like grip, ensuring I looked into his eyes. 'You're my queen, and I won't ever put you in that position. You understand?'

'Yes,' I whispered. My lips crashed onto his, as I went up onto my tiptoes to match his height, pushing myself into the kiss. His beard tickled the way I liked it, and his lips pushed against mine with equal fervour.

'Promise me that you won't do anything rash,' he said, pushing me back by my shoulders, his gaze assessing me, looking for deceit.

'I promise,' I replied, giving him a blank stare as I added, 'to try my best.'

'Guess that's the most I'll get from you.' He accepted that I would do what I could to not react poorly, but that I didn't want to promise anything I could potentially break and get whipped for later. 'Want me to tell you about her?'

'About Violet?' I rolled my eyes, a war raging inside me. I knew I wanted to hear the story, but I also knew I didn't want to come off as over eager. Even just the thought of her boiled by insides, to the point where they were probably leaking bile into my intestines or some shit. Poisoning me.

Violet was the wife I hated the most. It probably had to do with the fact that I personally knew her. Knew what kind of a person she was in life.

Vindictive. Bitchy. Rude.

A total cunt to everyone that crossed her path.

'Yes.'

'Fine,' I said with a huff, getting up from where I was sitting on the edge of our bed and moving to the sofa in front of the fireplace. May as well be comfortable while he told me about her. 'But give me the Cliffs Notes version, please.'

Baron came to sit beside me on the couch, his large hand splayed across my knee firmly to hold me in place. As if he could ever truly hold me in place for long.

'As you heard from Emily, I showed up one day and told her and Emmy that I was in a new relationship. After a while, I let them in on the fact that I was engaged to be married to a lovely young lady named Violet. Emily knew I meant her sister from the start. But she couldn't say anything. As she pointed out, she was aware that Emmy was dead to everybody out in the real world, and she didn't want to ruin her belief that everything would get better for her.'

'So, Violet,' I insisted, moving him along. I loved Baron's stories, but at times he wanted to relish in all the details, and all I wanted was for him to get to the point. I didn't have the focus or the mental faculty to wait hours to hear something that could be told in a matter of minutes.

'Well, you knew Violet.' I nodded. 'She was a bitch, but she served a purpose. I knew she was Emily's sister the whole time, having studied Emily's family before I took her. Knew that Violet would be impressed by my wealth and status and that she'd jump on the chance to further herself.'

'How did you meet her?'

'I introduced myself to her during a search for Emily.'

'Of course you did,' I said, laughing for the first time in a while. The meeting flitted into my mind, and I could envision exactly how it went down. Baron, acting his charming self, wooing her, and Violet, pretending she wasn't a massive raving bitch, acting coquettishly and thoroughly enamoured.

'Well,' he continued, laughing with me, 'nobody was going to think I took her while I searched for her, were they?'

'You do have a handsome, kind face, I suppose.'

'You suppose?'

'Well, there are those times, you know...' My words trailed off. Baron didn't say anything, but the hand he had gripped on my thigh tightened to the point of pain. 'When you look rather like the devil.'

'It was only six months later that we got engaged and married. I didn't even lust after her. Didn't want to lie with her. I only wanted to spite Emmy and Emily. The two of them had become quite the unit, and I wanted to unnerve them.'

I leaned into Baron's side, grabbing his hand to place it around my waist, and got comfortable.

'The weekend before I planned to hand over the key, Mrs Peters came to me with news that she'd found at least ten positive pregnancy tests in Violet's waste bin in her bathroom. So, I waited. Waited for her to come tell me her news. But she never did. And that was when I had her followed whenever she left the mansion.'

'She was allowed out?'

'Darling,' he said, lifting my chin with his finger so he could look into my eyes. He chuckled, his eyes light and happy. 'You're allowed to leave, too. You just don't want to.'

'Oh.'

'The men that followed her reported back to me that she was visiting an important gentleman. I contacted him, and he told me everything. The two of them were having an affair—had been before I ever met her—and she was adamant she was pregnant with his child. Because he was happily married, and an affair would've ruined his reputation, he ignored her and kept sending her away, hoping she'd get the picture. She'd become a nuisance, and he wanted her gone. I told him I may have a solution for all his problems.

'I went ahead with my plan, but not before I had her sign an annulment. I confronted her, and she blurted the truth to me. Tears poured down her face as she lied through her teeth, telling me of her remorse.'

'Then what happened? How'd she end up missing?'

'I showed her the keys and took her to the room. Once inside, she saw her sister and wept. That was when I gave her an ultimatum.'

'What was it?'

'Either she could take her sister's place, *or* she could flee.'

'Let me guess,' I said, my tone dry. 'She chose to flee.'

'She did. And she died because of it.'

It seemed to me like she'd deserved it.

BARON

My wife had taken to her new role in the most delicious way.

Like a phoenix rising from the ashes, she'd shed the old and become something fiery and new. Something better than I'd ever imagined or expected her to be.

But since our prisoner went missing two days ago, she'd become something else entirely. Something I feared equally as much as I revered.

Her eyes were wild, bloodshot, and I knew she'd barely got any sleep. Neither of us had. Because we both knew we needed to find Emily—and soon.

'Have you spoken to the police?' she asked, her voice shrill.

'I've called the chief,' I told her, placing my tumbler down on the coffee table. There was no way to escape her these days. Even in my rooms, sitting on my sofa, enjoying a whiskey while pursuing the papers, she interrupted me. 'Explained the situation. If he or his force finds her, we'll be the first to know about it. Her family has lost all hope for both their daughters, so I doubt they'll still be out looking.'

'But what if they are?' She flew at me and sunk her nails into my arm. 'We have no way of knowing that. Why can't we just throw them off the scent? Have them find Violet's body?'

'And implicate us further?'

'It wouldn't implicate *us*,' she sniffed.

'You seem so certain about that.'

'I am.' She sat down next to me and draped her body over my lap, drawing my eyes to her. 'They've done it before. Plus, she wasn't your wife anymore when she went missing.'

'No, but they'll find her dead and pregnant.'

'If she was even telling the truth about that.'

'Tell me, my queen. Why would she have lied about that?' He raised his eyebrow. 'And what, would she have faked the tests, too?'

'She would lie because she wanted to get far away from you. The man that was holding her sister captive in a cage hidden deep within the house. Those tests could've been anybody's.' Her face contorted into a sneer. 'Most women wouldn't accept it the way I did.'

'Yes, but as we've established already...' I lifted her hand and placed a kiss on her palm. 'There aren't many others out there like you.'

'You're right,' she said with a wide smile. 'I'm a rare gem.'

'You're a pain in my arse,' I told her, my smile matching hers. It amazed me how fast her moods could change. How one moment she could be bitter, or solemn, and then the next, she could be happy and delirious to the point of mania.

'Ah,' she sighed, pulling my arm so it wrapped around her, 'but you wouldn't want it any other way.'

'Keep telling yourself that, sweetheart.'

She pinched my arm, and I gave her no reaction. It was best not to. A reaction just made her want to do something more. Whether good or bad.

I knew it wouldn't be long until my queen went too far with our captive. Or at least, if we still had our captive, she probably wouldn't have been left on the earth much longer.

But now that she was missing, she had no outlet. No way of getting out her anger and frustrations. The staff was taking the brunt of it.

'Fine,' she huffed. 'I'm bored, Baron.'

Pleasure ran through my veins whenever she used my name. It sounded perfect coming from her plump lips. Lips that looked best around my cock.

'What do you wanna do?' My hand began to trail up her body, over her breasts, and down her stomach, until it rested on her protruding hip bone.

The spot tickled her.

'I don't know.' Her bottom lip jutted out in a pout. 'Maybe we should go look for her. You know that whole saying, *don't ask some-body to do a job when you could do it better*?'

'And you think we could do it better?' My tone was amused. She didn't even know the first thing about these woods. Had never ventured into them. And if she had, she hadn't been there alone.

'Be fun to try, wouldn't it. It could be our own little adventure.'

'Then lead the way.'

The snow on the ground crunched underneath my feet as I slowly stalked behind my prey.

My light.

My life.

Up ahead, my wife was searching the trees, or at least that was what she was pretending to do. Really, she was waiting for me to catch her.

Hadn't I made it clear that the thrill was in the chase rather than the catch?

I'd tired rather quickly of those I caught in the past, except maybe my sweet Emmeline, and I didn't want that to happen with *her*.

Because she was it for me. The end. My one and only and all the other nonsense phrases that The *Beurre Banner* was using to write about our relationship.

'These trees go on forever,' she whined, coming to a halt, stomping her foot on the ground like a petulant teenager.

'I told you it wouldn't be easy.' I laughed at the recurring pout forming on her luscious lips. 'How about we liven up this expedition?'

Her mouth tilted up, but she masked the flicker of amusement as quickly as it appeared. She wanted to hold on to her fury. Her boredom. Hell, whatever mood she was in that day.

No matter what I did to combat it, she held steadfast to the emotion she'd decided was hers for that moment.

'What do you propose we do?' she asked, a wicked smile covering her face.

'I think...' I trailed off, raking my eyes over her from head to toe, taking in the way she held herself. It had changed in the short time our paths had crossed. 'That you should run.'

Her eyes lit up, and before I could say another word, she

turned and bolted away to run through the trees, stumbling on the branches and snow that lay on the ground.

My queen was willing to play. And I wasn't going to disappoint. I also wasn't planning on going easy on her.

I counted down from ten in my head, letting her get a head start on me, but also knowing she wasn't going to get very far. I wouldn't let her get very far.

She was mine.

My eyes tracked her movements, and the adrenaline rose inside, waiting to be unleashed on her. The white sheet of snow covered the ground and the branches of the trees, creating a picturesque wonderland. I loved these woods. Alongside the chamber, the large expanse of trees surrounding my property were the reason I bought the manor.

'Ten!' My voice boomed out, echoing through the trees to wherever my life was running or hiding. She'd run off with gusto, but I knew her. She wouldn't be running at her full power because she wanted to be caught. We'd never taken part in rape play before, but it was something that I'd wanted to try with her for months. We had spoken about it back when we discussed our limits and safe words; that we were happy to forgo safe, sane, and consensual in favour of risk aware consensual kink.

Now was the perfect opportunity.

My feet took off after her in the direction she left in, and with my large strides, it didn't take me long to catch up with her.

I closed the gap between us, grabbing her by the hips, and shoving her front forward.

'Where do you think you're going, my queen?' I breathed into her ear, coming up behind her and placing my body up against hers, pushing her into the tree. 'You didn't truly think you could get away from me, did you?'

'N-no, Sir,' she stuttered, sucking in a large breath.

'Do you want my cock? Do you want me to ram my dick inside you and tear you apart?'

'No,' she said, her refusal at odds with the tone of her voice. 'I don't want that.'

'No?' I pressed into her more forcefully, my hard cock resting in between her arse cheeks, and the side of her face pressed into the tree trunk hard enough to leave an imprint. She wiggled beneath me, and her distress only spurred me on.

I grabbed both of her wrists and slammed them above her head, pushing them up against the bark of the tree, as her breaths came out in short, little pants.

'Don't move,' I commanded. My eyes were drawn to her brand and my dick throbbed in my trousers at the sight of it. 'If you do, it'll only make your pain worse.'

I lifted the skirt of her dress out of the way and all but yanked off her knickers, needing them gone so her bare pussy was available for me.

She winced beneath me, now exposed to the cool air, and I smiled at her reaction. She was trying not to move, fighting with her instinct to fight back and play and her need to obey me, but I knew she wouldn't stay still the whole time. She couldn't. It just wasn't in my girl's nature.

'Please don't do this,' she whispered. 'I don't want you to.'

'No?' I growled in her ear, biting her earlobe gently. I was no longer holding her hands above her head, as my hands were placed on her hips, keeping her in place.

A scream tore from her lips as her elbow jolted backwards and connected with my ribs. Pain shot through me from where her elbow had connected, and I hissed in air through my teeth, her defiance only spurring me on more.

She flew off, a couple of low-hanging branches tugging at her dress as she went, catching her arms and tearing the skin. Like an animal, I could smell the blood as it rose to the surface of her flesh.

My ears pricked, and I chased after her once more.

It wasn't long before I had her in my arms again. She wasn't great at escaping me. If she was, she would've escaped me before our first date. But we both knew that above all else, she wanted to be caught.

'No!' Stop.'

I ripped open the fabric of her dress that covered her breasts and took one roughly in my large hand. Her tits were the perfect size, firm and perky, and I loved that they filled my palm. I pinched her nipple between my thumb and forefinger, hard, until she moaned.

'Stop. I don't want this.'

I dug my nails into her nipple and a scream tore itself from her throat.

'I'm going to rip you apart,' I whispered in her ear. 'You're going to come all over my cock, and you're going to enjoy it.'

'No, no,' she muttered, trembling in my arms, her knees weakening.

I moved us close to a large tree and turned her around, placing her back up against the bark.

'This time you're going to be a good girl and stay where you are,' I told her, watching her tongue dart out to lick her bottom lip. Her words may be telling me no, but her eyes... her eyes were telling me all I needed to know and more.

Her bared breasts caught my attention, and I leaned down to lick them, taking my time with each nipple. Nipping and biting and licking. All the actions I knew my wife went crazy over. She whimpered, her moans growing in volume the more I sucked her.

'Please,' she pleaded. 'Please.'

I looked at her face and saw a tear trailing down her cheek. I pushed my body up against hers so she couldn't move, my knee trapping her, and I licked the single tear before it reached her chin.

'Even your tears taste like heaven.'

It was as if my words opened the dam within her. Tears began to fall thick and fast, and every one made my dick throb to the point of pain. Making sure she couldn't get away from me, I unzipped my trousers, making quick work of unleashing my cock from the confines of my boxers.

Then, in another swift motion, I moved her underwear out of the way. I grazed her folds, feeling how soaked and ready for me she was.

She may be saying no, but her body wasn't.

Even though I knew she could stop this with one word, it still thrilled me. The forbidden air to it all. I loved it.

I thrust inside her in one roll of the hips.

Her body squirmed beneath me, but my strength was too much for her. It overpowered her, and there was no way she was getting free.

My cock was buried deep, and I loved watching where it disappeared inside her cunt. The way she took me in, wrapping me with her tight walls, made my eyes roll to the back of my head.

It was going to be hard, rough, and quick. Recently, it seemed rare that we had a soft, slow, and loving session. My wife was in the mood for a certain flavour, and I wanted to deliver.

My thrusts picked up speed.

'Stop,' she whimpered in my ear, and the more she whimpered, the faster I moved inside her. The slickness of her pussy meant I eased in with no problem, and feeling how much I turned her on only spurred me on more.

'Oh, no,' she moaned, and I knew she was close. I pulled my chest away from hers and took a small globe in my right hand, rubbing my thumb lightly across her nipple.

Her breath came in small pants, and I slowed my thrusts, transfixed by the gorgeous expression that covered her face as she came. Her eyes widened, and her mouth opened as a moan ripped from her throat.

Once she came down from her high, I pulled out of her and flipped her around, pushing her face up against the bark.

My cum covered her arse cheeks, and I loved the paleness of her skin, the cum coating it, and the snowy wonderland that surrounded us.

Fuck.

I was the luckiest man alive.

The two of us righted our clothing—or at least I did. My wife did her best, but I gave her my coat that swamped her. A wave of possessiveness washed over me. I would do anything for that woman. *Anything.*

We didn't find Emily, but we definitely found something else.

My wife's willingness to play the way I dreamed about.

AFTER OUR TIME TOGETHER IN THE WOODS, I FELT
sated.

An animal that had been fed. Somebody with an owner who
understood what they needed to stay sane. A feeding of the soul
and the mind all at once.

I craved Baron's touch. His control. The need to submit to
him, and him only. But in everything else, I wanted to be just as
dominant as him. Just as in control. Powerful. Persuasive. Revered.

The phone rang in the hallway, and I waited for a member of
staff to pick it up.

After a minute of muffled voices, I heard my name being called
from the hall.

I stormed from my bedroom, livid that I was being hollered at
like some commoner that was passing in the street. The moment I
stepped outside my bedroom door and looked in the direction of
the phone, I snapped.

'What?' I demanded, looking at the young girl who was

holding out the telephone in my direction. For some reason, it was one of those old-fashioned ones where the phone itself was attached by a cable to the holder. I joked with Baron about it, but neither of us had done anything to change it. It was black and quite quirky. A random phone on a random side table.

'It's for you, ma'am.'

I nodded, confused at who would be ringing me on the home line.

'Hello?' I answered, placing the cold handset to my ear, the stud in my lobe pressing into the hard skin behind it, the point sharp and painful.

'Queen,' Baron answered. I gulped. Even down the crackling phone line, his voice was treacle, sticking to every surface, sweet and rich. 'I need your help.'

'Where are you?'

'Outside.'

'Outside...' Did the man want to be any more vague?

'In the woods,' he clarified. Then the next words that came down the line made me shiver. 'I've found her.'

'Who?' I spat. There were two possibilities that jumped to my mind within an instant, but for all I knew, there could be other women roaming in our woods that I was yet to meet.

I wondered if Baron had some kind of wood cabin on the grounds somewhere...

'... she was stumbling around near the road. Thank fuck she didn't go any further.'

'Huh?' I asked, only having heard the end of Baron's sentence, the luring thought of a wood cabin to trap people inside too much for my brain. I struggled with multi-tasking. It was a thing.

'Emily,' he repeated. 'I found her wandering around in the woods, dazed and confused, and dehydrated.'

'Oh!' My ears perked up, and I stood straighter, excitement rushing through me. 'Well, that's good news, then.'

'I thought you'd be happy.'

'I am.' I smiled, even though he couldn't see me. 'Are you bringing her back now?'

'She won't come back with me.'

'What?' I spat. 'Of course, she won't come back with you *willingly*. That's why you have to force her.'

'She wants you to come get her.'

'For fuck's sake, Baron, do I have to do everything around here?' My temperature was rising, and even though it wasn't his fault, my mind instantly wanted to blame him. He was the one talking to me, so he was the one that would be getting the full brunt of my anger. Unless... 'I'll come.'

'You changed your tune pretty quick, my queen. Anything I should know about?'

'Nope,' I responded flippantly, popping the *P* in an irritating way I hated in others but loved to do myself. 'Where abouts on the grounds are you?'

'Get one of the staff to drive you down to the end of the driveway, then head left. Should only be around five minutes until you reach us.'

'What if she tries to run away?'

'She's a bit tied up at the moment.' It always amazed me how you could tell somebody's mood by the tone of their voice. Even through a phone. And I could sense Baron's amusement. Just knew that he was enjoying every moment of capturing her. As long as he hadn't captured her the same way he had me in the woods, I didn't care what he did.

'I'll be there as soon as I can be. Don't start without me.

'Wouldn't dream of it.'

I hung up the phone and looked around me, hoping there would be a staff member flitting around somewhere nearby.

The girl that called me to the phone—who I was still rather mad at—was inside my bedroom fluffing the pillows on my bed. Who gave her permission to do that?

I needed to have a talk with Mrs Peters. Find out where on earth she was acquiring her new staff from and make it clear that they needed to be trained better. They were all impertinent.

'You,' I commanded, my tone cutting through the air, accusation in the word. 'Get me a car arranged now. Don't keep me waiting.'

'Yes, ma'am,' the terrified girl replied, falling into a small curtsy. 'Right away.'

The girl, and her fear, left my room as fast as they could, rushing off to do my bidding. I fucking loved it when people obeyed me without question. There was something about it that tasted like the most delicious dessert. The sweetest of wines. The most potent of potions.

It didn't take long for me to throw on a large faux fur coat from my wardrobe and make my way out to the front of the house, where a car was already idling for me.

I fucking loved it when staff acted competent. It was a thrill for me.

Within minutes, I was at the end of the driveway, and I headed left, taking my time as I didn't want to stumble over any fallen branches or ice patches that were being hidden by snow.

I grumbled to myself the entire time, pissed that I'd listened to Baron. Angered that I'd allowed Emily to get me out of my nice, warm home to come and drag her back. But my curiosity had won out. What on earth could she want to say to me?

She had a chance at freedom, and she blew it.

Guess I'd forgotten to mention to her that our portion of the woods was hemmed in by a large electric gate to keep out unwanted guests. My bad.

'Ah,' Baron called when they came into view. 'There you are, darling.'

'Yeah, yeah,' I replied. 'I'm here. Let's get on with this shit.'

'Is the car waiting for me?' he asked, and I shrugged. He hadn't told me to keep it waiting for him, so why would I have known to? I hated it when people assumed you knew what they wanted, when really it wasn't that obvious a request to begin with.

'I'll take it from here,' I told him, nudging my head in Emily's direction. Baron had tied her wrist to his, so I moved closer to them, knowing that he wanted my wrist to replace his, but not being overly thrilled about it. I hated getting too close to her. It was different in the chamber. She wasn't free to hurt me, and if she did, she paid for it.

Baron kissed my head, before attaching the rope Emily was tied to onto my wrist.

'Any trouble,' he said, tilting my chin up to look at him with his calloused forefinger, 'then ring me straight away.'

I nodded.

'I will,' I replied, trailing kisses from his cheek to his chin to his lips, standing as tall as I could on my tiptoes. Ignoring the fact that Emily was at my side, watching the whole display. 'You're my forever.'

'And you are mine.' He placed one last kiss on my lips, the softness in his eyes causing a sensation I could feel in the points of my toes as they curled in my boots.

He left the two of us standing there, watching his retreating back, and it was only once he disappeared into the tree line that Emily spoke to me.

Or, should I say, hissed at me.

'You didn't tell me there was an electric fence!'

'I didn't?' I said, playing innocent, but the smile covering my face made my true intentions known. 'Must've slipped my mind.'

'No,' she deadpanned. 'It didn't.'

I shrugged, and her arm moved, too. I began to walk, and she had no choice but to follow me.

'I'm impressed, though. You've somehow managed to survive for nearly three days wearing only your underwear in the snow.' Then I looked at her properly. 'Or not.'

When I arrived, I didn't look at her. She didn't matter to me enough for my brain to compute that she wasn't wearing the same thing I'd left her wearing in the chamber. Somehow, she'd managed to come across a fluffy jumper of mine and some leggings. I rolled my eyes. Of course, she'd stolen from me in the process of escaping from my clutches.

'It's been freezing,' she whispered. 'I didn't leave as soon as you did.'

'Why?'

'I thought it was a trap. Didn't believe you'd actually let me leave. I was certain I would've walked out the hallway to find you and Baron waiting there to punish me for ever thinking I could be free.'

'Huh,' I muttered, walking at a brisk pace. I wanted to be back in the warmth of the library. 'You've surprised me. Fancy that.'

'You've got to leave him.'

'What?' It was like ice cold water had been dumped on my head. Her words poisonous and deadly.

'Master,' she clarified, then shook her head, her whole body shaking with her, and it travelled down my arm. I could see the pain on her face as she blurted out his name. 'Baron. You have to leave him.'

'Why would I do such a thing?'

'Because he'll kill you. You know it, and I know it.'

'I think you're confused about your role here,' I told her, ignoring her sentence. There was no way Baron would kill me. I wasn't like the others. That was my power. 'It isn't your place to judge my decisions.'

'You're making a mistake. Look at what he did to my sister. Look at what he did to Emmy!'

'What did he do to Emmy?' I asked, raising an eyebrow in her direction. 'Because she was dead in the chamber the first time I found you in there, and you said she'd been dead for two weeks. That was when we got back from our honeymoon.'

'Yes.' Her face calmed, as if me asking for a story meant that she wasn't about to die a painful death in the middle of some trees. Which I supposed it did. Baron hadn't told me how Emmeline died, but then again, I'd never asked. 'While you were away, Emmy was beside herself. When he married my sister, she thought it was all a part of the plot to make me obey. But then after they got an annulment and Violet went missing, she began to realise that she was never getting out the way Baron told her she would.'

'Can imagine that didn't go down well.'

'Ya think?' she asked, rhetorically. 'She was beside herself. All she would do all day was pull her hair out in clumps, or hurt herself with her nails. Sometimes she'd scratch at the door for hours on end, begging for Baron to return. It broke my heart to see her so sad.'

I could hear the pain in her words. It was clear to me that Emily had grown to love Emmy. That a connection of sorts had formed between them, and that it hurt her.

Which only made me happier.

The snow on the ground—and the fact that we were tied together at our wrists—made the journey a hard one, and there were a couple of times when Emily was too frail and had lost her balance, nearly taking me down with her.

She fell, and I pulled her up again, nearly yanking her arm from its socket with the force.

'But how did she die?' I asked, wanting her to jump ahead. Why was it that nobody could just tell me what I wanted to know? It was as if nobody could tell a story without constant embellishments. Little additions that suited the narrator's needs with no thought of the reader.

'Baron came to our room the night before your wedding. Told us that he had a new wife now, living upstairs in the manor, and that we would need to fend for ourselves for a little while. Left enough food and water for a couple of days, said Mrs Peters would be coming to give us more, and then fucked off. If I thought Emmy acted crazed before that, then I was living in a delusional daze, because the moment he told us he was going on his honeymoon, she flew into a rage like I'd never seen before.

'When he came home, the night you returned from your honeymoon, she flew at him in a jealous cloud. I'd never seen her act that way with him before. It was as if every submissive thought or action had piled up within her, and she needed to be the one in charge for a time. And at first, Baron let her rage. Let her scratch and claw at his clothes, scream in his face, tell him he was an evil man. But then he snapped. Threw her to the floor like she was an old rag doll nobody wanted to play with anymore.'

She stopped talking, her eyes glazed over, her footsteps small and unsure. I tugged the rope, pulling her onwards, not wanting to give her a chance to stop and attempt to reel me in.

'I watched, cowered from my cage, as he beat her. Kicking her ribs, punching her face. It was the most vicious I'd ever seen Baron be, and I'd been down there for over a year. He would hit us when we misbehaved, but never that savagely. He wanted her dead.'

'So, she died,' I jumped in, ready to get to the bit I was meant to give a shit about. 'Baron killed her, blah blah. Then he left her corpse there to rot for two weeks, right?'

'Yes,' she whispered. 'She just festered in the corner, and I couldn't even reach her. Couldn't close her eyes and give her the respect she deserved. The smell was horrific—you smelt it that first day you entered and found us. For two whole weeks he left me there with her, only showing up each day for five minutes to change my water, give me some food or clean out my bucket.'

'It was pretty bad, yeah,' I agreed absentmindedly. I think *pretty bad* was a rather large understatement. It was fucking vile. I'd nearly been sick the moment it entered my nostrils. I couldn't imagine sitting within it for as long as she did.

'Why didn't you recognise me?' she asked, her voice soft, almost carried off with the wind that was picking up and whistling through the trees.

'Huh?'

'On that first visit. You didn't acknowledge that you knew who I was. Your eyes gave nothing away. I thought you didn't know it was me.'

'I knew,' I said, my admission surprising even me. 'Of course, I knew it was you. But if you haven't realised it by now, I guess I'll spell it out for you. I don't like you. Hate you, in fact. I didn't want you to know I recognised you, in case Baron came to you first and started asking about me.'

'What did I do to you to make you hate me? If you want to hate anybody, it should be *him*.' Her tone was filled with derision towards me.

'You ditched me,' I told her. 'At school, back when we first started at Hollowdale and you befriended the popular bitches. You didn't have the time of day for me from then on.'

'That's not true. We stopped talking before that because you were ashamed of where you lived and how your mother earned a living.'

'Do not talk about her!' I screamed. A bird call echoed throughout the trees as it flew from his branch, startled at my outburst. 'You have no right.'

'I–'

'No!' I seethed. 'You've lost your right to talk.'

For the rest of the walk, she stayed silent, adhering to my command. She was a good little prisoner, really, for the most part. Except for the whole running away thing. That she would need to be punished for. I couldn't have her repeating her mistake.

Even though it was a trap all along. Just not the trap she thought it was.

We stepped out from the trees and came upon the house looming up ahead. The light was fading, and the manor looked impressive, all lit up with decorations and lights for the holidays.

It was how I dreamed it would look and it made me happy beyond belief that my life had changed so much in such a short period of time.

The two of us made our way up the stairs at a snail's pace. Emily—according to her—was too weakened to climb quicker, and I snapped and told her that had she not run around out in the snow for the last three days, then maybe she wouldn't be so fucking weak.

There were no staff in the halls when we entered. Somehow, everybody was elsewhere. Maybe they were preparing the meal for the next day. I hoped they were.

It would be my first Christmas with Baron, and I wanted to make it a good one. And I couldn't have a misbehaving prisoner interrupting it.

She had to go.

We made our way through the house, slower still, as there were even more stairs up to the West Wing. If I wasn't enjoying her pain, I would've picked her up and carried her just to make the journey quicker. But the weaker she was when she entered the room, the better for my plan.

Finally, we made it to the door.

It was unlocked and left slightly ajar for us. Baron was already inside. Waiting for us. Waiting for her.

I slammed the door behind us once we were inside the hallway, then we made our way to Baron, who was standing in the centre of the room beside the hanging single lightbulb, looking every bit the devil.

My thighs clenched at the sight of him.

He wore a tight white shirt, with his sleeves rolled up to his elbows. The top couple of buttons undone to show the sprinkling of dark hair on his toned chest. Fuck, he was hot.

It pissed me off that Emily was also privy to the sight before me. It made me want to gouge out her eyes with a hot spoon, so she could never lay her eyes on him again.

Baron untied me from her, and took the rope attached to her wrist, holding it firm in his grip, before looping it around a large metal ring that was fastened to the stone wall.

Emily looked from Baron to me, and I knew she hoped I would step in. Her eyes pleaded with me to save her. But hadn't I already tried to help her? And she'd wasted it. Threw it back in my face. If Baron knew I was the one who let her free on purpose, then he may be mad at me. And the last thing I wanted to do was instil anger into Baron.

'Please,' she whispered, staring into my eyes.

I gave her a small shake of my head. She wasn't going to get mercy from me. If anything, she'd sealed her fate on the walk back. She tried to poison me against my love. The best thing that ever happened to me.

'Where shall we start?' I asked, turning to face Baron, who was standing in front of a wooden table ladened with tools. I rubbed my hands together with glee.

Baron meant business if he'd set up a table of torture implements.

'What would you like to do, my queen?'

'Let's start with her fingernails,' I said, my top lip curling up into a pleased grin.

'Want to do the honours?' Baron asked, holding out a pair of pliers to me.

My heart soared. Everything about the moment was exactly how it should be. Baron was handing me the reins, and I wanted to show him how good I was. Show him that he had chosen correctly the day he met me in the coffee shop.

I took the pliers in my hand, surprised by their weight, and took a step closer to Emily.

'Wait,' I said, looking at her from head to toe. 'She needs to be naked.'

Small steps took me over to the table, and I glanced at the variety, then found the shears that were laying there and picked them up.

'P-please,' she whispered, tears springing into her eyes. 'Please don't do this.'

'Shut up!' I growled, losing my patience with her. 'I'll do what I want.'

The shears made quick work of her clothing.

Once she was naked, I felt a sense of peace overtake me. By shedding her clothes, I'd shed something about myself. Something hidden for years, only now unleashed because of Baron's love and generosity.

Her finger was long and bony. Gripped in mine, I held her in place as I pulled her nail from its bed.

The scream that tore from her throat pleased me. As did the trickle of liquid that trailed down her leg when she realised that there would be no reprieve.

No way out.

'Sweetheart,' I whispered, my breath fanning across her tear-streaked face, her eyelashes clumped together, her eyes wide. 'I'm just getting started.'

Emily died.

The torture was too much. Guess she was too weakened from the lack of food and water to withstand much.

A sack of bones was useless to me. To *us*.

I told Baron as much.

'Darling,' he replied, a deep-rooted sigh following his one word response. 'They have to be weak. Emily escaped. She would have succeeded had she been stronger. Strong enough to survive in the woods without us finding her before anyone else.'

He was right, of course. He was always right.

And I loved him for it.

Even if he did piss me off to the core.

RECTIFY

THE DEATH OF A PRISONER STUNG AND SMARTED MORE than I ever thought it would.

Her beaten and bloodied corpse discarded in the corner of the room, disrespected in death the way she was in life. If it wasn't for the smell, I'd opt to keep her there. But trust me, there was nothing quite like the smell of rotting flesh to turn the stomach.

Baron's team of cleaners were scheduled to come, but because of Christmas and the New Year, they were unable to come straight away. What they did with her was of little importance to me. They could violate her for all I cared. She meant nothing to me.

The only true loss I suffered was that I was now a queen without a subject, without an audience. Who would I torment with her gone?

It was only a week after her passing that Baron and I turned our minds to a *new* prisoner. With a week to reflect on our married life without somebody to torment, we both decided it would be for the best if we introduced another outlet for our anger and frustrations.

'We need somebody younger,' I told him with a nod. I'd already decided on that. And no, of course, I didn't mean somebody under the age of sixteen. Even I drew the line somewhere.

'Anna?' he asked, his voice a deep rumble.

Her image filled my mind. I pondered and turned it over before responding. It couldn't just be anybody. Not just *any* girl. But the *perfect* girl.

'Anna could work...'

Mrs Peters rushed into the kitchen, her severe face filled with a fear I'd never seen before, distracting us both from the topic.

'Sir. Sir.' She bowed her head at Baron, then begrudgingly did the same in my direction. 'They've found her.'

'Found who?' I snapped. As far as I was aware, we didn't have a prisoner anymore to be found. Unless she was talking about Emily's body? I didn't know where that was, but seeing as Baron had always done the right thing by his previous wives—except Emmy—I doubted he'd left her lying around for anybody to find.

'Violet!' she shrieked. 'They've found *Violet.*'

Huh. I hadn't expected that one.

I shrugged, watching Baron's face closely for anything to give him away. He told me he had nothing to do with her death and I believed him. Or *had* believed him. Whatever he did now would let me know the truth.

If he didn't have anything to do with it, then why had Mrs Peters flown into the room looking so distressed?

I noticed the paper in Mrs Peters' hand and demanded she hand it over.

Of course, it was The *Beurre Banner.* The headline read: **Body found in search of missing wife**

The article stated that the body of Violet Brown was found in the woods at one a.m. in the morning and that the newspaper was the first to break the news. Ridiculous, really, that the local paper got the jump on national news outlets, but the death of Violet probably didn't matter as much in the city. Which made no sense either, because Baron was a well-respected businessman who brought a lot to the city with his hotels and the work they provided.

It always irritated me when the papers called Violet Baron's *wife*. How could she be if I was now? They'd covered our wedding and engagement, for fuck's sake.

I was Mrs Henrick, and no fucker was going to take that away from me. Dead or alive.

I handed the paper over to Baron, and when he took it, our fingertips grazed against one another, sending a spark through me. Even just the brush of his hand caused me to go giddy as a schoolgirl.

He scanned the page, and his eyebrows climbed higher on his forehead the more he read.

'What is it?' I asked, frustrated that he was just letting me watch his face darken without telling me not to worry. 'What does it say?'

'They've found Violet.'

'Funny that. I can read the headline.'

'The papers reckon the police are planning to interview people, and rightfully, they think I'll be the first person the police want to talk to.'

'You had nothing to do with it.'

'I know that. But the person who *did* have something to do with it isn't exactly going to walk into the station and announce himself, is he?'

'Well, who is he?' I asked, exasperated. If he knew who killed her, then he should just say it and be done with it. Unless...

'It was David Carroll.'

'The politician?' That was the last name I expected him to say.

He was at our wedding, if I remembered correctly, but that was all I knew about him. Politics wasn't something I gave a shit about. I didn't even understand what each party stood for. All I knew was that I was poor, and the government hadn't helped us any.

'The very same,' Baron stated, and I could sense he was going to continue talking, so I lifted my spoon and went back to eating my bowl of cereal. Baron told me most mornings that I was clearly a psychopath because I didn't have milk with my cereal. Apparently, only a monster did that. 'He was the man she was having an affair with.'

'Why didn't you tell me that when you told me the tale of Violet?'

'Because it wasn't important. I didn't think her body would ever show up in *my* woods. He told me he'd dealt with it.'

'Well, he clearly dealt with her life... Think he's trying to frame you?'

'Yes,' Baron replied, his voice grave. 'I think he might be.'

'But what would he gain?'

'The chief of police in his back pocket. Seems to me that John is being coerced, most likely by a lot of fucking money.'

'Can't we just offer more?' I asked, pretty naïve to the world I'd stumbled into. Money spoke, but it didn't make much sense to me how they decided who was in charge and who was in whose pocket. Seemed pretty fickle and tentative if you asked me. 'If John has a price, and is willing to ditch us for more, then surely we can try harder to keep him on our side.'

'When did you become so smart?'

'Oh, puh-lease,' I scoffed. 'None of that was smart. You were already thinking it.'

He smirked, and my nipples hardened underneath the thin material of my dress, the look on his face exuding such sexual magnetism.

'You know what else I was thinking?'

'What's that?'

'That you and I should go upstairs and...' His voice trailed off, and he left me to fill in the blanks with whatever I wanted. But before I could stand up from my chair, the sound of the door knocker reverberated throughout the house.

'Looks like the police are here already.' Baron sat up straighter in his chair and resumed eating his breakfast omelette as if nothing was going wrong. As if his ex-wife's body hadn't been found on our property without our knowledge an entire eight hours ago. Pretty fucking fishy.

Talking of fishy shit, Mrs Peters hurried from the room, her wide frame waddling with the motion, and I held in a laugh at the sight of her. She reminded me of a penguin, and now that I'd thought it, I couldn't ever unsee it.

'Goody,' I said, sarcasm flowing thick.

She returned in a moment with a short, large man that reminded me of that stereotypical kids' TV show policeman. One that was as wide as they were round. His face was red, and squashed, like a pug's. I picked up my glass of water and took a sip to cover up the laugh that was bubbling up my throat. But then the water went up my nose the wrong way and I started to choke.

Wonderful.

It was the first time the man my husband bribed to hide his sketchy shit met me, and there I was, dying because I snorted some water and it went down the wrong hole.

If my eyes weren't bugging out of my head while I coughed, I would've rolled them.

'Mrs Henrick,' the pug said, holding his hand out to me. 'It's a pleasure to meet you.'

I spluttered in his face, and held my hand out to shake his, feeling like a fool. Once my coughing fit subsided, I chanced a glance at Baron, who was so fucking amused at the entire thing that I wished I could wipe the look off his face with a knife.

'Pleasure to meet you, John,' I replied, pulling out the chair next to me at the table. 'Please, do sit.'

'Bit of bad business this, Baron,' he said, looking across the table at my husband. Baron, as usual, looked stoic and uninterested. Above it all. Nothing ever fazed him. He ran with the punches, rolled with the flow. 'The girl showing up in the woods outside your property line doesn't look good.'

'No,' Baron agreed. 'I suppose it doesn't.'

'Sorry if this seems dim to you intelligent men,' I began, looking at them both wide-eyed. 'But wouldn't it look worse if she was found within our property boundary? Wouldn't it be rather silly to leave a body *outside* of our gates?'

'Mrs Henrick, I can assure you that I'm not accusing your husband of anything. I just wanted to make it clear how it looked to the rest of the town.'

I nodded, my face the picture of somebody lost deep in thought. A meek female surrounded my big strong alpha males who knew so much better than little old me. I didn't need the chief of police to know that I was just as intelligent as Baron. He could learn that later down the line, but for us to make sure the problem of Violet Brown disappeared, I needed to act like a damsel in distress.

'Oh, of course, Sir,' I said, reaching out to touch his hand. His papery skin was wrinkled and spotted, showing his age, and the way it felt under my fingertips unlocked a memory inside me.

It was of my great grandmother, who was long dead, when I was a child. I was fascinated by the skin on the back of her hands. I would spend hours pulling it up and watching it as it slowly fell back down. The older she got, the longer it stayed airborne, and I was captivated by it.

When she died, it was one of the things I missed about her most. The way her smile would light me up from the inside as I pulled her skin as hard and as high as I could.

'...you remind me of my daughter.'

I caught the end of John's sentence and recoiled. The sick fuck. I saw the way his eyes lit up when I called him *Sir*. I knew the thoughts that were running through his head about me. The way his eyes lingered on my breasts for a little too long, and the way he held my hand for longer than necessary when we shook hands.

But without realising it, he'd just given me an in.

'You flatter me,' I said, letting out a playful titter. I had no idea what he'd said before his daughter comment, but I was certain it held no real importance. When my brain let me down like that, sometimes I was pissed off about it, and wondered what it would be like to have a brain like everybody else. Or maybe not everybody else, because I was pretty sure it was normal for brains to all be different.

Obviously, I'd missed a large chunk of the conversation because my brain had gone off on a tangent about how brains—especially mine—went off on tangents.

I laughed out loud, drawing the attention of the room back to me.

'I'm sorry, fellas, I was just thinking about how silly I was, interrupting you men on business. I should leave. I won't be of any use to you here.'

'To the contrary,' Baron said, smiling at me. 'I think you're of great use, darling.'

Of course he did, the cheeky bastard.

'Stay, Mrs Henrick,' John said, placing his hand on my knee to keep me in place. 'Your husband and I were just discussing who could have wanted to harm Violet.'

'I have a theory,' I whispered, sticking out my bottom lip in a pout. 'But I don't think it's a good one.

'I'm sure it's a good one,' John said, rubbing his thumb on my knee. I held down the gag I wanted to let free and smiled at him, batting my eyelashes.

'Well, I read the paper this morning,' I stated, pointing at the copy of The *Beurre Banner* Baron had discarded on the table. 'And it said that Violet was pregnant.'

'She was,' John concurred, nodding his head.

'Well, as you and I both know, the baby wasn't Baron's.' I nudged my head in my husband's direction but kept my eyes locked on John's. 'Which is why Baron was given the annulment.'

John kept nodding, like a bulldog bobblehead they had in those adverts.

'I have a feeling that whoever got her pregnant is the person you need to be looking for. And they're framing my darling husband on purpose.' I took a deep breath, ready to go in for the kill. 'But I know you, John. And I know that you never want to see injustice take place under your jurisdiction.'

I leaned forward, bringing my face closer to his, hoping that he'd notice the way my tight top highlighted my breasts.

'I have my utmost faith in you, and I respect your opinion, and if you think the case against Baron needs to go further, I'd understand. But we both know, John, that some mean man out there is trying to harm *us*.'

He gulped, his Adam's apple moving with the motion, and my eyes focused there. His neck was short and fat, and pretty saggy. The man repulsed me more and more the longer he was in my home, but I knew that he had to leave knowing that we would continue the special relationship he and Baron had already established.

'I wouldn't want anything to change with the way things are,' I said, blinking at him, praying he understood me. Praying he got what I meant. Because fuck, I couldn't say much more to persuade him other than maybe blurting out that I'd let him come on my used underwear if he continued to help Baron when he needed him.

I clenched my thighs together, and he felt it through his hand that was still firmly placed on my knee. Our eyes were locked, and I watched as his large, bulging eyes darkened and dilated.

'I think I understand you perfectly, Mrs Henrick. And I agree. The father of Miss Brown's baby is most likely at fault.' He turned to face Baron, removing his hand from my knee, finally. 'I may need to question you further, but it will all be a formality. You understand these things, Baron. Gotta keep it all above board.'

'I understand, John. And I thank you. I'm happy that our *relationship* can continue as it has been.'

The men both nodded at each other, and John stood up, straightening his trousers with his hands. All three of us ignored the fact he had a semi in his slacks, and he shook our hands before he left.

Wouldn't surprise me if the dirty bastard jerked himself off the moment he got back to the car.

'If you don't mind, Baron, I'm going to use your restroom before I leave.'

I coughed, amused that he couldn't even wait until he reached his vehicle.

Baron smirked and murmured, 'Of course.'

'Goodbye, John,' I called out once he left the room.

The moment Mrs Peters had shown him to the bathroom, I burst out into giggles. It was either that, or I vomited on the spot.

I inhaled through my nose, wanting to scrub myself clean, but knowing that I did what I thought was best.

'Come here, you,' Baron said, as he pulled me from my chair and placed me on his lap.

We both laughed and I could feel his hard dick through his slacks. I smiled at the reaction I instilled in him.

'You,' he whispered, placing a kiss on my forehead, then my nose, then my lips, 'deserve a medal.'

'I'll settle for a really good fuck,' I said with a laugh, and I loved Baron's reaction. I loved watching Baron's pupils flare when I said something so unexpected.

'You, my queen, are a pleasure to have around.'

'I've already decided I'll suck your cock, so there's no need to gas me up.'

We both chuckled, and I couldn't help the wide smile that covered my face. He smiled back just as wide and I knew that we were both on the same wavelength, about so many things.

Maybe my life was on the up and up.

Maybe I was about to live out the rest of my life happily. With the man of my dreams. With no worries, and no family outside of the mansion to worry about.

My mind soared with the possibilities.

'SISTER!'

The word confused me for a moment. The word foreign and unfamiliar. Like an owl, my head swivelled in the direction of the voice, to see my younger sister barrelling towards me at a faster speed than I'd ever seen her move in before.

'Hello!' I called back, enthusiastic. Hoping I sounded as happy to see her as she did me. Because inside, I was seething. Fury filled my veins.

I hadn't invited her here.

And I doubted Baron would've done so without me telling him I'd be okay with it. Not so soon after Emily's death.

We were in a state of mourning. The house was draped in black. Our clothes sombre. Our mood even more so.

'Oh, I am so happy to be here!' She opened her arms wide, and I stepped into them, embracing the hug as best I could without peeling her fingers from my body and snapping them in two. 'It's been so long since I saw you last!'

'It can't have been that long,' I told her, my tone slightly scolding. She was making it out like I hadn't seen her, or invited her to my house, in well over a year.

Baron and I had met only six short months ago, married for three. Wasn't exactly a lifetime. But then again, my sister was only fifteen—with her sixteenth birthday soon approaching—and much too young to understand the true depth of a relationship like the one I shared with Baron. Too innocent to know how such a short period of time could truly change every aspect of your being. Could change the way you see both yourself and others.

I'd always known I was different. That my head hadn't been put together by the same person that everybody else's had. But seeing my sister in front of me, a relic of my old life, standing in the centre of my new life, turned my blood ice cold.

She didn't belong here.

'Okay,' she conceded, bouncing up and down on her toes. 'It wasn't that long ago at all. But it *feels* like forever, I can tell you that much.'

I nodded. The poor soul was now stuck in that shitty apartment with only our slut of a mother for company.

'Sorry if this comes out wrong,' I said, pushing her away from me and gripping her hands in mine. 'But who invited you here?'

She laughed, her fringe falling into her hazelnut-coloured eyes.

'You did, silly!' Her sweaty hands squeezed mine, the infectious —*irritating*—smile planted firmly on her face that I wanted to slap away. 'You wrote to me.'

'Oh.' I gave a nervous laugh. 'Of course I did. How silly of me to forget. Have you got it here with you?'

I wanted my hands on that letter. Note. Whatever the fuck you wanted to call it.

Was it Emily who sent it? Her last act from the grave. What

were the odds she'd got the chance to post a letter, though? If she'd got anywhere near town, she would've been discovered. Saved.

And she wasn't. Not by anybody that wanted her *safe*.

Or maybe that shrew-faced bitch, Mrs Peters? She'd never liked me, and it'd amuse her to get a rise out of me by inviting my sister to the house without me knowing.

'I do. I'll show it to you when you show me your library.'

'My library?'

'The one you mentioned. You wrote about all the science books that I would love, remember?'

Her face scrunched up and I could see her assessing me. Scrutinising my every feature.

She let go of my hands, dropping them like hot coals, and rubbed her damp palms on the skirt of her dress.

A dress that was, up until six months ago, *mine*.

'Of course I remember.' I hit my forehead with the bottom of my hand. If she questioned my actions, she didn't say anything. I wasn't goofy. Had never been the kind to act stupid or be overly forgetful. I remembered every face and every name. I was one of those people who remembered everything that happened ten years ago but would probably forget what they'd done the morning before.

I'd thought it before, and I would probably think it again, but fuck me, a therapist would have a field day with my mind.

My hand reached out to hers, and I gripped it in mine, trying to pull her away with me. She paused and picked up a bag that I hadn't noticed sitting at her feet.

'You're not just here for the day?' I asked, a stone dropping to the bottom of my stomach. Just what the shit had I said in my supposed letter?

'Why would I only come for the day when you invited me for the weekend?' She chuckled, and I matched her, forcing my eyes not to roll into the back of my skull. *The weekend?* Now I knew for sure that it was Mrs Peters who sent that letter.

The woman would do anything to knock me down a peg or two.

But you could fucking bet that the moment my sister was gone, I'd make her life hell.

The weekend passed surprisingly slowly when you had company that you couldn't really stand.

Oh, my sister did her best to be charming, and it was exactly that quality of hers that pissed me off the most. She charmed everybody. Including Mrs Peters.

And the more people she charmed, the more I imagined her dying a slow, torturous death.

I'd never had that charm. Had never appealed to people merely from smiling at them. Or from my witty conversation, or, well, *anything* I did.

'Do you really love Baron?' my sister asked as the two of us sat in the library, listening to Beethoven while we both sat in the large armchairs, a book in each of our laps.

'What makes you ask that?'

'I need to know.' She shrugged. 'I need to know that you're happy here. With him.'

'Of course I am,' I affirmed, brushing it off. Inside, I bristled at her questions. Why wouldn't I be happy? I had more money than I could spend in my lifetime. I had a larger bathroom than our old apartment, and I had a loving husband who cared about me. Wanted only my happiness.

My sister was too young to understand all that. She may be

nearly sixteen, but she hadn't experienced much of life. Not in the way other girls her age got to.

She was sheltered, really.

Hidden away from life's true ugliness, even if she had to live with the shame of having a mother that prostituted herself out for a measly tenner.

'There are plenty of rumours in town about him, you know?'

'There always have been.'

'No, they're getting worse,' she said, her tone insistent. 'Ever since Violet's body was found, people have been beside themselves. Remembering things that they repressed.'

My cackle was high and grating.

'Repressed?' I closed the book I was reading with gusto, the pages thumping together with a dull thud. 'What kind of memories have these people *repressed*?'

'People that have gone missing,' she whispered, leaning closer to me, nearly toppling the lamp on the table in between us. 'Loved ones who have moved to the mansion as staff, and then never returned.'

'Maybe they're still working here?' I shrugged.

'What?' she spat. 'And just have never contacted their families again?'

'Do you have any proof?' I asked. 'Any names?'

She shook her head. Her bangs moved with the motion, and I wondered when she'd decided to get them. They looked like mine.

Her whole look did, now that I had time to assess her. Maybe it was the fact she was wearing all my old clothes, but I felt like I was staring in a mirror at age sixteen.

'Not exactly. But they were all women. Every single one of them.' Her piercing eyes looked into my soul. The room went cold, and I pulled my cardigan tighter around me. My sister's words were unsettling—but not for the reason she hoped they would be.

No. They unsettled me because they were true. Or at least I assumed they were true. Emily wasn't the first girl in the chamber. She also wouldn't be the last.

'Women can decide to leave their families and disappear, you know? It happens.'

'It's pretty unbelievable, actually. But when it comes to Baron Henrick, it becomes downright absurd.'

'Leave my husband alone.' My eyes narrowed back at her. 'You have no proof except for some town folks' bullshit comments. And since when did you start talking to people, huh? Or, let me guess, these are things Mum heard from her clients?'

She winced. God, she was so transparent. All of her emotions written plain as day on her face for all to witness. To know what was going on in her know-it-all mind.

I bet it killed her, not having the proof she needed. Not able to say for definite whether my husband was killing innocent girls. Causing them to never return to their families.

'You have to admit that there's something shady about him!'

Why was it that people always went red in the face when they got mad? Was it the rush of blood, or maybe it was the body's way of showing how you felt inside on the outside.

'I don't have to admit shit to you!' I shouted, losing my cool. The way she sat there and needled at me, as if she was holier than thou, grated on me more than it should. Even though I was the older sister, she'd always treated me like I was the younger—more stupid—one.

'Because you know I'm right.'

'I know that Baron's a good man and a good husband. I know that people are full of lies and are spiteful to those they're jealous of. Baron's wealthy, has a mansion filled with staff, and people just can't stand it.'

'Or maybe it has nothing to do with jealousy. Maybe it has everything to do with his previous six wives all winding up dead!'

'He's told me all about them.' *And you're only partially right about the winding up dead bit.*

'And?'

'And there's nothing there to analyse.' I swept my fringe away from my face and tucked it behind my ear. My sister did the same with hers. 'It all happened the way we knew from the papers.'

'You're certain he isn't lying to you?'

'I am,' I asserted, my tone softer. I needed her to believe me. Needed her to put it all behind her and forget her vendetta against Baron. Because she couldn't continue spouting these lies. Especially now that I knew they weren't *complete* lies. If anything was investigated, *I* could be implicated. And that shit wasn't going to fly with me. 'Baron would never lie to me.'

'What makes you so sure?'

'Just call it a hunch, okay?'

'Only if you're sure you're safe.'

'I would tell you if I wasn't. I promise.'

A sound came from the doorway. A cough and a deep chuckle. I looked up to find Baron standing there, staring into the library, taking both my sister and me in.

I wondered how long he'd been standing there. Had he heard any of our conversation before announcing himself?

And if he had, would it piss him off that my sister was spurting things that could get her killed?

'Hello, girls,' he greeted in a dark tone, the chuckle still ringing through his words. 'Light spot of reading?'

'Something like that,' I said with a laugh, trying to convey with my eyes that I needed him to follow my lead. Hoping that our connection was strong enough for him to receive the brainwaves I was sending in his direction. 'My sister was just telling me the craziest story.'

Her head whipped around to face me, the force of it causing her bangs to dislodge from behind her ear and cover her face once more. The accusatory glare she gave me was enough for me to pause—just for a second—before I continued.

Served her right for sticking her large nose where it wasn't wanted.

'Do tell.' He regarded her with impassive coldness, his tone lighter than the air surrounding him. He stepped into the room and headed over. I got a short burst of energy when my sister shivered in his presence. It was the first time since she arrived that she'd seen Baron. He had kept to himself, mostly trying to utilise all his wealth and power to make sure he made his way off Violet's suspect list. With the police in his pocket, it was unlikely they would arrest him, but they still had to keep up the pretence that they were doing all they could to find her killer.

A killer that, I felt pretty certain, also had the police in *his* back pocket, but that was all part of the fun.

Large hands landed on my shoulders. The weight of them both grounded me and sent a wave of fear through my bones. I trusted Baron. I loved Baron. But there were still times when I was scared of him. Scared of the person he could become if a person nudged him in the right direction.

He loomed behind my chair, a shadow that I ignored, as I continued talking to him.

'She said there are rumours swirling around town.'

Like in a play, people knew their parts. They knew the moment they were to enter stage left, and even when to laugh on cue. Baron was one of the greatest actors I knew. Even without a script, he played his role to perfection. Never missing a beat. Always knowing when to enter, exit, and, most importantly, laugh.

'What kind of rumours?' Pressure on my shoulders and thumbs digging into my shoulder blades made me sit up straighter. Taller. Somebody in control of the situation.

'Oh.' I laughed, flipping my hand in the air, waving the words away. 'Silly ones. About people coming to work here and never returning.'

'I can assure you, Miss Smith, that there are no staff disappearing on my watch. No more wives disappearing, either. Your sister is safe here with me.'

The room groaned.

The books on their shelves seemed to sigh with Baron's declaration, as if they'd seen enough to know that he was bending the truth. Maybe they had.

The library was for Emmeline, after all.

This entire house was for Emmeline.

And if Emmeline was still alive... I would kill the bitch for being such a threat to what I now had with Baron.

'Only if you're sure,' my sister muttered, not looking up at Baron, but still looking at me, biting down hard on her bottom lip. Her hand gripped mine. The urgency of her touch conveying the words she was too frightened to speak. She was scared. Terribly so. With no good reason. Rumours could kill. And she'd walked blindly into our home, expecting the worst. And by expecting the worst of Baron, she also thought low of me. Because who could stay married to such a vile man under their own free will?

Or maybe she thought I was being trapped. Coerced into staying here and loving a man who was all wrong for me.

My anger at her only grew. Who did she think she was? A loving sister here to protect her older sister from the big bad wolf?

Didn't she know my old life was the stain? The poison?

I'd released the old me. Like a snake shedding its skin, ready for a new life. A new look. The ultimate power move.

'Of course I'm sure,' I said, my tone demure. Like the mild-mannered wife I sometimes pictured myself to be in my head. I leaned forward, placing her fringe behind her ear, a smile wide on my face.

My sister gasped.

Her eyes filled with tears.

And she covered her mouth with her hand. The other, she ripped out of my grasp, and with a shaky pointing finger, pointed at my collarbone.

Ah, fuck.

'YOU HAVE TO LEAVE HIM!' MY SISTER WHISPERED LATER that evening, when Baron had left the two of us alone and we'd made it back to my rooms.

'What? Why?'

I knew she saw my mark earlier. Knew she saw Baron's name burned into my collarbone. She'd gasped when I leaned forward, and within seconds had tried to cover up her reaction.

But we both noticed it.

Baron's hands squeezed into my shoulders even harder, and we were in sync enough to be thinking the same thing.

My sister had to leave the manor.

She was too young, too pure. Plus, the way she was trying to emulate my style irritated me, to say the least. What was she trying to do?

For somebody that spoke so poorly of Baron, she seemed to be trying to get into his good favours—or at least before she glimpsed my brand.

My know-it-all, insufferable brat of a sister would never under-stand the true meaning behind my mark, though. To her, it was something ugly. Something to be hidden.

Fuck. Maybe it was even abuse in her eyes.

But I knew the truth. *We* knew the truth.

It was far from abuse.

It was love. Devotion. Power. Control. Trust. All of the things people dreamed of in a relationship. We were equals when it mattered. And far from equal when we wanted to be.

We defined us.

Nobody else did.

And that was what mattered to me. Which was why I was struggling to face my sister with a straight face and listen to the nonsense spurting out of her mouth.

'*Why?*' she screeched, incredulous. 'He's branded you!'

Self-consciously, I covered my collarbone with my cardigan, pulling it tight around myself once more. I should've worn a better outfit. A dress that came up higher on my chest. But I quite liked having the mark so close to the surface. Loved toying with my clothing around Baron to tease him.

The moment he saw his name imprinted into my skin, he couldn't control himself.

'He hasn't branded me, silly,' I scoffed, rolling my eyes.

My sister's face was horror personified. Filled with a disgust deeper than the disgust she had when our mother brought her work home with her.

'Then what the hell is that on your chest?' Hands tugged at my cardigan, then yanked away to show my burnt flesh hiding underneath. I could deny it until I was as blue in the face as Baron's beard, but a fat lot of good it'd do me. My sister had eyes on her face. A brain in her head.

But even while looking at a simple math equation of one plus one, she would still come up with four. Because she didn't understand.

'You just don't get it!' I screamed, pulling myself away from her grabbing hands. 'Baron and I are in love. *This*'—I pointed at my collarbone—'is a sign of that love.'

'It's sick,' she whispered, tears filling her eyes. 'You're sick.'

'And who decides that?' I spat. '*You?* Little miss I've never had a date.'

'He's manipulated you. Turned you into something I don't even recognise.' Tears stained her cheeks. Her face crumbled with every word. 'Can you even hear yourself?'

'Of course I can.' I scoffed at her implication. How dare she suggest that Baron had manipulated me?

I hated that.

Hated it when people told me that my own thoughts and feelings weren't my own. Were the invention of somebody else. That I couldn't possibly have thought something without it being put there first.

Why did people want to think the very best of you when you knew deep down that you were the worst?

And why was it that those people believed you were being defeatist and negative about yourself when you owned up to the terrible thoughts? Why couldn't they just accept that you were a realist, and knew yourself better than anybody else ever could?

But also, it was fucking rich to think that Baron had manipulated *me*.

We were both as manipulative as the other. We both wanted the marriage for different reasons. I wanted to escape my life, and he was the easiest way out. He wanted a new wife he could lead into the darkness, that would live with him there, a safe space.

We both got what we wanted.

'I think it's time you left, don't you?' I stated, posing it as a question, but we both knew it wasn't. It was a command.

She was in my home, and she wasn't going to disrespect me in my space. Back when we both lived together and shared a bedroom, I let her get away with disrespecting me because I didn't know better. Or I didn't care about her enough to correct her.

'I'm going!' she spat. 'But when you realise what I can see as plain as day, you'll need my help. And maybe then you'll say sorry for the way you've treated me.'

I rolled my eyes again at her dramatics.

I didn't say any more as she stormed from the room, off to grab her things I assumed, choosing to stay where I was, crossing my leg over my knee and clasping my hands together in thought.

'Mrs Peters!' I called out, and when the little woman didn't rush into the room, I picked up the tiny silver bell I'd taken to carrying with me wherever I went, ringing it for her assistance. Or any staff member's assistance. I wasn't fussy. 'Mrs Peters!'

The woman in question came waddling into the room, a bruise forming on her right cheek from where I lost my temper with her the day before.

'Could you please get my maid to run my bath,' I told Mrs Peters, not looking at her but keeping my eye on the book in front of me. It was one of the books by Marquis de Sade I'd found in the library, back before I discovered the room—and myself. 'And then I want the sheets changed on the bed in my bedroom.'

'But Mrs Henrick,' she said, and I could hear her feet shuffling on the ground, irritating me. 'We changed the sheets on your bed two days ago.'

'So?' I asked, putting the book down and slowly raising my head to look at her face. 'What's your point exactly?'

'The sheets are clean. You haven't stayed in the room since they were changed.'

'And?'

'And I wasn't sure if you knew that, ma'am. Because I'm certain that if you knew, you wouldn't have asked.'

'Oh,' I said, standing from my chair to tower over the dumpy woman. 'You're certain, are you?'

Terror washed over her face.

'I'm sorry,' she muttered, stumbling over her words, backtracking. 'I didn't mean any offence.'

'I think you meant every offence.' I seethed at her display of disrespect. She'd been pissing me off for some time, always questioning my commands and trying to override my wants and needs.

She opened her mouth to reply, and I slapped her, my palm connecting with her right cheek, the sound reverberating through the library.

A red handprint formed there rather fast, and her eyes were wide with shock.

It was the first time I'd struck her, even though I had fantasised about it for some time. She was impertinence personified, and I fucking hated her.

'Now,' I said, taking my seat once more, picking up my book and taking my eyes from her back to the page I'd left off on. 'Please, could you change the sheets on my bed? I want them changed to the bright white satin ones. That will be all.'

My mind came back to the present, and I looked at Mrs Peters' waiting face. If she was annoyed that I didn't instantly make my demands known, she didn't let on.

'Yes, Mrs Henrick?' It seemed she'd learned her lesson, slightly, as her tone was respectful of me, but the underlying hatred simmered beneath the surface. Mostly, I saw it in her eyes. Her little beady eyes that assessed my every move. 'You rang?'

'Can you assist my sister in leaving the property, please? Arrange for the car to take her home as soon as she's ready.'

'Would you like to say goodbye to her?'

'No,' I grated out. 'I would not.'

'As you wish.' She bowed her head and left the room, leaving me there to stew in my dark thoughts. I wanted my sister to suffer for humiliating me in my own home. For making me question the best thing that had ever happened to me.

Baron and I were meant to be.

I knew it. I could sense it in every fibre of my being. And he knew it, too. So for her to come here, supposedly invited, and try to convince me to leave, she had some fucking nerve.

But who had invited her?

I forgot to ask to see the note, and now she would be leaving with it in her bag, and I would be none the wiser. Why would anybody take it upon themselves to invite my sister here?

It just didn't make any sense.

Hours passed as I sat in my chair, thinking of all the things I could do to hurt my sister if given the chance. Was it morbid? Sure. But did it make me feel better? Fuck yes.

I couldn't explain why my brain worked that way. All I knew was that others didn't experience it. Most people loved their family. Wanted to be kind, and all that good jazz.

Whereas I just didn't have any fucks in me to care. It was as if the invisible cord between us was severed when I was younger. Maybe it was because my mum always compared us four, with me always drawing the short straw in her estimation.

Maybe it was because I never had a father figure, what with me and my brothers being too close in age for them to step up in that capacity for me. Plus, they left the first moment they could.

And then maybe that was it. The true crux of my issue. I felt abandoned by those that were meant to care about me. Those that were meant to keep me safe, and warm, and loved.

I screamed in frustration, all the repressed emotions from my sister's visit leaving me in one long roar, my brain snapping at the strain it was under. At the thoughts that never went away, no matter how somebody treated me.

I needed to find Baron. Needed him to hold me in his arms and show me the love I craved desperately in that moment. He didn't even need to say shit. Just be.

My feet took me from my room in search of my husband.

And I knew just where I would find him.

The room felt wrong now that nobody occupied it.

'Hey,' I said, entering and coming up behind Baron, placing my arms around his waist and hugging him tightly. Needing his strength, his power, to stop me from falling apart.

Because my brain was holding on by a thread. A thin piece of string, unseen by others, that helped to hold me in the real world as opposed to the world I fantasised about daily.

In the world in my head, everything went. Nothing was forbidden, or wrong, or frowned upon. People like my sister were treated the way they deserved; the law be damned.

'Where's your sister?' he asked, turning in my arms to face me. Baron's height made me smile. It always did. He towered above me, and I always felt like a small, cherished thing under his watchful gaze.

'She left,' I stated, blinking up at him. His jaw tensed and his eyes narrowed. Baron always could tell when I was lying. 'Or, should I say, I sent her away.'

'And why did you do a thing like that?'

'Because she hurt my feelings. Pissed me off. Acted superior.' The more I spoke, the more worked up I got. My words began to fly out harsher and with more anger the more I said. 'Who does she think she is? A little brat who doesn't understand the real world.'

'What did she say?'

'Well, you saw her!' I spat, gripping his forearms in a tight squeeze. 'She spotted your name while we were in the library.'

'She did, yes. And I'm assuming her reaction was less than favourable?'

'Less than favourable?' I repeated, my tone mocking. 'Less than fucking favourable?'

My tone was shrill, and if I was looking into a mirror, I knew I would see my entire face contorted with rage. Growing up, I wished I was better at acting. I always thought my expressive face would be good for that sort of thing. Everybody told me they knew what I was thinking because my face gave me away.

Huh. Maybe that was how Baron had seen through me all along.

Or maybe I was a better actress than I believed.

'Okay,' he said with a low chuckle, gripping my hips and holding me still, 'she was more than a little shocked, then?'

'To her, it confirmed every bad thing she's ever read about you. Every warning she gave me. This only confirms that she was right, and you know how much she loves to be right.' Baron nodded, and I continued, 'She told me to leave you. Get out while I still could. Who the fuck invited her in the first place?'

'I did,' Baron replied, a soft silver glint flashing in his eyes.

'You did?' I whispered, keeping my temper in check on the surface, but inside, I was livid. Horrified. Why would he make such a decision without consulting me first? Without even asking if I would be okay with it. Just lumping her on me like a bad surprise that I never wanted or asked for. 'Why would you do that? And why wouldn't you tell me first?'

'If I told you, you would've said no.'

'Damn straight!' I threw my hands up, exasperated. 'And with good reason.'

He shrugged at that, not confirming or denying my point. There must be a reason why he invited her here. Because there was one thing I knew for certain.

It wasn't for me.

Baron hugged me close, and I wrapped my arms around him, slotting perfectly into the gap he'd created for me.

I pressed onto my tiptoes, and I placed a firm kiss on his lips. His beard brushed against my lips, a slight scratch on my skin, and it felt like home.

A buzzing sound entered our ears, and Baron looked questioningly at me, but I shook my head. It was rare I carried around a mobile, and if I did, I definitely didn't have it on loud or vibrate. The sound overwhelmed me. I couldn't understand how people were happy for their phones to be making noise constantly. It wasn't even like I received enough messages or calls for it to be an issue, though. I mostly heard from Baron, and it was rare that he wasn't somewhere in our large home. Since we married, and connected fully as one, Baron barely worked away on business, instead sending employees to his many hotels and resorts dotted around the globe.

We agreed that eventually I would start to travel with him, but for the time being, we wanted to adjust to living together in the manor.

'Who is it?' I asked as Baron took his phone from his pocket and glanced at the screen. His face contorted in confusion, not moving to look at me. When he still hadn't responded after a minute, I shook him by the waist a little. 'What's going on?'

'It was an alert from the gate,' he replied, his forehead wrinkling. 'A car's coming up the drive.'

'Surely, you didn't just allow any old car into our property?' I asked, my voice shrill. There were times when Baron's decisions didn't make sense to me. Him letting randoms into our property was one of them.

'I did,' he said, not sounding worried in the slightest. 'I have a feeling, though, that we know our visitors.'

'*We* do?'

'We do,' he confirmed, pulling me closer. 'I think you might recognise them.'

He turned his phone so I could see who was at the gate, and the moment my brain computed the image, I grabbed the phone out of his hand to zoom in. Shock zapped through me, my mouth agape, gobsmacked at who was in the car coming up our driveway.

'Fuck,' I mumbled.

'So you do know them, then?' Baron questioned, a hint of glee in his voice. The sound caused my head to tilt upwards to assess his features, and I was met with a smirk playing on his lips.

'Of course I do!' I snapped. 'They're my brothers.'

'What the fuck are my brothers doing here?' I asked nobody, because deep down, I knew the answer.

My good-for-nothing bitch of a sister must've told them something.

But how did they get here so fast? As far as I was aware, they were still away, nowhere near Beurre. The two of them hadn't even attended my wedding because they were too busy.

'Maybe they're just here to check on you. Your sister's probably more than a little worried about you.'

'I told her not to be!' I said with venom in my tone, irritated at the drama she'd brought to our door. 'If she'd just listened to me, then maybe she wouldn't have started acting superior about some-thing she didn't understand! I could've explained it. Or at least tried to get her to see it all from my point of view. But now, she thinks you're an abusive husband who's harming me without my consent.'

'That brand would get me arrested,' he pointed out, the words filled with truth. I hadn't even thought of that before. 'In the eyes of the law, I am an abusive husband.'

'Well, it's a good thing I don't leave the house right now, isn't it?' I asked, a small smile playing on my lips. 'Whatever the law thinks, I consented, so fuck them. Fuck all of them. How dare they judge us? How dare *she* judge us!'

'Calm down, my queen. We don't know what they're here for.'

'I highly doubt they're here for some tea and biscuits, Baron!' My voice was shrill, and I was starting to lose my cool. Our driveway may be a mile long, and the staff would probably waylay them for a moment, but we didn't have much longer until they stormed the castle, so to speak.

My brothers had always been hard-headed. Ran into situations before they looked at all the facts. Before they inspected all escape routes.

I couldn't understand how they were on my property. The two of them were in the military and had been ever since they finished school. The two of them wanted out of Beurre so badly that they enlisted "to be free", whatever that meant to them.

They never came home. Not for anything.

The knock on the double doors that covered the entrance to our home reverberated throughout the open hallway and travelled up the stairs to the landing we'd made our way to after Baron showed me the picture.

'Open up!' a voice hollered through the door. 'We know you're in there!'

'What do we do?' I asked, turning to Baron. 'We're going to have to let them in.'

'Mrs Peters will open the door in a moment. Just watch.'

Like clockwork, the penguin waddled into the hall and opened the door. My oldest brother stood there, his fist raised to pound the door again, a snarl covering his face.

'Can I help you?' Mrs Peters asked, her tone no-nonsense, as if it was a normal occurrence to open the door to an imposing six-foot-three male.

'We're here to see Baron Henrick,' my other brother stated, poking his head into the open doorway. Both of them had military haircuts and reminded me of cartoon thugs with their muscular builds.

'Master is busy,' Mrs Peters responded, not at all intimidated by the two of them, even though they towered over her. If I wasn't so pissed at it all, I would've laughed. 'If you don't move from his property within the next minute, I'll have to contact the police.'

From our vantage point at the top of the staircase, I could see my brother pull a knife out of his pocket, something that was hidden by the door frame for Mrs Peters.

Before either Baron or I could warn her, she slumped to the ground in a heap.

My heart leapt, mostly with irritation, but a tiny part of me was amused to see Mrs Peters hurt. I hoped she didn't die, though. I wouldn't be able to boss her around if she was in a grave.

'What is the meaning of this?' Baron called, making his way down the stairs towards the entrance hall. My brothers had stormed inside, climbing over Mrs Peters, and were looking around for where the voice had come from.

Their eyes locked on Baron.

'You!' my older brother, Tom, roared. 'You owe us an explanation!'

'I do?' Baron asked. His stance was wide, his arms nonchalantly hanging at his sides, and I knew he was portraying his idea of calm. On quick feet, I made my way down the steps to come and stand beside him.

I wasn't going to watch them stab my husband and do nothing

to try to intervene. To stop the inevitable. Because even I could see that the turn of events was pretty dire, even if unexpected.

'Sister!' Tom yelled, his face splitting in half when he saw me. The joy on his face confused me. 'You're okay?'

'Of course I am,' I told them, my tone bristly. 'Why wouldn't I be?'

'Because we got a phone call from–'

'We thought you were dead!' The younger of the two, Daniel, blurted out. 'She said she wasn't sure what would happen once she left.'

'Why would she say that?' I asked, my entire body shaking at the implication. As if Baron would kill me. *Could* kill me. 'As you can see, I'm perfectly fine.'

My sister had a lot to answer for, that was for sure.

'Show us your neck,' Tom demanded, pointing his knife at Baron. I rolled my eyes at the two of them. They were the least likely pair of wannabe vigilantes I'd ever come across. The only ones I'd come across. 'That will tell us all we need to know.'

'I doubt it,' I deadpanned. I looked at Baron, tilting my head in question, and he nodded once. If he wanted me to show them, then I would. I wasn't ashamed of my claiming. It bothered other people more than it did me.

There were times when the staff looked at Baron's name blazoned on my collarbone, and I always smirked when I saw their reactions. It amused me that my flesh made people uncomfortable. That a true love like ours could bother people so profoundly.

My fingers trembled as I lifted them to the collar of my dress, curling them around the neckline, and pulling the fabric down to expose my skin to their beady eyes.

Was it wrong of me to enjoy the way their faces contorted with horror?

Was I meant to feel wrong, or ashamed, or abnormal? Because I didn't. If anything, I felt victorious. Like I'd found my place on the earth at Baron's side.

'What did you do to her?' Tom growled, taking a step closer to Baron. 'You're a monster.'

'He is not a monster!' I shouted, spittle flying from my mouth and landing on the ground in front of them. I covered my brand, pulled my collar to rights, and stared my brothers down. 'How dare you storm our home uninvited and disrupt our day.'

'You can't truly be happy here, sis,' Daniel piped up, the more reasonable of the two.

'I can assure you that I am,' I said. 'I'm the happiest I've ever been. And I don't appreciate the two of you trying to ruin that happiness. Don't I deserve it after everything that's happened in my life?'

'You're delusional,' Tom spat. 'You're only eighteen. You don't understand what's happening here. This man'—he looked Baron up and down—'is grooming you.'

'Grooming me?' I laughed. How funny. 'Big word for you, isn't it?'

My hand reached out to Baron's, and I held it in mine, grounded by the electricity that travelled from his skin through me. That ever apparent connection between us was forever present.

'Don't be clever. We can see right through this marriage, even if you're too stupid to.'

'Too stupid to?' An unusual twinge of disappointment made its way through me. I felt like a scolded child. Somebody overlooked. Underappreciated. 'Too stupid to understand what, exactly?'

'What this man is doing to you?' Daniel said, his gaze sympathetic. 'It's a textbook case.'

'Is it? Find me the textbook and then maybe I'll believe you,' I scoffed. 'Now you can both leave. This is my home, and you're not welcome here any longer.'

'But–'

'No!' I moved in between my brother and Baron. Neither of them had moved, and I rolled my eyes at them. Men made me die sometimes. As if standing there, chests puffed out, slightly touching, was showing anybody anything of note.

'Let's go, Tom,' Daniel said, grabbing our brother's shoulder and pushing him backwards away from Baron. They both looked at us, standing united against them, and frowned. 'This isn't over. We will do everything we can to get you out of here.'

'Just like you did everything you could to get me out of Mum's apartment?' I gritted my teeth, pissed that all of a sudden, they cared about me when they hadn't for so many years. 'Go bore somebody who gives a shit about your guilt.'

'Queen.' Baron spoke for the first time since they'd started talking to me. He turned to me, and I looked up at him, taking in his dark eyes. 'You know you're free to leave with them, don't you?'

I nodded, my eyes wide. Of course *I* knew that. But his words weren't for my benefit. God, I was obsessed with him.

'So you see,' Baron affirmed, turning back to address my brothers, 'my wife isn't being held captive and is free to leave whenever she wishes. Now, if you don't mind, the two of us were about to have dinner. I have to ask you to leave, or like Mrs Peters said, I'll have to call the police.'

My gaze went to where Mrs Peters was lying on the floor, surrounded in a pool of her blood. My heart twinged—a shock to me, too—at the sight of her.

'You better leave,' I told them, 'or I'll tell the police it was you who killed our dear Mrs Peters.'

For good measure, tears sprung to my eyes. The old woman

would be shocked that I had so much emotion for her if she could see me.

'We didn't. We haven't,' Daniel stated, his lower lip jutting out, fear flashing in his eyes.

Tom, on the other hand, didn't look scared. No. Instead of fear, his face was covered in triumph.

'If we've killed the old lady, then what's one more?' he asked, raising his eyebrow, an evil glint in his eye.

In a flash, he pulled a gun from his back pocket and aimed it at Baron's chest. Before I could move, he pulled the trigger, the sound louder than anything I'd heard before. I'd never been close to a gun firing. One had gone off once back at my old apartment block, but it had been four floors below us, and the sound was somewhat muffled.

Baron fell to the floor. Face down.

'Thomas!' Daniel screamed. 'What the fuck do you think you're doing? You're gonna put us both in prison.'

'If you leave now, you won't,' I said, my tone surprisingly calm. 'If you leave now and head straight back to your unit, I won't tell a soul. I'll cover for you until my dying day. As long as you go and never come back to Beurre.'

'You don't want to leave with us?'

'What?' I huffed with a laugh, waving my arms around me at the hall we were standing in. 'Now that I've inherited all this? No. Thank you.'

'Are you sure?' Daniel asked, as Tom was pulling him back. Clearly, Tom knew what was best for him.

'Positive,' I said coldly. 'Now go. Go and you'll be long gone by the time the police arrive.'

'Okay!' Daniel agreed, finally understanding the gravity of the situation.

'Oh,' I added, before they left the wide-open front door. 'One more thing.'

'What's that?'

'You can never contact me again. Or Mum. Or our little sister. She doesn't need to be dragged into this. She's only fifteen. She doesn't need this hanging over her head forever.'

They both nodded, a sombre expression on their faces.

I smiled inside, but kept my face stoic for them.

'Goodbye,' Daniel said with one last blink in my direction.

I nodded.

I listened to their car start and peel away, heading down the driveway to the gate at the front of the property. I considered leaving it locked, so they'd still be trapped when the police arrived, but I thought better of it. It suited my purpose more to let them go.

'You can get up now.' I kicked Baron in the shoulder. He spluttered, and I rolled my eyes at his theatrics. Like I didn't know the man had a bulletproof vest underneath his suit. There was no way he would've been so eager to meet my brothers if he hadn't.

'I may not have been shot, my love, but this is going to bruise like a motherfucker.'

'Yeah, yeah,' I muttered, pretending I wasn't bothered, but deep down I was thrilled he was okay. My gut had told me he was still alive. That was why I didn't break down in tears the moment the gun went off. If Baron's soul left this plane, I would know about it. My brothers hadn't noticed the lack of blood leaking from Baron's body, but I had. It was one of the first things I noticed. After all, Mrs Peters was a metre away, bleeding out like an animal carcass, while the tiles around Baron were as bright and shiny as ever.

I took a deep breath.

'Shall we ring the ambulance and police for her?' I asked,

nudging my head in Mrs Peters' direction, even though Baron still hadn't moved from his spot on the ground.

'Leave her,' he said. 'It was only a matter of time until you killed her anyway, so maybe this was all for the best.'

The man had a point.

I crouched down beside him and moved his hair away from his face so I could see his dark pupils with their silver flecks and check that he really was okay.

'Least my family will no longer be an issue,' I told him, raising my eyebrow in satisfaction. 'Going forward.'

'That's good, darling. Now come lay down beside me until I'm ready to move.'

'Yes, Sir,' I whispered, instantly moving my body against his. I placed a kiss on his cheek, breathing in his scent, and I smiled.

Could life be any more perfect?

Ever since my brother's visit, I knew what I needed to do. I'd known before they came, but the way they barged in here trying to disrupt my life only confirmed it to me.

Baron was my true family.

The one that mattered above all else.

Who knew that the key Baron gave me would open up my world to so much more. Not only had becoming his wife changed my life in so many ways, but his love, and the dynamic we'd established between us, made me see myself completely anew. I wasn't born to be meek, submissive, or subservient. Well, not outside of our marital bed, at least.

No.

I was born to be the queen. To be the one with all the power.

Because, unlike the first eighteen years of my life, I wouldn't let anybody take my power away from me again.

I deserved more than that.

I deserved the life for myself that I'd always envisioned. One where I called the shots. Was in charge of my own destiny and all that good shit.

And now Baron and I were heading into the next chapter of our time together. The next chapter of our fucked up fairytale.

I rubbed my stomach, soothed by the constant warmth that lived there these days. My small, rounded belly was another part of the fucked up dream. We hadn't planned it. Had never discussed children. But everything in our lives was falling into place.

It was time to go get our new girl. Our new captive. One who would come easily. Or at least, *easier*. The cage was prepared, the room ready for a new inhabitant.

Anna.

Hadn't I already promised her, back on my wedding day, that I would save her if I could?

Yes. My mind hissed. *She would come willingly.*

It was time to go get my sister.

Acknowledgements

Okay, so, who to thank this time?

Megan, thanks for weathering this storm with me. I know things will only get better, and I know one day we'll be laughing about this. Maybe not any day soon, though.

Billie, thank you for always being there, no matter what. I am so ready for the future with you by my side, and one day we'll look back on this time from that beach, smug as fuck.

My girl Els, thank you isn't enough. You are a star, and I love that you love my words and want more of them. I can't wait to repay the favour... if you get my drift.

Fi, thank you for always having faith in me.

Tay, I'm so glad the world put us in one another's path.

Jess and Jess, the dynamic duo, thank you for everything you do. This is our year.

Thank you to the fam, as always.

To Leggett, who has put up with my whining about a certain book for years and is happy I've written my own version, so I'll shut up.

To my ARC and street teams, I say thank you! You're all bomb and I'm super thankful for such a great team.

I also need to thank you, the reader, for picking up this book and, hopefully, enjoying it.

About the Author

Katie Lowrie is a twenty something year old Brit who loves to write the many things that pop into her head on the daily.

A list in no particular order of her greatest loves:

- Henry VIII and the Tudor era
- Her baby cat, Cress
- Musicals
- Disney
- Cheese

She loves to stalk people online (in a good way) and understands if you do too.

instagram.com/katielowrieauthor

goodreads.com/katielowrieauthor

facebook.com/katielowrieauthor

bookbub.com/authors/katie-lowrie

Also by Katie Lowrie

Hawthorn Academy Series:

Disorder

Disease

Disturbed

Dispose

Re-Imagined:

Key of Cunning

www.ingramcontent.com/pod-product-compliance
Lightning Source LLC
Chambersburg PA
CBHW050802190726
48285CB00005B/1758